The One Right Thing

Bruce Coville

edited by Deb Geisler

The NESFA Press
Post Office Box 809
Framingham, MA 01701
2008

FIRST EDITION, February 2008

International Standard Book Number:
1-886778-72-8 (trade)

The One Right Thing was printed in an edition of 800 numbered hard-cover books, of which the first 125 were signed by the author and artist, bound with special endpapers and slipcased. Of these 125 copies, the first 10 are lettered A through J and the remainder are numbered 1 through 115. The trade copies are numbered 116 through 790. No other copies will be printed in hardcover.

This is book __163__

Publication History

"The Stinky Princess" first graced the covers of **Odder Than Ever,** Harcourt Brace, 1999.

"I, Earthling" and the poem "Just Like You" were originally published in **Bruce Coville's Book of Aliens: Tales to Warp Your Mind,** Scholastic, 1994:

"Guardian of Memory" first appeared in **A Glory of Unicorns,** Scholastic, 1998.

"A Life in Miniature" was originally published in **Swan Sister,** Simon & Schuster, 2003.

"The Troddler" first trod the pages of **Unexpected: 11 mysterious stories,** Scholastic, 2005.

The World's Worst Fairy Godmother *(illustrated by Katherine Coville)* first appeared in 1996, published by Aladdin.

"The Box" first appeared in the anthology **Dragons and Dreams,** Harper & Row, 1986.

"My Little Brother is a Monster" first appeared in **Bruce Coville's Book of Monsters: Tales to Give You the Creeps,** Scholastic, 1993.

"The Giant's Tooth" was first printed in **Odder Than Ever,** Harcourt Brace,1999.

The poem "Ragged John" first appeared in **The Unicorn Treasury,** Doubleday, 1988.

"Saying No to Nick" was published in **Twice Told : Original Stories Inspired by Original Artwork,** Dutton, 2006.

"Clean as a Whistle" appeared first in **Oddly Enough,** Harcourt Brace, 1994.

"With His Head Tucked Underneath His Arm" first appeared in **A Wizard's Dozen,** Jane Yolen Books/Harcourt Brace, 1993.

"Wizard's Boy" was published in **Bruce Coville's Book of Magic: Tales to Cast a Spell on You,** Scholastic, 1996.

"The Metamorphosis of Justin Jones" appeared in **Bruce Coville's Book of Magic II,** Scholastic, 1997.

contents

Introduction

by Tamora Pierce

What do you call a man who feels short stories are an unnatural writing form, and yet has written nearly fifty of them, in addition to editing numerous anthologies?

You call him Bruce Coville.

Bruce paraphrases Walt Whitman, often saying that he is vast; he contains multitudes. He does. He will say "that's it" to a writing piece at one moment and give it thirteen drafts in another. He will write a tense, dark tale of a long-laid plot for the destruction of an entire race, and stop in the middle to fashion a short adventure tale to be told with the backing of a symphony orchestra. While crafting antic books about the misadventures of a daffy wizard, he runs a full cast audio book company, directing and acting in many of its productions. He speaks at schools and conferences across the nation, leaving bewildered, delighted audiences in his wake.

He creates truly hideous puns at the drop of a hat, and—like Stonewall Jackson—he will drop the hat himself. He readily tells writers and parents alike that it is hard to fail in a book for younger readers if one is not afraid to use the words "booger," "fart," "naked," and/or "underwear." He has written many, many illustrations of this maxim. He is criminally fond of alliteration. (I am not.)

Jane Yolen, the Queen of Children's Literature, says, "Bruce is his inner nine-year-old."

And yet.

He has written over ninety books, from picture books to books for teens. He taught school for a number of years: grades kindergarten, two, and four. He was on the board of the Society of Children's Book Writers and Illustrators. He started *two* audio book companies. The first, Words Take Wing, recorded works by the likes of Philip Pullman and Patricia

Wrede before it was bought out by Random House. The second, Full Cast Audio, is just beginning its sixth year of recording books by writers like Bruce himself, the magnificent Paula Danziger, James Howe, Gail Carson Levine, Sid Fleischman, Kathe Koja, Shannon Hale, Kenneth Oppel, Geraldine McCaughrean, and, well, me. He retells the stories of the Shakespeare plays to make them accessible to very young readers and has begun to do the same with the Norse myths and legends. He has edited, with painstaking care, a large number of anthologies with contributions by outstanding writers who are delighted to get the chance to work with him. Bruce is a patient editor with a sharp eye for improving a story without working it to death.

He is quick to encourage new writers who are making their first steps on the professional stage. He gives them advice on the world of publishing, on the process of making a career in writing, and on maintaining their self-esteem during the long and often heart-breaking process of getting first books sold. He is a careful and considerate director of nervous actors and actresses of all ages, giving them the confidence to face a microphone or an audience to deliver performances they had no notion they were capable of giving.

But it is as a writer that Bruce has the greatest weight of my respect. For years I viewed him as a light, "fun" writer, until the loss of my father, and the choice of my comfort reading, made me see him in a very different light. In those days after my dad's passing, I read Bruce's *Ghost* books (*The Ghost in the Third Row*, *The Ghost Wore Gray*, and *The Ghost in the Big Brass Bed*) over and over, not just because I like ghost stories, but because the solid relationship between Nina and her dad gave me such comfort. Then, in seeking citations for a speech I regularly give on how fantasy writers include reality in their books, I discovered what a subversive my friend Mr. Coville really is.

In this book you will find depths of meaning in stories that, on the surface, appear to be paeans to sheer silliness. "I, Earthling," begins with boogers and farts. In the end Bruce not only makes a pitch for us to pay less attention to body functions and more to what takes place in the mind, but he makes a serious case for setting aside parochialism. In our time, as people turn to smaller and smaller groups, what idea is more meaningful to tuck into a story all people, not just kids, will enjoy?

At a time when publishing is offering us a plethora of pleasing, pretty princesses (four p's in a row—Bruce will be so proud!), Bruce performs something else he does quite often: he stands the trope on its ear. In "The Stinky Princess," he gives us just that—a princess of character who smells unpleasant. His ugly monsters are not always nasty and brutish, as you will find. Sometimes they are. Bruce never lets you take him for granted, either. And his values shine through without preaching: keep your word. Fight for those who can't fight back. Treat those who are different with respect. And now and then, howl at the moon.

Just when you think you know all about the man, you'll plunge into something powerful, like "Guardian of Memory," with its lush descriptions and epic tale. "The Box" reminded me of the old poem "Abou ben Adem" in its serenity and its ability to draw echoes from the soul. In stories like these we learn of the oddball's quiet heroism.

For years I have heard people dismiss children's literature and those who write it as "simplistic," "saccharine," and "shallow." They should read Bruce Coville. *Really* read Bruce Coville. Once you swim out of the depths, shaking your head with bewilderment, you'll know Bruce really is vast. He really does contain multitudes.

Tamora Pierce
December 2007

The Stinky Princess

Once there was a princess named Violet who didn't smell very good.

This was an unnatural condition for a princess, of course, and it did not reflect well on her parents. On the other hand, it had nothing to do with either her birth or her upbringing. In fact, she had started out smelling just fine. When she was born, she had smelled as a rosebud does when it is just beginning to open on a misty morning in early June. When she was a little girl she had smelled of mischief and mud pies (it was a small kingdom, and she had an understanding nurse) as well as cinnamon, apples, and sunny afternoons. And when she was just becoming a young lady she smelled of clear mountain streams a moment before the rain comes, of lilacs, and of a small red blossom called dear-to-my-heart that grew on the castle grounds and nowhere else.

So, all in all, she smelled just as a princess should and her parents were pretty well satisfied. More satisfied than the princess herself, certainly. Violet found her own smell boring, and often declared that there must be many far more interesting scents in the world, a statement that always gave her mother a bad case of the quivering vapors.

It did not improve matters any when Bindlepod the goblin came to visit.

If it had been up to the king, he would never have allowed the goblin into the court to begin with. Alas for him, Bindlepod was not merely a goblin, but an ambassador from Goblinland, with which they had recently been at war. So the king was obliged not merely to let him in, but to offer him hospitality.

Bindlepod's skin was the color of rotting toadstools. His bare feet slapped on the stone floors of the castle like dirty dishrags. The pupils of his oversize yellow eyes did not stay still, but instead swam about like tadpoles, which made it very distracting to try to hold a conversation with him.

But the most distressing thing about him was his smell. Nobody could say exactly **what** it was he smelled of. But everybody agreed it was distinctly unpleasant, and somehow made them think of dark and distant places.

Everybody, that is, except the princess.

She thought Bindlepod smelled quite interesting.

"You must be joking, darling," said the queen, speaking through the handkerchief she was holding over her mouth and nose.

"Of course I'm not joking," said Violet.

"But he's…**revolting**," sputtered the king.

"I don't think so," said Princess Violet calmly.

"I can't stand this!" cried the queen, and she fled the room, shedding copious tears as she went.

"There," said the king. "Now see what you've done?"

"What?" asked Violet, who was totally baffled. "What have I done?"

"As if you didn't know," sniffed her father bitterly.

Later that day the princess was walking in the castle garden when she spotted Bindlepod's frog, which was nearly as tall as she was. It was wearing its saddle, as if Bindlepod had just returned from a ride, or was about to leave on one.

A little farther on she spotted the goblin himself. He was perched on the stone wall, gnawing a raw fish.

She walked over and looked at him for a few moments. He nodded at her, but said nothing, preferring to give his attention to the fish.

"My parents don't like you," she said, partly because she was annoyed, but mostly to see how he would respond.

The goblin took another bite from the fish, smacking his lips as he did. Then he said, "I'm not surprised. Are you?"

"I think they're pains," said the princess, surprising herself with her bitterness.

"That doesn't surprise me either," said Bindlepod. He cleaned the last of the flesh from the fish's spine, sucked out its eyes, then tossed the skeleton over his shoulder. It landed in the moat with a tiny splash.

"My parents are not merely pains," said the princess, warming to her topic. "They're royal pains."

"That's appropriate," said the goblin, who privately thought of Violet as "sweet, but dangerous."

She climbed onto the wall and took a seat next to him. "What's it like in goblin land?" she asked.

Bindlepod shrugged. "Nice enough, if you're a goblin. It's a bit darker than here, but that's mostly because it's underground. It's damp, too. We call it Nilbog, by the way, not 'goblin land.' That's rude. It would be like calling your kingdom 'people land.'"

"Is Nilbog smelly?" asked the princess.

Bindlepod closed his eyes, and seemed to be remembering something. "Yes," he said at last, with just a hint of a smile. "Very."

"Let's go there," said the princess.

"You," said the goblin, "are walking trouble, a danger zone with feet."

"Does that mean no?" asked Violet.

"It means never in a million years!"

Then he hopped down from the wall, whistled for his frog, and rode away.

Every day for the next two years, Violet asked Bindlepod to take her to Nilbog, and every day the goblin told her no. This was not because he did not like her. Actually, he had come to find the princess fairly interesting. He had even begun to like her odor, which was not nearly as boring as that of her parents. But much as Bindlepod liked the princess, he liked his own skin even better. More specifically, he liked his skin exactly where it was, and preferred to keep it there rather than have it peeled from his bones while he was still living — an event he was fairly sure would occur were he to run off with the king's daughter.

At the end of the second year it was time for Bindlepod to return to his own land. As he saddled his frog to leave, the princess once again asked if he would take her along.

"Not for all the jewels in your father's treasury," said the goblin. "Nor all the fish in his moat," he added, hoping to make the point more clearly.

Princess Violet wrinkled her nose at him. "You're not very nice!"

"I never claimed to be," replied the goblin. "And you're something of a stinker yourself, when it comes right down to it."

Then he went to say goodbye to her parents.

Halfway back to Nilbog Bindlepod's frog stopped in the middle of the road and said, "I am not taking another hop until you get that princess out of the saddle bags."

"What are you talking about?" cried Bindlepod in alarm.

"The princess," said the frog patiently. "She's in the saddlebag, and I'm getting tired of carrying her."

"Why didn't you say something before now?" asked Bindlepod, torn between exasperation and despair.

"She bribed me," said the frog. "With Junebugs. You know I can't resist Junebugs."

Bindlepod groaned and climbed down from his steed's spotted green back. Poking the saddlebag he said, "Princess, are you in there?"

No one answered.

Even so, the shape of the saddle bag was distinctly suspicious. So Bindlepod unstrapped it and opened the top.

Out tumbled the princess.

Bindlepod sighed. "What are you doing here?"

"Going to Nilbog," said Princess Violet, picking herself up from the road and brushing the dust from her backside.

"You most certainly are not," said Bindlepod.

For a moment, Violet considered telling him that if he tried to take her back she would claim he had kidnapped her to begin with, then had a change of heart, but only after he had done unspeakable things to her, and so on. She decided against this tactic, mostly because she had always hated the girls who acted that way in stories. It was a cheap way to get what you wanted.

"Well, if it's not Nilbog, it will be somewhere else," she said. "I'm not going back, and you can't make me."

"She's got a point," put in the frog. "Even if you took her back, they probably wouldn't let her in on account of...well, you know."

"I know," said Bindlepod. "The smell."

This conversation alarmed Violet considerably. Despite her wish to escape from the palace, she had done so assuming that she could return any time she wanted. "What are you talking about?" she demanded.

"The smell," said Bindlepod again. "You've been in my saddlebag for three hours already. By now the smell will have worn deep into your skin. Your parents may have put up with goblin smell on me, but they certainly aren't going to accept it on their daughter."

"Well, I'll just wash," said Princess Violet indignantly.

"Goblin smell doesn't come off with mere soap and water," said Bindlepod. He sounded offended at the thought.

"What does it take?" asked the princess, indignation turning to alarm.

"A dip in Fire Lake, if I remember correctly," said the frog.

"Good grief!" cried Bindlepod. "We can't expect her to do that! There's no telling how she might come out."

"What does that mean?" asked Violet, more alarmed than ever.

"Never mind," said Bindlepod. "Be quiet. I have to think."

"Never an easy task for him," put in the frog with a smirk.

"Shut up!" snapped the goblin.

The frog winked one melon-size eye at Violet, but said nothing more.

An hour later Bindlepod stood, stretched (a movement that created an odd series of pops, clicks, and crackles), and said, "We're turning back. Even if the princess's parents don't let her in, we have to let them know what's happened. If we don't, they're going to assume I stole her anyway, and before you know it we'll be at war all over again."

He climbed onto the frog. "Come on, princess, hop up here behind me. And no complaints from **you** about the extra load," he added, digging his heels into the frog's side to get him moving again. "If you'd said something to begin with, we wouldn't be in this mess."

They had only traveled about a third of the way back to the castle when they found the king coming in their direction. His brow was dark, he was dressed for war, and he had a hundred knights riding behind him.

Violet, who had not expected this, was both frightened and thrilled.

"Hail, King Vitril!" said Bindlepod, springing down from the frog.

The king said nothing.

"I have your daughter," said Bindlepod, gesturing to where Violet was perched atop the frog. "I was just bringing her home."

"Why did you take her to begin with?" demanded the king.

"He didn't!" cried Violet, scrambling down from the frog's back. "He didn't, Papa! I snuck into his saddle bags, because I wanted to see the world. I longed for new sights and sounds and smells. I'm sorry if I caused you any worry."

She raced to her father's side. But when the king dismounted to embrace her, he made a terrible face.

"Euuuw!" he cried. "You stink of goblin!"

And, indeed, the princess—who had once smelled of apple blossoms and spiced muffins—now had a distinctly strange odor about her. A quick sniff was more apt to remind you of wind-wild October nights and distant caverns than of dew on the grass and freshly washed laundry. A deeper inhalation of the scent was apt to bring to mind secrets better left unspoken.

The king looked at his daughter sadly. "I can't take you home like this. It would never do, not at all."

Violet's eyes widened in astonishment. "You can't be serious, Papa!"

"Alas, I am utterly serious," said her father. "What do you think your mother would say if she got a whiff of you now? The smell would break her heart quite in half." He turned toward Bindlepod. "Had you taken my daughter against her will, I would have cleft you in two, fed both halves to my dogs, then ridden in vengeance against your people. As she chose to go with you, I leave her to you."

With that he bade his daughter farewell, told her to be wise and good and to write as often as she was able, apologized for not embracing her, then climbed onto his horse and rode for home.

The astonished princess stood in the road, blinking back tears as she watched her father gallop away. It is, after all, one thing to run away from home. It is another thing entirely to run away and discover that they don't want you back.

She stood watching until the army had galloped completely out of sight, and neither Bindlepod nor the frog said a word to disturb her. Finally, when she could no longer see even the smallest cloud of dust from beneath the horse's hooves, she sighed and turned her face toward Nilbog.

Bindlepod still said nothing, simply held out one clammy hand and helped her onto the frog's back.

Toward evening on the third day of their journey, they came to an opening in the side of a hill.

"This is the entrance to Nilbog," said the goblin. "Are you still sure you want to go in with us?"

Violet looked at the dark hole, then glanced back toward her old home. After a while she nodded. "I'll go in."

Bindlepod and Violet dismounted, for the entrance was too low for the frog to carry them through. He took the princess by the hand, and led the way into the cavern.

It was darker than Violet had imagined possible.

"How can you see?" she asked, as she picked her way forward on the stony path. She was holding tight to the goblin's hand, and secretly terrified that if he let go of her she would never find her way to the light again.

"There's enough light, replied Bindlepod. "It's just that your eyes are too small."

"It gets better soon, anyway," added the frog.

And indeed, after another five or ten minutes, she could see a dim glow ahead of them, which was like food to her light starved eyes.

The glow turned out to come from some greenish mushrooms that grew along the cavern walls. It was sufficiently bright to let her walk with confidence, though not bright enough to cast shadows. Violet noticed that it gave an odd tinge to Bindlepod and his frog. Then she held up her hand and realized that the light made her look strange, too.

Narrow stone bridges took them across dark chasms. Winding passages with many tunnels branching to the sides carried them deeper into the earth. And at last they arrived at the entrance to Nilbog—or, at least, one of the entrances. It was carved in the shape of a great mouth.

Within that mouth, barring their path forward, were dozens of spiky stone "teeth."

An enormously fat creature who looked something like a goblin, though not entirely, was leaning against one side of the entrance, cleaning his navel with a sharpened bone. When he saw them coming he opened his yellow eyes a little wider, but made no movement.

Bindlepod stopped a respectful distance away. He stuck out his long tongue by way of salute, then said, "Greetings, Frelg. I return from the land above."

"Not alone, I notice," said Frelg, shifting his huge bulk to the side just a bit.

"Princess Violet wished to see our world," said Bindlepod, not referring to the fact that her father had banned her from returning home.

"Come here," said Frelg. "Not you, princess! Just Bindlepod."

The goblin stepped forward. Frelg lurched to his feet, and the princess shuddered to see that he was twice the height of Bindlepod. Bending forward—not easy, given his enormous bulk—he began to sniff.

Sniff. Sniff sniff.

A frown of disgust, which Violet found truly terrifying.

"Whooie!" cried Frelg. "You stink! You smell of quiet rooms and cramped hearts, tiny minds and tiny places. You smell small and nasty."

Hearing this, the princess grew nervous. "Does that mean he's not going to let us in?" she whispered to the frog in a quivering voice.

"If I sent you away, then I would have a tiny little mind too, wouldn't I?" asked Frelg, who had heard her in spite of her caution. (No surprise, really, given the size of his ears.) "You may enter. Just don't be surprised if people are not particularly happy to smell you."

With that he wobbled his way from in front of the gate, and gestured for them to enter. At the same time the stone teeth slid out of sight, leaving the path clear.

With Bindlepod leading the way, they passed through the gate, into a long, dark tunnel that led down at a steep angle. After about an hour the tunnel widened once more and they came out on a ledge overlooking a stone city. It was lit all about by that same glowing fungus.

Bindlepod sighed with pleasure. "Home."

Not for me, thought the princess sadly, wondering what was to become of her.

They followed the stone path, which was sometimes dry, sometimes slimy, down to the level of the city. As they drew closer to the city, the path widened into a road. Now Bindlepod and Violet climbed back onto the frog. As they hopped toward the city they occasionally saw other travelers, goblins all. Some of them merely waved. Others, recognizing Bindlepod, greeted them with respectful bows. But all of them, even the goblins who bowed, stayed at the far side of the road, sniffing suspiciously.

Their reception at the court of the goblin king was no more encouraging than Violet's last interview with her father had been. The goblin king—a huge creature with leering eyes, fantastical warts in several colors, and a tongue as long as his arm—was sympathetic, but disturbed. "I am glad to have you back, Bindlepod," he said. "And your young lady friend is welcome to stay as well, of course. But really…"

With that, his voice trailed off, and his eyes rolled around, as if he were searching for exactly the right word.

The goblin queen, who had been plucking out a tune on the back of a strangely-scaled creature, looked up and said, "Your father is troubled, son, on account of the princess's smell."

"Son?" asked Violet in surprise. "You didn't tell me you were the **prince** of Nilbog!"

Bindlepod shrugged.

"And what's wrong with my smell anyway?" continued Violet indignantly. "My father thought I smelled too much like a goblin to go home. So I would think I would smell just fine for you."

"You do smell of goblin," said the king wearily. "But you also smell of the world above, of something lost and distant that it pains us to remember. We will give you shelter, of course. But I fear my people will not be jolly in your presence."

"I fear not," said the queen, striking a particularly melancholy chord on the back of the lizard-thing.

Time proved the queen to be correct. Though everyone in Nilbog was polite to Violet and Bindlepod—at least, polite by goblin standards—no one seemed terribly **comfortable** in the presence of either of them.

The result, not surprisingly, was that Violet and Bindlepod spent more and more time alone together.

The result of that situation **was** surprising, at least to those who think goblins and humans are more different than they really are.

Bindlepod and Violet fell in love.

It happened—or, at least, they became aware it had happened —one afternoon when they were sitting beside an underground river, basking in the gentle light of the glowing fungus. Bindlepod had just caught a fish, and was trying to convince the princess to try a bite.

"Princesses don't eat raw fish!" she said tartly.

"You have done many things princesses are not supposed to," replied Bindlepod, speaking a little tartly himself.

Violet pursed her lips in exasperation, but couldn't think of a good answer for this. "All right," she said at last. "I'll try a bite. One. A small one."

Bindlepod cut a bit of flesh from the fish with his knife, then took it between his fingers and held it out to the princess. As she bent forward to take it in her mouth Bindlepod found himself, much to his own surprise, running his finger gently along her lower lip. Though he drew his hand back in shock, the bigger shock was the one that had passed between them, a jolt of recognition that made it impossible for them to ignore what their hearts had known for a long time.

From that moment on they knew that they were in love.

"I can't say we were made for each other," said Bindlepod, later that same afternoon. Violet was reclining in his arms, dreamily gazing at the waterfall. "Even so," he continued, "I am glad we found each other."

"And why weren't we made for each other?" she asked, reaching up to pat his sallow cheek.

"Well, my stinky little sweetie, our smells are, to say the least, incompatible."

"Oh, fiddle," said Violet. "You smell fine to me."

"And I've grown quite fond of your odor as well," he replied —which was not what you would call a ringing endorsement, but satisfied the princess nonetheless.

But as the days and weeks wore on, Violet began to realize that Bindlepod was right. Though they were utterly happy in each other's company, the world around them—or, to be more specific, the other goblins—were most uncomfortable with their relationship. And, though Bindlepod claimed this did not bother him, Violet was perceptive enough to see that he missed the company of other goblins, missed their easy teasing, their wild energy, their bizarre games.

Finally she decided to seek help for their situation, and, after a bit of asking around, made her way to the wisest of goblins, an incredibly ugly female of astonishing age. Her name was Flegmire, and she lived in a cave at the edge of Nilbog.

Violet did not tell Bindlepod where she was going, simply asked if she could borrow the frog for a time.

Bindlepod agreed, on the condition that she not be gone for long.

Violet and the frog hopped away.

Flegmire's cave was deep and dank, and hung about with moss. Snakes lounged around the entrance, as well as some other creatures that were like snakes, only stranger.

Standing at the front of the cave, Violet called, "May I enter, O Wisest of the Wise?"

"Yeah, yeah, come on in," replied a gravelly voice.

Picking her way around assorted slimy creatures, Violet entered the cave.

Flegmire sat on the floor, which meant that her knees were considerably higher than her ears. She was playing with a collection of colored rocks that had been carved into various shapes. Violet recognized the game—she had seen the goblin children playing it fairly often—and wondered if coming to see Flegmire had been such a good idea after all.

Her doubts increased when the ancient gobliness held up her hands, cried, "Wait! Wait!," and then farted with such violence that it raised her several inches off the floor.

The smell caused Violet to gasp in shock, and she grabbed a nearby stalactite to keep from falling over. Flegmire, however, sighed in contentment and said, "Well, now that I can think again, tell me what was it you wanted."

Eyes watering, the princess explained her difficulty.

"A sad story," said the gobliness. "But I still do not know what it is you want of me."

"You are the wisest of your kind," said Violet. "Don't you know anything I could do to rid myself of this smell?"

Flegmire hooked a curved green fingernail over her enormous lower lip. "You can't think of anything yourself? No hints you've had along the way?"

The princess started to say "No," then stopped. She swallowed nervously. "Well, Bindlepod's frog did mention something about…Fire Lake."

Flegmire spread her arms as if the whole thing had been the essence of simplicity. "Well, there you go! If you already knew about that, why did you come here to bother me? I've got games to play, you know."

"But the frog said the lake would change me," said the princess.

"There are worse things that can happen," said Flegmire. "Not changing isn't so good, either."

"But *how* will it change me?"

"What do I look like?" asked Flegmire. "A prophet? You want to get rid of the smell, you go in the lake. How you come out, that's no concern of mine."

"Well, can you at least tell me how to get there?" asked Violet.

Flegmire smiled. "Sure," she said. "That's easy."

That night—night and day being pretty much the same in Nilbog—Violet rose from her bed in the little stone cottage behind the palace grounds that the goblin king had given her to live in. She put on her riding clothes, then slipped out the door, with the intention of saddling up the frog and riding off to Fire Lake. But she hadn't gone more than ten paces from her door when Bindlepod stepped from behind an enormous mushroom and said, "Going somewhere, my darling?"

Violet jumped and gasped. "What are you doing here?" she cried. Then, spotting the frog, who was crouched on the far side of the mushroom, she hissed, "Blabbermouth!"

The frog merely shrugged.

"He does have his loyalties," said Bindlepod. "As do I. If you are going to do this thing, then so am I."

"You can't!" cried the princess.

"Piffle," said Bindlepod. "There's no point in only one of us taking the risk. If we're going to change, we might as well change together."

And nothing the princess could say would dissuade him.

So together they rode to Fire Lake, a journey that took them ever deeper into the earth.

At the end of the second day they crossed a field of bubbling hot springs, and the frog narrowly escaped scalding his rear quarters when a geyser erupted behind him. "You're going to owe me a lot of Junebugs when this is over," he said bitterly.

At the end of the third day, the horizon began to glow. Nervously, they climbed to the top of a slippery hill. Ahead lay Fire Lake, its flaming waves lapping idly against its scorched shore.

Violet tightened her hand on Bindlepod's arm. "I'm frightened," she whispered.

"You should be," croaked the frog, who was standing next to them.

"Whatever happens, we're in this together," said Bindlepod.

They started forward again.

In a few hours they were standing at the edge of Fire Lake. The blazing waves hissed and crackled as they rolled against the shore.

Bindlepod took Violet in his arms. He held her close, burying his nose in her neck.

"You know," he murmured, "I like the way you smell."

"And I like the way you smell," she replied.

"Then what are you going to do this for?" cried the frog, who had been growing more alarmed as they approached the lake. "Are you out of your minds? What do you care what the others think? It's none of their damn business! You love each other the way you are. Who are you going to change for?"

Violet blinked. Bindlepod stared at her. "Do you care if they think we stink?" he asked gently.

"I don't care if you don't care," said the princess.

They both began to laugh.

Princess Violet and Prince Bindlepod never did step into Fire Lake.

What they did do was build a home for themselves in a giant oak tree halfway between the gates of her father's kingdom and the entrance to Nilbog. Part of the home was in the branches, and part beneath the roots. It smelled of sky and leaves, of stone and soil, and they loved it nearly as much as they loved each other.

Though they never went back to either kingdom, their home was always open to anyone who cared to visit, and who would take them as they were.

As the years passed Violet and Bindlepod had seven children, who brought a great deal of jolliness to the home in the tree. They were an odd group: goggle-eyed, pale-skinned, and full of mischief. They adored the frog, who taught them to swim, and always called him "uncle."

The frog adored the children, too, and often said to visitors, "They're really sweet." Then he would chuckle deep in his throat and add, "For a bunch of little stinkers."

I, Earthling

It's not easy being the only kid in your class who doesn't have six arms and an extra eye in the middle of your forehead. But that's the way it's been for me since my father dragged me here to Kwarkis.

It's all supposed to be a great honor, of course. Dad is a career diplomat, and being chosen as the first ambassador to another planet was (as he has told me more times than I can count) the crowning achievement of his career.

Me, I just want to go home—though to hear Dad tell it, Kwarkis **is** home. I'm afraid he's fallen in love with the place. I guess I can't blame him for that. What with the singing purple forests, the water and air being sparkling clean (which **really** makes me feel like I'm on another planet) and those famous nights with three full moons, this truly is a beautiful place.

But it's not home. The people aren't **my** people. Most of the time I just feel lonely and stupid.

According to Dad, the first feeling is reasonable, the second silly. "You've got cause to feel lonely, Jacob," he'll say, standing over me. "And I'm sorry for that. But you have *no* reason to feel stupid."

A fat lot he knows. He doesn't have to go to school with kids who can do things three times as fast as he can, because they have three times as many hands. Even worse, they're just basically smarter than I am. **All** of them. I am the dumbest one in the class—which isn't easy to cope with, since I was always one of the smartest kids back home.

3

I'll never forget my first day at school here. My father led me in and stood me next to Darva Preet, the teacher. She smiled that strange Kwarkissian smile, reached down one of her six arms to take my hand, then turned to the room and cried: "Class! Class! Come to order!

I want you to meet our new student—the alien you've all heard so much about!"

I began to blush. It was still hard to think of myself as an alien. But of course, that's what I was: The only kid from Earth on a planet full of people that I had considered aliens until I got here. Now that I was on Kwarkis, the situation was reversed. Now I was the alien.

The kids all turned toward me and stared, blinking their middle eyes the way they do when they are really examining something. I stared back, which is what I had been taught to do on the trip here. After a moment one of them dug a finger into his nose, pulled out an enormous booger, then popped it into his mouth and began to chew. The sight made my stomach lurch, but I tried not to let my disgust show on my face. Fior Langis, the Kwarkissian diplomat who had been in charge of preparing me for this day, had taught me that Kwarkissians feel very differently about bodily functions than we do.

"Greetings," I said in Kwarkissian, which I had learned through sleep-tapes on my way here. "I am glad to be part of the class. I hope we will have good times together."

Everyone smiled in delight, surprised that I knew their language. Then they all farted in unison. The sound was incredible — a rumbling so massive that for a moment I thought a small bomb had gone off. I jumped, even though Fior Langis had warned me that this was the way Kwarkissians show their approval. What she **hadn't** told me about, prepared me for, was the tremendous odor.

My eyes began to water.

I had a hard time breathing.

I fell over in a dead faint.

When I woke, I was in the hospital.

Since then the kids have referred to me as *Kilu-gwan*, which means "The Delicate One." I find this pretty embarrassing, since I was one of the toughest kids in class back on Earth. It doesn't really make that much difference here on Kwarkis, where no one fights. But I don't plan to live here forever, and I'll need to be tough when I get home to Earth. Back there you have to be tough to survive.

3

The only one who doesn't call me Kilu-gwan is Fifka Dworkis, who is the closest thing I have to a friend here. Fifka was the first one who talked to me after my embarrassing introduction to the class.

"Do not worry about it, Jay-cobe," he said, pronouncing my Earth name as well as he could with his strange oval mouth and snakelike green tongue. "The others will not hold your oversensitive olfactory organ against you."

He put his arm around my shoulder. Then he put another arm around my ribs, and another one around my waist!

I tried not to squirm, because I knew he was just being friendly. But it sure felt **weird**.

To tell the truth, it wasn't just the weirdness that bothered me. It was also that I felt pretty inadequate having only one arm to offer back. Kwarkissian friends are always walking down the street arm in arm in arm in arm in arm in arm, and I wondered if Fifka felt cheated, only getting one arm back.

Whether or not he felt cheated, he doesn't spend a lot of time with me. He's always kind when he sees me, but he has never stayed overnight, or anything like that. Sometimes I suspect that the reason Fifka is nice to me is that his mother has told him to be. She's part of the Kwarkissian diplomatic team that works with Dad.

The only real friend I have here is my double-miniature panda, Ralph J. Bear, who I brought with me from Earth. In case you've been living on another planet (ha, ha) the new double miniature breeds are only about six inches long. Ralph can easily fit right in my hand.

I like to watch him strolling around my desk while I do my homework. (Yes, I still have homework; I guess some things are the same no matter where you go!) And he's so neat and clean that Dad doesn't object to my letting him eat off my plate at the table. I love him so much I can hardly stand it.

The Chinese ambassador gave me Ralph at the big going-away party the United Nations threw for Dad and me. The gift was a surprise to everyone, since the Chinese are still pretty much holding on to the miniatures.

(Of course, between the fact that there are so few of them available, and the fact that they are so devastatingly cute, there is an enormous demand for them. People were wildly jealous of me for having Ralph, but I figure I ought to get **some** benefit from being a diplomat's son. I mean, none of those people who were so jealous of Ralph were being dragged off to live on another planet!)

As it turns out, Ralph is one reason that the Kwarkissians made contact with Earth in the first place. Well, not Ralph J. Bear himself. But the breeding program he came from was part of a major last ditch effort to save the pandas. According to Dad, the Kwarkissians have been monitoring us for a long time. His contacts say that one thing that made them decide we were worth meeting was when we started taking our biosphere seriously enough to really work at saving endangered species, such as pandas.

Anyway, Ralph is the only real friend I have here. So you can imagine how horrified I was when I was asked to give him away.

"What am I going to do, Ralph?" I said, trying not to cry.

The genetic engineers who created the miniatures have enhanced their intelligence, too. Ralph J. Bear is very bright, and he always knows when something is bothering me. Waddling across my desk, he stood on his hind legs and lifted his arms for me to pick him up.

I set him on my shoulder, and he nestled into my neck. Normally that would have made me feel a lot better. Now it had the reverse effect, because it only made me more aware of how much I would miss him if I had to give him away.

3

I've been avoiding talking about how I got into this mess, because it is so embarrassing, but I suppose I had better explain it if any of the rest of this is going to make sense.

It started while we were having a diplomatic dinner here at the house.

According to my father, diplomatic dinners are very important. He says much of the major work in his profession happens around dinner tables, rather than at office desks.

The big thing he is working on right now is a treaty that has to do with who gets to deal with Earth. See, what most people back home don't know yet is the Kwarkissians aren't the only ones out here. But since they were the first to make contact with us, according to the rules of the OSFA (Organization of Space-Faring Races), they get to **control** contact with us for the next fifty years.

My father was not amused when he found this out. He thinks the Kwarkissians shouldn't be able to do that. He feels they're treating Earth like a colony, and that it should be <u>our</u> choice who has contact with us. But he doesn't want to make the Kwarkissians angry. For one thing, they've been very good to us. For another, we suspect they could probably turn us (by "us" I mean the entire planet) into cosmic dust without much trouble.

So the situation is very touchy.

Dad is dealing with this other planet called—well, I can't actually write down what it's called, because no one ever says the name; it's against their religion, or something. Anyway, this planet that shall remain nameless is interested in making contact with us. But to do so they have to go through the Kwarkissians.

Dad is all in favor of it; he says the more trading partners Earth has, the better. So he was throwing this dinner, where we were going to get together with a bunch of Kwarkissians, including Fifka's mom, and a bunch of dudes from the nameless planet, including their head guy, whose name is Nnnnnn.

Dad asked me to be part of the dinner group because (a) people usually want to meet your kids, no matter what planet you come from, and besides (b) it's good diplomacy, because it usually softens people up. I know Dad felt a little guilty about using me like this, but I told him not to, since I am glad to be of some help—especially here on Kwarkis, where I feel like such a doof.

Diplomatic dinners are always a little tricky because you want to keep from offending anyone, which is not so easy when you have people from three different cultures sitting down to eat together. This is true even on Earth, so you can imagine what it was like for us to have representatives from not three countries, but three **planets**.

"Look, this is going to be a delicate situation," said Dad. "The Kwarkissians want to have you around tonight. They were quite insistent on it, in fact; they're very fond of you, you know. But Nnnnnn and his group don't like children—partly because in their culture childhood barely exists."

"What do you mean, 'childhood barely exists'?"

Dad frowned. "On Nnnnnn's planet children are hatched. They come out of the egg looking much like two-year-olds do on Earth, and mature very rapidly thereafter. Even with that, they're pretty much kept out of sight by their nurses and teachers until they're ready to join adult society. On Nnnnnn's world someone who looks as old as you do might well have gained adult status, which is a thing they take very seriously. They are going to consider you not as a child, but as an equal —so for heaven's sake be careful."

He handed me a computer printout on their culture and told me to read it. "There's a lot here you should know," he said. "Study it. The main thing to remember is, whatever else you do, don't compliment them on anything they show you."

He got up to leave the room. Stopping at the door, he added, "You'd better keep Ralph locked up for the night, too."

Then he told me how he wanted me to dress, and hurried off to tend to some details for the dinner.

3

I don't know about you, but when someone hands me something and tells me to read it, my mind immediately starts thinking of other things I need to do instead. It's not that I didn't want to learn about the new aliens; it's just that my brain rebels at being told what to do. So I put the printout aside and started to do something else.

A few minutes later my message receptor beeped. I pushed the Receive button, and a holographic image of Fifka, about four inches tall, appeared in the center of my desk. Ralph skittled away in surprise —he still hadn't gotten used to the Kwarkissian version of a phone call. I pushed the Send button, so that Fifka could see me as well.

We started to talk about the dinner. He was excited because his mom was coming. I almost got the feeling he was jealous of her. That surprised me. When I thought about it, I realized that I had never actually invited Fifka to come visit; I had only thought about it, and waited for a good opportunity. Maybe he was more genuinely friendly than I had thought.

We got talking about something that had happened at school, and then about a game we were both working on, and by the time we were done I had pretty much forgotten about the printout Dad had given me. Next I did a little homework. Then I spent some time fooling around with Ralph J. Bear.

Before I knew it, it was time to get dressed.

That was when I noticed the printout lying on my bed.

I sighed. The thing had to be twenty pages long. No time to read that much before dinner. I would just have to be on my best behavior.

The flaw in that plan, of course, was that what one culture considers good behavior can get you in a lot of trouble somewhere else...

3

The dinner party consisted of Dad, me, three Kwarkissians (including Fifka's mother), and three beings from the planet that shall remain nameless. These guys only had two arms, which was sort of a relief, but they were bright green and seven feet tall.

The first part of the dinner went pretty well, I thought, if you set aside the fact that eating dinner with a bunch of Kwarkissians is like going to a symphony in gas-minor.

I had had a long talk about this with Fifka one day.

"Biology is biology," he said. "What is it that you people find so bad about it, anyway? Good heavens, think what life would be like if your bodies **didn't** process all the stuff you take in; if your bodies **didn't** do their jobs! The important choices have to do with the mind and the heart, Jay-cobe, not the stomach and the intestines. I hope this won't offend you, but most of us feel that if your people paid more attention to ideas and less to biological by-products, you would all be better off."

When he put it that way, it was hard to answer.

Still, it was a strange thing to sit down to dinner with some of the most important people on the planet and have them punctuate their conversation with gaseous emissions.

I had no idea how the guys from the planet that dares not speak its name were taking all this, since they barely talked at all. But they've been dealing with the Kwarkissians for centuries, so presumably they cope with it just fine.

The real trouble started **after** dinner, when we all went into the water room for dessert.

Every home on Kwarkis has a water room. It's one of my favorite things about living here. Basically it's a huge room with a multi-level stone floor. Clear water runs down one wall then flows through stream beds into the pools and ponds that dot the floor. There are even a few small waterfalls. Some of the ponds have fish—well, they're not really fish, but that's close enough for you to understand. Also, there are a lot of plants and a few flying things that are sort of like birds.

The Kwarkissians spend a lot of their free time in the water rooms; they're a great place to chat and relax.

Well, we went there for dessert—at least, Dad and I were having dessert (gooey chocolate pie, to be precise). The Kwarkissians were chewing purple leaves, which was what they liked to do after dinner. The guys from Planet X were just sort of watching us. I got the impression they didn't do much of anything for fun on that planet.

While we were sitting there, Ralph J. Bear wandered in. I flinched, remembering that Dad had told me to keep Ralph in my room that night. I glanced at Dad. He didn't seem upset, but this didn't give me any useful information; Dad's training as a diplomat makes him *very* good at masking his real feelings. Certainly his face gave me no clue as to the kind of trouble I was about to get myself into.

When our guests saw Ralph they all wanted to pick him up—which seems to be an almost universal reaction to the little guy. At Dad's suggestion, I showed him around. Everyone liked him; even the guys from the planet with a secret name seemed to lighten up at the sight of him.

A little while later Nnnnnn tucked one long green hand under his robe and pulled out something that looked like a picture frame, the kind that you can open like a book. He opened it, looked inside, nodded, smiled in a sad kind of way, then started to pass it around. Each person who looked into it first appeared startled, and then— well, a strange look would cross his or her face. Sometimes it was happy, sometimes sad, but in all cases it was intense.

I couldn't wait for it to come to me.

I was sitting next to Fifka's mother. I had taken off my shoes, and we both had our legs dangling in the water. (Kwarkissians don't wear shoes, since the soles of their two-toed feet are like leather.)

When the thing from the nameless guys came to Fifka's mom she looked into it and sighed. Then she passed it on to me.

Dad moved forward, as if to stop me from taking it, then settled back against the mossy stone on which he was sitting. He looked worried, a slight slip in his diplomatic mask. That should have been a warning to me. But I was too eager to see what was inside the frame, so I ignored the expression on his face.

Big mistake.

Taking the frame, I opened it, and cried out in shock when I saw my mother looking out at me. Mom had died six years earlier, in a brush war in Asia she had been covering for *The New York Times,* and I mostly tried not to think about her, because it hurt too much. Now she was smiling at me as if she had never been gone.

I closed my eyes.

"The heartmirror sends a signal that generates an image from the brain," said Nnnnnn. "It pulls from the mind that which is deeply buried—that which you love, or fear, or wish most to see. What you see in the frame comes from yourself."

I opened my eyes again. My mother's face was still there, smiling at me. "It's wonderful," I said.

Nnnnnn's eyes narrowed in his green face. He made a sharp gesture, almost as if he were angry. "It is yours," he said gruffly.

My stomach tightened as I remembered Dad's warning: "Don't compliment them on anything they show you."

Suddenly I wished I had read that printout. What had I just done?

The room was silent, a heavy kind of silence that I found very frightening.

"Thank you," I said at last, nodding toward Nnnnnn.

More silence, then Nnnnnn said, "Your pet is wonderful, as well."

"Thank you," I said again.

For a time the only sound in the water room was that of the water rolling down the wall, across the floor. The tension among the beings who sat around me was distinctly uncomfortable. I got the sense that they were waiting for something. I also had an idea **what,** but I tried to convince myself that I was wrong.

Finally Fifka's mother leaned over and whispered, "Nnnnnn is waiting for you to offer him your pet."

I felt as if she had hit me in the stomach.

Nnnnnn just sat there, staring at me.

Jumping up, I grabbed Ralph and ran from the room.

3

I was lying on my bed, holding Ralph and staring up through my ceiling—which I had set on "clear"—when my father came in. His face was dark with anger.

I ignored him and continued to stare at the moons. They were all out, one at full, one at the half, and one no more than a tiny crescent.

"Jacob, did you read that printout?" he asked.

I shook my head. A tear escaped from the corner of my eye. I was half embarrassed at crying, half hopeful that it might get me out of this mess.

Dad sighed.

"Why can't we just give Nnnnnn back the heartmirror?" I asked, trying to fight down the lump in my throat.

"If we do that, it will mark us as unworthy trading partners. Jacob, we have to follow through on this. It is a matter of honor for Nnnnnn and his people."

"So you want me to give Ralph to this guy just because he thinks I'm an adult and I got caught in some weird ritual that I didn't even know was going on? Forget it!"

I had overplayed my hand.

"If you had read the information I gave you, you would have been well aware of the custom," Dad snapped back. "Even ignoring that, you knew you were supposed to keep Ralph in your room. If you had done as I asked, none of this would have happened!"

He had me. I decided the best tactic was to ignore that fact and move on.

"Well, they can just go back to the nameless place they came from," I said defiantly. "I'm not giving Ralph to Nnnnnn. For all I know the guy just wants to eat him!"

Ralph whined and snuggled closer, and I felt a twinge of guilt. No one is sure just how much human language the little guys can understand. I hoped I hadn't scared him.

"Jacob, listen to me. Forging a good relationship with Nnnnnn and his group is—well, it could be a matter of life and death. The implications for Earth are overwhelming, and we simply can't afford a diplomatic incident right now. I'm sorry, but I have to insist…"

I knew he meant it.

I also knew that I was not going to give Ralph to some weirdo from a nameless planet.

Which meant I also knew what I *was* going to do.

I remembered what Fifka had said about the important choices, that they had to do with the mind and the heart.

My mind and my heart were both telling me the same thing right now. I didn't like what they were saying, but when I thought about it, it wasn't a choice at all. Running away was my only option.

3

The trees were singing their night song as I slipped into the forest. The sky was darker now because the full moon had set, leaving only the two partial moons.

A buttersnake slithered around the base of one of the trees and stared at me in astonishment. (It wasn't really a snake, of course—that's just what Dad and I call them. They're bright yellow, and can spread themselves out so flat they look like melted butter. They can go from flat to round in a half second when they are startled or angry. I tried not to make this one angry.)

Ralph J. Bear clung to my neck, looking around with bright eyes and whimpering once or twice when shadows moved too close to us.

"It's all right, Ralph," I whispered. "We'll find someplace where we can hide until this blows over. Or maybe we'll hide out forever," I added, thinking that I couldn't see any good reason to go back at this point. I was tired of being the alien, the weird one, the outcast.

I remembered Toby, and wondered if this was how he had felt.

Toby had been the dumbest kid in my class, back in the last school I had been in before Dad and I moved to Kwarkis. He was okay, but he just wasn't with it. Some of the kids were mean to him, which I thought was stupid. Most of us pretty much ignored him.

I felt bad about that now. I wanted to go back and put an arm around him, like Fifka had put three arms around me, and tell him that I liked him. Which was true, now that I thought about it. He was a nice kid and never did anything to hurt anyone. I had always figured that he didn't add anything to the class, but now that I thought about it, I realized that just his being there had been important. He was part of who we were, and we would have been different without him.

I wondered how the kids in Darva Preet's class felt about me. Did they think about me at all? Would they miss me, now that I was gone —or would they just be relieved that they didn't have a two-armed gimp around to deal with anymore? Did I make the class more or less than it had been when I came to it?

I was so wound up in my thoughts that I hardly noticed where I was going, hardly noticed Nnnnnn standing in my path until I almost bumped into him.

"Do you think this is wise?" he asked, his voice deep and solemn. He didn't sound mean, but there was something very frightening about him. I think it was simply that he was so sure of himself.

I stared at him, unable to speak.

He knelt in front of me and looked directly into my eyes.

"Are you an adult, or are you a child?" he asked.

My throat was dry, my stomach tightening into a knot of fear and despair. I remembered what my father had told me about the way Nnnnnn and his people felt about kids. Running away was one thing —Dad might have been able to skinny his way out of the mess without me around. (Though when I stopped to think about it, I realized he would have turned that forest inside out to find me, no matter what it meant to the deal.) Face-to-face defiance of the diplomat from another planet was something else altogether.

The silence lay thick between us. Nnnnnn continued to stare into my eyes. I realized that there was no way I could lie to him.

"Are you an adult, or are you a child?" he repeated.

I swallowed hard, then told him the truth.

"I'm both."

Nnnnnn nodded, which seemed to mean the same thing on his planet as on ours. "I suspected as much. Come with me."

He turned and walked away. I could have run in the other direction, but I didn't. I followed him.

We left the forest. The purple trees were singing the song they sing when the sky is clear. I cradled Ralph in my arms.

Nnnnnn led me to the bank of a stream. We sat and looked up at the stars.

I knew what he was showing me, or at least I thought I did. He was showing me the community that Earth was being invited to join, or might be invited to join, if I didn't screw things up.

Are you an adult, or are you a child?

The question burned in my ears. My father had given me the printout. He had told me to keep Ralph in my room. He had warned me not to compliment our guests on anything they showed us.

Every bit of the trouble I was in now was my own fault.

"Will you take good care of Ralph?" I asked, my voice thin and whispery, like dry leaves sliding against one another.

Nnnnnn was silent for a moment. At first I thought he was trying to decide how to answer the question. Later, I realized that what he was debating was whether to answer it at all.

Finally he nodded.

"I will," he said.

Trying hard not to cry, to keep the part of me that was an adult in charge, I lifted Ralph from my neck. Pressing him to my cheek, I wiped my tears against his fur, then passed him to Nnnnnn.

I wanted to say, "You don't know what this means." I wanted to say, "I am so lonely, and he is my closest friend." I wanted to say, "I hate you."

I said nothing.

Nnnnnn took Ralph from my hands. He placed him in his lap and stroked his fur. The water rippled past Nnnnnn's green feet. The stars filled the sky, the clear sky of Kwarkis, in an abundance we never see through the soiled air of Earth.

"Over there, that way, is my home," said Nnnnnn. "It is a sacred place, of great beauty. I do not like to be away from it."

I wondered why he was telling me this, then realized that it was a kind of gift. In saying this he was speaking to me as one adult to another.

He turned to look directly at me. "We have things that will bring your world much benefit, Jacob—things of beauty, things of value. We have medical technology, for example, that will mean that many who might have died in the next year will live instead."

I thought for a moment. "If I had known that, I would have given you Ralph without so much fuss. I would have hated you for it, but I would have given him to you."

"Of course you would have. That was not the issue. We are a trading race. It was not your compassion for your own kind that mattered to us, it was your honor. Can we trust you? That was what we needed to know."

"Can you?" I asked, my voice small. "I had to be pushed."

He stopped me. "Your impulses are good," he said softly.

We sat in silence for a moment. Finally Nnnnnn moved his green hand in a circle, indicating the stream, the forest, the city. "I know you feel like an alien here," he said softly. "But that is because you are thinking too small. Yes, you are from another world. So am I. If we think of ourselves only as citizens of those worlds, then here we are indeed the aliens. But think in larger terms, Jacob." He swept his hand in a half circle across the sky. "Look at the grandness of it. You are a part of that, as well. Your planet, my planet, Kwarkis—they are all a part of something bigger. If you think in terms of planets, then here you will always be an alien. But you and your people can be more, if you choose. You can be citizens of the universe. If you see yourself that way, you will never be an alien, no matter where you go. You will simply be—one of us."

Lifting Ralph from his lap, he handed him back to me.

I looked at him.

"It was not necessary that I **have** the animal," he said. "What was important was that you fulfill your responsibility to me. I am glad that you did. It will mean much for your world."

He put his hand on my shoulder.

Ralph snuggled into the crook of my arm and went to sleep.

The stars shimmered above us.

I stared out at them, wondering how many I would visit.

3

Guardian of Memory

A Tale from the Unicorn Chronicles

The banging at the door woke Grimwold, keeper of the Unicorn Chronicles, from his nap.

Naturally, this made the old dwarf even more crotchety than usual, and he grumbled mightily as he headed down the long, wood-paneled tunnel that led to the outside world.

The banging continued.

"I'm coming!" he shouted as he stumped along. "I'm **coming!**"

The banging went on, unabated. He could tell from the sound that it was made by a hoof.

"Bang, bang, bang," he muttered. "Dratted nuisance anyway." When he finally reached the door he yanked it open and snarled, "Well, what do you want?"

The unicorn standing outside looked slightly startled. "It is time for the changing of the guard," he said quietly. "The queen has sent us to escort you to the ceremony."

Grimwold groaned. He had completely forgotten the upcoming ceremony...not that he was about to admit such a lapse to this unicorn.

"All right, all right. No need to kick the door down! I was just getting my things ready. Come in while I finish." He glanced past the unicorn, and sighed when he saw four others waiting behind the one he had been speaking to. "You can **all** come in," he grumbled.

Quietly, on hooves that could cross a field of flowers without bending a stem, the glory of unicorns entered Grimwold's underground home. They passed through the door like a sudden surge of moonlight, all shimmering manes and tails, their horns like spears made of pearl and ice.

"I'll be with you in a moment," said Grimwold. Padding back through the tunnel, which was lit by soft lanterns, past the paintings of unicorns and mermaids and humans who had played a part in Luster's history, the dwarf made his way through the story room to the chronicles themselves. Going to a wooden rack, he selected the proper scroll—though it was hardly necessary, since he knew the story by heart. He stopped in his living quarters long enough to grab a fresh robe and splash some water on his face, then returned to where the unicorns were waiting.

"You're Dreamhorn," he said, looking at the leader. "Son of Ayla Forestfriend. Am I right?"

Dreamhorn nodded. "You keep very good track of us."

"Have to," muttered Grimwold. "Queen insists. Part of the job. Well, what are we waiting for? If I have to do this, I have to. Let's get going."

Dreamhorn looked toward the others and nodded. They turned and went back through the door, which Grimwold had not bothered to close earlier.

The little man was the last to leave. He pulled the door shut behind him, sighed, then climbed onto Dreamhorn's back. Riding a unicorn was supposed to be a great honor. Grimwold, however, preferred to walk. He rode only because he was too old to travel the entire distance to the gathering place on foot, a fact which annoyed him no end.

The journey took two days. Grimwold and the unicorns traveled peacefully, with no sign of any of the delvers that were the unicorns' main enemy in Luster. Autumn was on the land, and the forest was rich with the reds and oranges of the season. The wind moved occasionally through the fallen leaves, stirring and rustling them. The unicorns' silver hooves made no sound at all.

The gathering was to be held at a large grotto, where a high waterfall tumbled into a silver pool. Not all the unicorns of Luster were required to come, of course, but there would be a good number of them—including all who might be chosen to become the new Guardian of Memory.

Though they reached the grotto two days before the ceremony was scheduled to begin, Arabella Skydancer, Queen of the Unicorns, was waiting for them.

Grimwold closed his eyes for just a moment when he spotted the queen. They were old friends, and it hurt him to see how thin she was becoming. Not thin in the sense of gaunt or bony. Her thinness was that of one who was fading away; someone who would, all too soon, leave this world behind. Though he would not want to admit it, Grimwold would miss her.

The queen bowed her head in greeting when she saw him enter the grotto. Grimwold returned the gesture, fighting down a surge of emotion as he remembered all they been through together over the years, the dangers they had faced, the boons she had granted him in return for his service.

"The time has come again," she said softly, when he was standing close by her side.

"As it always does," said Grimwold. "All too swiftly."

"Not too swiftly for the current Guardian," said the queen, sounding amused.

Grimwold nodded. Though twenty-five years had passed since the last changing of the guard, he remembered vividly the ceremony at which Night Eyes, son of Manda Seafoam, had been chosen.

It had been a surprise. But then, it was always a surprise.

He was glad he was not the one who had to make the choice.

"You have been well?" asked the Queen, interrupting his thoughts.

"Well enough."

"And busy?"

"Too busy," growled the dwarf. "If your subjects would stop having adventures for a year or two, I might be able to catch up on my work, Arabella. As it is, I fear I shall never be current."

The queen laughed, a sound like water on smooth stones, like wind passing through daisies. Grimwold's complaint was an old one; he had been making it for over two hundred years.

"I'll see what I can do," she said.

Grimwold snorted, which is not considered an appropriate response to a queen, but was ignored because of their long friendship.

The time until the ceremony passed rapidly—more rapidly than Grimwold would have liked, since several unicorns came to him with stories that needed to be told and recorded. He slept at night on a bed of ferns they had prepared for him. It was comfortable enough, but he preferred his cave. The sky above him was too big, and it made him nervous.

He was woken the first morning by a unicorn standing at the foot of his bed. She made no sound, simply stared at him. But the old dwarf felt her presence, even in his sleep. Opening one eye he glared at the unicorn and growled, "Leave me alone."

"I have to speak to you," said the unicorn urgently.

With a heavy sigh, Grimwold sat up. "About what?" he asked,

sounding even grouchier than before. "Not a story, I hope. I don't take stories this early in the morning. Lots of others ahead of you anyway."

The unicorn shook her head. "I want you to tell me how I can be chosen as the next Guardian."

Grimwold blinked in astonishment. "Have you been drinking moonbeams? No one **wants** that job. Do you have any idea how appalling it is?" He narrowed his eyes. "Who are you, anyway?"

The unicorn started to answer, but Grimwold raised his hand. "Wait, let me see if I can figure it out. Never saw you before, but I know that flow of mane. The horn—yes, the horn would be…Turn around!"

The unicorn did as asked, making a full circle for the dwarf.

Grimwold snorted in triumph. "You're Cloudmane, daughter of Streamstrider. The queen is your grandmother."

The unicorn's large eyes widened in astonishment. "How did you do that?"

"It's my job to keep track of you unicorns—even young and foolish ones like you. Now, why in the world do you want to be chosen as Guardian? Oh, never mind. It doesn't make any difference anyway, you silly thing. Only stallions take that job. It's not for mares—and a good thing, too, dangerous, thankless task that it is. It's more than those fools you creatures are doing it for deserve. Let them get on without you, that's my stand on the matter. But the queen insists it has to be done. Says it's important. Says something in them will die without you." He narrowed his eyes. "So why is it **you** want the job? Out to prove something? Running away from something? Some young stallion break your heart?"

Cloudmane's nostrils flared, and her enormous blue eyes flashed with a fire and a strength that surprised the old dwarf. "My reasons are my own," she snapped, her mane bristling. "I ask only for some advice."

"Then I'll give you some. And I hope you'll take it. Forget the whole idea. The job of Guardian is not for you—not for any unicorn in its right mind. It's not a job you volunteer for, it's a job you take only because you have no choice."

"We'll see about that," muttered Cloudmane. Spinning on her silver hooves she trotted away from him, her sea-foam tail whisking angrily behind her. She made not a sound as she crossed the carpet of dried leaves that covered the forest floor.

Grimwold closed his eyes and tried to go back to sleep, but it was impossible. The rising sun was too bright, the conversation too upsetting. And he missed the comforts of his familiar caves. Feeling even crankier than usual, he rose and went to the stream to get a drink and wash his face.

The unicorns arrived in ones and twos at first—mostly those who had traveled the farthest and wanted to make sure to be there on time. As the day wore on they appeared in larger groups. Some of the groups were simply those who had met along the way and decided to finish the journey together. Others were made up of unicorns who had been traveling together for some time, usually those out on border patrol. Late in the afternoon a group of a dozen young stallions arrived, laughing and boisterous, and so full of loud energy and mock battles that at one point the queen herself had to call them down.

And all through the day as the unicorns arrived Grimwold fretted about his conversation with Cloudmane, and wondered if he should speak of it to the queen. But she was busy with her duties, with preparation for the ceremony and with greeting old and honored friends, and had little enough time for him to bother her with nonsense from a young mare that, in the end, would come to nothing anyway.

Many of the arriving unicorns made it a point to seek out Grimwold—some to tell him that they had new stories for him to record in the chronicles, others simply to greet him and to inquire after his health, a kindness that pleased the old dwarf in spite of himself.

He kept an eye out for Cloudmane, but did not see her again.

Aside from Grimwold, only a handful of two-legs were invited to the ceremony. One of them was a girl named Ivy, who had the queen's blessing. Another was a painter named Master Chang, a handsome man with almond eyes and long, dark hair who sometimes made pictures of important events in Luster, pictures which were stored with Grimwold in the Cavern of the Chronicles. A third was Madame Leonetti, an old woman who wore a dark blue robe and gazed out at the world from beneath its hooded robe with eyes so sharp and bright it seemed they could start a fire of their own accord.

Ivy came to stand beside Grimwold as he was watching the unicorns gather. She fussed with her red hair for a moment, then asked shyly, "Did you finish my story?"

Grimwold, who was no taller than the girl, shook his head, and gave her a sad look. "I have finished writing down what happened to you so far," he said. "But it will be many years before your story is finished." *Many long, hard* years, he wanted to add. But he bit back the words.

Ivy nodded. "May I stand with you for a while?"

"It would be my pleasure," replied Grimwold, who was starting to feel nervous about the ceremony and his part in it, and was glad of a distraction.

After a while the dwarf and the girl climbed a narrow path that led to the top of the cliff over which the waterfall flowed. Evening passed softly into full night, and still standing together, high above the ceremonial ground, they continued to watch the unicorns gather.

It was like watching moonlight collect in a bowl, save that it seemed there were as many shades and tones of whiteness as there were stars burning in the vast, clear sky above them.

"Never this many at home," said Ivy, looking upward.

"Unicorns, or stars?" asked Grimwold.

"No unicorns at home at all," said Ivy sadly.

Grimwold snorted. "That's not quite true, my girl. What do you think this ceremony is about, after all?"

"I don't know."

He turned to her in surprise. "No one has told you?"

"The queen said I would find out in good time."

Grimwold hesitated, then said, "This may be as good a time as any."

"Are you going to tell me a story?" Ivy asked eagerly.

"Might as well. Have to tell it down there in a little while. Good warm up to tell it to you now."

They walked along the edge of the cliff, going far enough from the waterfall so that Grimwold could speak without having to work to be heard above its sound. Ivy found a seat on a moss covered rock. Grimwold stood before her and cleared his throat.

"You know, of course, that long ago the unicorns lived on Earth."

"Of course," said Ivy solemnly.

"And that they came here because they were hunted so ferociously that they were in danger of extinction."

"Yes," said Ivy sadly.

"But do you know what happened to your world after they left?"

She shook her head.

"Then I shall tell you."

Ivy settled to the ground and made herself comfortable. Grimwold faced her, closed his eyes for a moment, then began to speak. His voice was deeper, softer, calmer than usual.

This is the tale he told:

In the long ago and sweet of the world, when things were slower but hearts were no less fierce, there came a time when the unicorns had to leave.

This was not done easily, nor was it done without grief. Earth was home to the unicorns, and they were part of it, horn and mane and hoof. But to stay was to die, for the hunting of unicorns by their enemies had become all too successful.

And so they came here to Luster.

The passage was not an easy one, and more than one unicorn gave its life to help in the creation of that first door.

And when it was over, and the last unicorn had left, it was as if the earth itself sighed with loss and sorrow.

For what is a world that has no unicorns?

That sorrow and that loss grew within the hearts of those who lived on earth. Even the ones who had never seen a unicorn, never heard of a unicorn, had felt the passing of something sweet and wonderful. It was as if the air had surrendered a bit of its spice, the water a bit of its sparkle, the night a bit of its mystery.

But only a very few knew why.

Not all felt the loss in equal measure, naturally. The coarse and the crude were but vaguely aware of something making them uneasy in their quiet moments. Most people simply felt a little sadder, a little wearier. But for the more sensitive ones, the ones most deeply open to the beauty of the world and all its joys and sorrows, there was an ache in the heart that grew greater by the day, until it seemed that grief would overwhelm them.

Painters painted only scenes of sorrow; singers and players made only mournful music; storytellers, sensing the loss, told tales that made their audiences weep long into the night, and offered them no light tales, no comedy, for relief.

Gloom enfolded the world.

And finally a child—it's always a child, you know—decided something had to be done.

She was the daughter of a storyteller, and seemed likely to become a storyteller herself. Her name was Alma, and she had a heart of steel and fire. She went to her brother, Balan, and said, "Something is wrong, and I am going to find out what. Will you travel with me, brother?"

And though Balan was more given to doing than to thinking, to fighting than to feeling, he agreed to go with his sister, for he did not want her to travel alone. She gathered some food and a few coins, which she carried in a pack on her back, and several of her father's best stories, which she carried in her heart, and set out. She went on foot, and Balan walked beside her, one hand always on his sword.

And he needed the sword, for the road was perilous. It had always been dangerous, even in the best of times. But with the passing of the unicorns, hearts had become hungry, and in some that hunger had turned to viciousness.

For three years Alma and Balan traveled through peril and pain, and many times Balan's sword saved them from disaster, and many other times Alma's stories gained them food and shelter, and sometimes even a clue.

Finally, weak and weary, wandering through a deep forest, they came upon the home of an old magician named Bellenmore. It was set in the side of a hill, and magic hung thick about it. When they first approached the door it began to sing, calling, "Bellenmore, Bellenmore! Wanderers two outside your door!"

Then a wall—or something like a wall, for they could not see it, only feel it—rose in front of them, and they could go no farther until the old man appeared.

"Well, what do you want?" he asked, in a voice that creaked with age. "If you're looking for Aaron, he's long gone. Great things doing. Great things. Probably couldn't help you anyway. Getting too big for his britches."

"We want to know what's gone wrong with the world," said Alma, her voice gentle, coaxing. "For three years now things have seemed flat and stale."

Bellenmore closed his eyes, and gave out a sigh so heavy it seemed to flow not from his body but from someplace deep in the earth itself. "I was afraid of this."

"Of what?" asked Balan, struggling to raise his sword, which seemed frozen at his side.

"Of exactly what this girl—your sister, I assume from the look of her—has just described. The unicorns have gone, and when they left they took with them something that is essential to the human heart."

"Where have they gone?" asked Alma anxiously. "And why? How did they get there? Can I follow them?"

"Hold, hold!" cried the old magician, raising his hands. "One question at a time."

He studied them for a moment, then made a small gesture with the little finger of his right hand. The invisible wall disappeared, and Balan gained control of his sword once more.

"You may come in," said Bellenmore.

Balan glanced at his sister. "Do you think its safe?"

"Nothing is safe," she said sharply. Then she stepped forward, toward the old man, and followed him through the door into the hill.

The inside of his house was warm and cozy, and slightly strange. A green fire crackled on the hearth. On the mantel above the fireplace stood a row of earthenware mugs with hideous faces. One of them winked at Alma, another leered and rolled its eyes, and a third stuck out its tongue and made a rude noise. Then they all began to sing a bawdy song, until Bellenmore waved a hand to silence them.

The tables and chairs were made of dark wood, and ornately carved—some with odd designs, others with scenes of dragons and unicorns. At one side of the room was a tall oaken stand; a thick book rested open upon it. The longest table held a glass cage with no top. Inside the cage was a lizard, which was resting its front legs on the upper edge of the cage and staring out at them with a curious expression.

"Sit," said Bellenmore, gesturing toward one of the chairs.

Alma sat. Balan stood behind her, both because he had not been invited to sit, and because he would not have sat even had he been asked. His hand rested on the hilt of his sword.

Bellenmore did sit, his robe shifting and whispering around him as if it were alive.

"Alas, the unicorns," he said sadly.

"What happened to them?" asked Alma.

"They were driven away. There is a family which holds an ancient grudge against them, and the hunting had become so fierce that it seemed they all might perish. Finally the unicorn queen came to me and asked if I might open a door for them, as I had for the dragons."

"The dragons?" asked Balan, confused.

The magician shrugged. "It was much the same thing. The world is changing, boy. Wildness and magic are in retreat before the rise of men. Better—much better—it would be for science and magic, order and wildness, natural and supernatural to live together. But that cannot be, at least not for now. So the dragons have gone, and the unicorns had to leave as well. I helped them open a door to a place that they have named Luster. It is a good place for them. But they did take a piece of our hearts with them when they went."

"Send me through the door," said Alma.

The old man looked startled. "That's not possible."

"Why?"

Bellenmore blew a puff of air through his shaggy white mustache, then looked down at his knobby hands. Finally he said, "The queen wouldn't like it."

"I don't like what's happened here," replied Alma firmly. "I must speak to them."

"They are not tame beasts, you know."

"I am not a tame girl."

Bellenmore sighed. "Wait here."

He stood and went to a door at the far side of the room. When he opened it and stepped through he seemed to disappear into a kind of shadowy gloom. Balan started forward, but Alma touched his arm, and he resumed his stance behind her chair.

When Bellenmore returned he was holding a golden chain, from which dangled a crystal amulet. Inside the crystal was coiled a long strand of white hair that seemed to glow with a light all its own.

"This amulet was a gift of the queen," he said. "There are only five such in all the world. It will allow you to pass into the land of the unicorns."

Alma took it from him. It felt warm in her hand.

The magician leaned forward and in whispered tones told her how to use it. Her eyes grew wide, and just a hint of fear showed in them, but she nodded to show that she understood.

"And what do I do when I get there?" she asked.

"That, my girl," said the wizard, "is entirely up to you."

"Come with me," said Alma.

The old man looked at her in surprise. He started to answer, paused, then shook his head. "This is for you to do," he said softly. "Alone."

Balan placed his hand on his sister's shoulder.

"She must go alone," repeated the old wizard.

Grimwold paused and looked at the sky. "I'm taking too long to tell this. They're going to want me down below soon."

"You can't stop now!" cried Ivy. "What happened to Alma?"

"Well she came through, of course. But you know how that goes. You've done it yourself."

"But what **then?**"

Grimwold glanced at the sky again. "Then you and I went back down the cliff," he said abruptly. "Because it is not a good idea to keep the queen waiting."

Ivy started to protest again, but he raised his hand. "I have to tell the whole thing down there anyway," he reminded her. "You'll hear soon enough."

She sighed, and turned to follow him back down the path. When she did, she gasped in astonishment. The gathering of unicorns was complete. There must have been a thousand or more of them waiting in the grotto below. And though the sky was settling into darkness, from their gathered horns came a glow that lit the night, a glory that brought a sharp sting of tears to her eyes.

"They **are** beautiful," said the old dwarf, and for a moment there was no hint of gruffness in his voice, only love and wonder.

Ivy nodded, unable to speak.

They made their way back down the trail, which was lit by the glory of unicorns, passing near enough to the waterfall on several turns that its spray dampened their clothes.

At the base of the cliff Cloudmane stood waiting for them.

"Let it be me," she said desperately.

"You're mad," replied Grimwold, brushing past her.

Ivy hesitated. She knew she should follow Grimwold. But the unicorn, who she had not met before, was clearly in great distress. She stopped, glanced uneasily at the dwarf, who did not look back to see if she was still coming, then put her hand on Cloudmane's neck.

"What is it?" she asked softly.

The unicorn simply shook her head and turned away, trotting silent back to join the others, melting into the glory so smoothly that Ivy lost track of her in just seconds.

Ivy sighed. Grimwold was far ahead of her now, and she started to scurry to catch up. Before she had gone ten paces, a pair of tall stallions barred her path.

"The two legs stand over there," said one of them, gently but firmly. "Only Grimwold goes on from here."

Ivy started to protest, then remembered it was a privilege to be here at all. She looked after Grimwold and suddenly realized that following him now would be like walking out onto a stage during a play—or rushing up to the pulpit during a church service. She turned in the direction the unicorn had indicated and saw a handful of humans and near humans standing together. They were gathered beneath a clump of blue-green trees that were almost like the pine trees of home, but somehow different, too, of course. She recognized Master Chang, the painter, and old Madame Leonetti; the others were strangers to her.

She went to stand with the group.

The ceremony began.

The queen spoke first, greeting the gathered glory with what was clearly great joy. Yet there was sorrow in her voice as well.

Then came a song that was made not of sound but of light, and which Ivy heard not with her ears but with her heart.

Then a tall stallion walked slowly to the front of the group. He stood for a moment, then trumpeted a call that pierced the night, seemed to split the sky itself. A deep silence, a quiet unlike anything Ivy had ever experienced before, fell over the clearing. Even the voice of the waterfall seemed to have disappeared.

The stallion spoke into that silence in a voice that was no more than a whisper, but that carried to the farthest edges of the glory. "We are here to choose the next Guardian of Memory. It is a position of honor and horror, of strength and sorrow, of glory and grief. He who fills it must be strong and swift, brave of heart and fleet of foot, able to endure pain and loss and the piercing joy of unexpected love that cannot last. To ready your hearts, listen once more to the story of the First Guardian."

Into the silence stepped Grimwold. He began to speak, telling them all that he had told Ivy and more, adding details of the unicorns' first passage to Luster and how it had come to be.

Though Ivy had just heard the story, she hung on every word, drinking it in, trying to understand more deeply.

Now (said Grimwold) when Alma had entered the land of the unicorns, she had—as should be no surprise—adventures strange and won-drous. She was captured by the delvers and held prisoner for three years. In her escape, she saved a young princeling named Windfoot, who was much beloved of his mother the queen. When the two made it back to the court together, the grateful queen offered Alma a boon.

Alma stood, small and quiet. Gathering her breath, and her courage, she said, "Come home."

A murmur of horror rippled through the unicorns.

"Come home," said Alma again, and this time there were tears coursing down her cheeks. "Something good is dying without you." She stepped toward the queen, and touched her, which was a great crime. Pressing her cheek to the queen's, burying her face in that mane that felt like spun cloud and smelled of the sea and the forest and something more, something that cannot be named, Alma whispered, "Hearts grow hard and weary. Pain spreads, and joy diminishes. Those who hated you hate you still, but those who loved you, or would have loved you, or wanted to love you but never had the chance are being scraped hollow by a loss they don't understand. Come home. Please come home. We are withering without you."

"The world is not kind to us, child," whispered the queen.

"It is even unkinder without you," replied Alma fiercely.

Then, her face pressed close to the queen's ear, the storyteller's daughter began to sing of all that the unicorns had left behind, the good and the bad, the oceans and the forest. She sang of all that she had seen in her three long years of wandering to find the unicorns. And pulsing through her song was all the sorrow she had felt with their passing, and beneath that the love of things unseen and mysteries unsolved— of untouched joy waiting just around the bend of the next moment— that had vanished with the passing of the unicorns.

And as Alma sang, the queen remembered all the humans they had loved over the years, humans who had fought and died for them, and had loved them back with open hearts. And she remembered the world that had given them birth, no more beautiful than Luster, but no less so, either. And she thought of her son, who Alma had saved from the delvers, and finally she said, "Peace, girl. Be silent. Here is what I will grant you. From this time forth, there shall always be one unicorn, one and one alone, who lives in the world of our birth. That unicorn will have to be enough, enough to remind you of what was, and what can be. He will live alone, in the high places. He will not be seen often, or by many. But his presence should be enough to keep something alive in you. He will guard the memory of what has passed to this world, and the sight of him will help to keep it alive. Those who know such things will know, and those who understand such things will understand, and it will be, if not enough, then something. Something."

Then she turned to her son Windfoot and said, "Will you be the first?"

And Windfoot agreed, and so it was, and so it will be. Windfoot returned to the land of the humans for five and twenty years, and when his time was up a glory of unicorns gathered to choose a new Guardian of Memory, who went to take his place. And again it was done, and again, and yet again, for these many centuries, though not all the Guardians of Memory survived their full five and twenty years. For the hunting still goes on, and the world is full of danger.

And now the night for choosing is upon us once more, and that is the tale of its beginning.

His story finished, Grimwold came to stand beside Ivy.

A deep silence filled the grotto.

Into that silence came the voice of the queen, sighing across the glory like wind through clover. "Willing hero, willing victim, child of strength and pain, the chosen one must walk alone in paths of sorrow for the sake of those we have left behind. Who will step forward to try the wheel?"

Silently, about a hundred stallions moved to the front of the glory. Then, to Ivy's surprise, Madame Leonetti stepped forward, too. In her hands was a wreath made of flowers that Ivy did not recognize.

She held the wreath to her side, at shoulder height. The first of the unicorns came forward, and took it with his horn. He held it for a moment, then—looking both disappointed and relieved—bent his head so that the next unicorn could take it from him.

In this way the wreath passed from horn to horn, with no decision being made.

"What are they waiting for?" asked Ivy. "How will they know?"

But Grimwold only shook his head and whispered, "Watch!"

From horn to horn passed the wreath, without a sign of change. Now only three volunteers remained, and though the queen appeared unworried, Grimwold was beginning to grow fretful.

When the last unicorn took the wreath a cry of astonishment went up. The reason for the cry was not that something had happened, but that it **hadn't**. No decision had been made, no new guardian chosen.

The queen looked toward Madame Leonetti. "What does it mean? Can the magic have failed after all these centuries?"

Madame Leonetti spread her hands. "I really don't—"

She was interrupted by an outburst from among the unicorns. "Let me try!" called Cloudmane, shouldering her way past a pair of stallions considerably taller than herself. "Let me try!"

The queen looked startled, but Madame Leonetti smiled, and extended the wreath.

Moving carefully, Cloudmane thrust her horn through its center.

For a moment the only sound was that of the waterfall. Then there was a crackle of power, and under it a murmur of astonishment from the gathered unicorns as the wreath began to vibrate. Light danced across its surface.

Madame Leonetti dropped her hold on the wreath and stepped back. Suspended in the air, Cloudmane's horn still at its center, the wreath began to spin. The light on its surface grew brighter, spiraling around the green leaves like mist made of fire. The crackle changed to a hum, the hum to a note like a bell. The wreath began to grow, and as it did, it became a window to the other world, the world the unicorns had fled; a window to Earth.

The view was that of a mountaintop.

At its peak stood Night Eyes, son of Manda Seafoam, who for twenty five years had walked the hills of Earth, a Guardian of the ancient memory of unicorns, a silent, unseen reminder of lost joy and the possibility of healing. He looked toward them, but obviously could not see them, as if his attention had been drawn by the sound, but the door had not yet opened.

Then there was a flash of light, and the door *was* opened, the worlds linked, the homeward path completed. With a trumpet of joy, Night Eyes leaped forward, bounding through the circle of light to where the glory of unicorns stood waiting.

But no sooner through than he stopped in shock. "Cloudmane!" he gasped. "You!"

"Who else?" she asked softly.

"Quickly!" cried Madame Leonetti. "The magic will last but a moment longer."

"But why?" asked Night Eyes, his voice filled with sorrow. "Why, Cloudmane?"

"I want to know what you know. Besides, brother—I was the one who most wanted you to come home. That's part of the magic, too."

And with that, she stepped through the glowing circle, onto the mountaintop where Night Eyes had stood but a moment earlier.

The circle closed with a rush and a snap. The wreath fell to the ground, no longer green but a brittle, burnt brown. Earth was gone. The door was gone. Cloudmane was gone.

A song rose from the unicorns, the prayer they always uttered for the Guardian of Memory. "Guide her and guard her, Powers that Be. Love her and watch over her on her journey. Bring her home safe to us." Soaring above all the other voices was that of Night Eyes. But on the last very last word he differed in what he sang, ending with a sob on, "Bring her home safe to **me**."

For a moment, all stood in silence. Then the first stallion who had tried the wreath stepped forward. He bowed to the queen, then asked in a deep voice, "How can this be?"

The queen shook her head from side to side, the tip of her horn inscribing an arc of light. "I do not know."

"I do," said Madame Leonetti. Her voice was frail, and she had to work hard to be heard above the waterfall. But the shape of the grotto brought her words to even the most distant ears.

"The answer is simple: you have forgotten the nature of the magic. The spell as first created called for the Guardian of Memory to be 'the unicorn with the deepest love for those left behind.' Clearly, that was Cloudmane."

"But how can that be?" asked the queen. "Since the beginning of our connection, the deepest ties between human and unicorn have been between the stallions and young maidens. And since the time of the first Guardian, young stallions are taught an understanding of humans, and compassion for them, in preparation for the possibility that they may be chosen to return to Earth. How could Cloudmane have more love for those left behind?"

At first no one answered. Finally Ivy said, "I think I know."

The queen turned to her. "Speak, child."

Ivy glanced around, trying to fight down a surge of panic. "When Night Eyes went to be the Guardian, Cloudmane was left behind. That's why she can love those left behind on Earth. She knows what it's like. She's felt it herself."

"As have I," said Madame Leonetti, moving to place a hand on Night Eyes' shoulder.

"You were left behind?" he asked.

"Actually, I have both left someone behind, and been left behind by him. His name was Balan, and he was my brother."

Ivy gasped. "You can't be—"

The old woman drew back her hood. Her face was lined with deep wrinkles, but in her eyes was something strong and wonderful. "Alma? Of course I am. With the blessings of the unicorns, one can live a long time in this place. Not, alas, without growing old. I left Balan behind when I came to Luster to beg the unicorns to return home, and left him even further behind when I chose to come back and live here. And now I have been left behind, too, because he is long dead, as are all the humans I knew when I was your age. It's been a good life, child. But it is lonely. To leave. To be left."

Ivy moved to stand beside her. Alma Leonetti wrapped one arm around the girl's shoulder, the other around Night Eyes's neck.

Together they looked toward the spark that still hung, flickering and fading, in the sky where Cloudmane had disappeared. A reminder of a reminder, it burned its way into their hearts, even as it vanished.

A Life in Miniature

Once a poor couple worked at a place called TTT, which stood for "Tomorrow's Technologies Today." They swept the labs, cleaned the windows, and generally picked up after the scientists, some of whom were astonishingly messy. The couple lived in a small cottage at the edge of the TTT industrial park, and would have been content with their lot were it not for one thing: they did not and could not have a child.

One dark and stormy night there came a knocking at their door. As they rarely had guests, this so frightened the wife that she threw her apron over her face. But the husband scurried to the door. There he found a tall man with fierce eyes, much bedraggled with rain and mud.

"My car has broken down," said the man. "May I take shelter here?"

Though he looked like a vagrant, the husband asked him in, partly because he had a kind heart, and partly because he knew security at TTT was such that no outsider could pass its gates.

What he did not know was that their visitor was Dr. Merrill Lyon, head of research at TTT.

After ushering their guest to the table, the husband dialed up some fresh coffee and hot bread, which the table swiftly delivered.

When Dr. Lyon had warmed himself a bit, both inside and out, he noticed the wife peering out from behind her apron.

"Come come, good woman," he said. "You've nothing to fear from me!"

After a bit more coaxing the wife lowered her apron and edged her way to the table. Yet still she seemed sad, and now that Dr.

Lyon saw it, he noticed that the husband, too, had eyes weary with sorrow.

"Why such long faces? Is TTT not treating you well?"

"Oh, no!" cried the husband quickly. "We love our jobs!"

This was not entirely true, but was probably the wisest thing to say under the circumstances, since he could not be sure that their guest had not been sent to spy on them. "It's just that…"

When his voice trailed off his wife jumped in with a vigor that belied her previous timidness. "It's just that we want a little baby boy, sir, and can't seem to have one. Oh, I want a child so much I wouldn't mind if he were no bigger than a mouse."

And that was how the whole thing started.

In his office the next day Dr. Lyon could not stop thinking about the wife's words; they almost seemed an invitation for him to test a bit of technology he had been tinkering with. Two days later he invited the couple to his lab, where they signed several release forms freeing TTT from all responsibility, then underwent numerous tests and injections.

Not many months after, the wive gave birth to a perfect baby boy. Well, perfect in all ways save one: He was barely the size of his father's thumb! Despite her comment to Dr. Lyon, the mother was not entirely happy with this. On the other hand, the tiny infant was so dear that her whole heart went out to him the first instant she saw him.

Word of the miraculous child quickly made the rounds at TTT. Before long many scientists had come to visit the baby, who Dr. Lyon dubbed "Tom Thumb." (Though Tom's parents were not entirely happy with this name, they preferred it to Dr. Lyon's first suggestion: "The Spacesaver 3000, Mark I.")

Eventually even the daughter of the man who owned TTT came to visit. The girl, Titania by name and but four years old herself, was immediately smitten with the baby. "Oh, the dear thing!" she cried. "Please, can I hold him?"

Tom's mother, being no fool, passed the child to Titania, who cradled him in the palm of her hand, and wept bitterly when it was time for her to leave.

The next day came a knock at the cottage door. Before either man or wife had a chance to answer, in swept the little princess (for that was what the people at TTT called Titania), bearing an armload of gifts for Tom.

From that moment on the baby wanted for nothing in the line of clothing, as it was Titania's delight to dress him as if he were a doll.

So it was that the child of the humble cottagers wore silks and satins, and shoes made of the finest Italian leather—though it must be said that their cost was all in the workmanship, since an entire wardrobe for the lad could be made from a mere handful of scraps. Titania came to visit often, and adored the tiny baby, though it did distress her that she often found him scrabbling around on the floor with the mice, who seemed to look on him as a special friend. Tom even trained one to carry him about on its back, as if it were a tiny horse. He named it "Charger," and the two made quite a sight.

Though he grew no taller, Tom seemed to mature rapidly, and when he was but a year old it was decided that he should join the children of the other TTT employees at their daycare facility.

This did not turn out not to be an entirely good idea, for he was constantly in danger of being stepped on by the other children. Moreover, Tom himself was the soul of mischief, and loved nothing more than to slip into some child's pita bread then stick his head out from behind a cherry tomato and shout "Boo!" just before the poor thing took a bite. These antics led to more than one case of hysteria, several parental complaints, and two lawsuits. Finally the vice president in charge of employee relations decreed Tom would have to be schooled elsewhere.

When Dr. Lyon learned of the problem he invited the wee lad to come live in the lab. Tom's parents were reluctant to let their boy go, but the doctor made so many promises about the fine education he would receive, and the splendid people he would meet that finally, with heavy hearts, they agreed. Tom agreed, too, though he insisted that Charger be allowed to come along with him.

Dr. Lyon had a dollhouse custom-made for Tom to live in. Though he mentioned it to no one, he also had the dollhouse fitted with cameras and microphones, so he could monitor Tom's life.

Tom loved being in the lab, for all the scientists who came through would stop to talk to him, and compliment him on what a fine lad he was becoming. In fact, by the time he was four Tom had the wits and skills of a ten year old. Dr. Lyon made many notes questioning whether this was a function of his reduced size.

Tom was enormously curious and he and Charger were always prowling the lab to see what Dr. Lyon was up to. Finally the scientist ordered Tom to stay on the table tops, saying he was afraid someone would step on the tiny boy if he was running loose on the floor. This so frustrated Tom, who now could not get from one table to another without being carried, that one of the TTT engineers created a system of towers and bridges for him. Soon each lab table had a five foot tower at each end, each tower being connected by a narrow bridge to the one at the next table, with the bridges sufficiently high that the scientists could walk below them with no problem. The kindly engineer added a system of pulleys, so all Tom had to do was climb into a little cup and then hoist himself to the top of the towers.

Now he could travel freely about the lab and was much happier. Most of the scientists soon became used to the sight of the thumb-sized boy scampering about overhead. Dr. Lyon, however, seemed to be somewhat nervous about having Tom move around so easily. And after a while Tom noticed that every night the doctor carefully locked his center desk drawer. The boy wondered what was in the drawer that Dr. Lyon hid it so carefully, but as the man always took the key with him, he was not able to find out.

The lab was a place of great fascination for Tom. He loved the bubbling test tubes and the crackling power sources and the strange smelling concoctions so much that even though Dr. Lyon repeatedly begged him to be careful around them he could not resist getting too close—which was how he happened to tumble into a small pot of something extremely disgusting one afternoon.

The goo, as it turned out, wasn't an experiment at all, but something one of the lab assistants had been cooking for lunch that had been left on the burner too long and gone bad.

Tom thrashed and struggled to get out, but the gluey stuff held him fast. Even when the lab assistant picked up the pot and scraped it into the garbage Tom wasn't able to make himself heard above the deafening music that the assistant was playing while Dr. Lyon was out of the office.

When the lid of the garbage can closed over Tom, he was sure his end had come. The darkness was so complete it was as if he had been swallowed, the papers in the can stuck to him when he tried to move, and every time he struggled too vigorously, he sank deeper into the trash. Twice someone opened the can to throw something in, but by that time Tom had sunk so far that the papers above him muffled his tiny cries.

He wept bitterly.

Finally the lid was lifted again—and stayed open. For a brief moment, Tom thought he would be saved. But swift hands tied the top of the plastic bag lining the can, sealing Tom in more completely than before. He felt the bag being taken from the can. He cried out more desperately than ever, but his voice was muffled by the jumble of trash. The bag was flung somewhere, moved, flung again. Tom was certain he would soon run out of air, or be crushed, or something equally terrible, and was sure his end was near. But he was not the sort to despair. With his tiny fingers he began to claw at the plastic that held him in. It was maddening work, for the plastic slipped and slid, but he finally managed to tear open a small hole. Thrusting his hand through, he waved it about, hoping someone would see him.

Someone did—an old seagull who was scanning the trash heap for something interesting. Landing on the bag, the gull quickly pecked it open and snatched Tom up. Off it flew, Tom dangling from its beak.

The boy struggled and squirmed, until he realized that if he **did** manage to get the bird to let go of him he would be dashed to his death on the rocks below. What a choice: be eaten by a bird, or plummet to a stony death!

But when the gull flew out over some water, Tom quickly swung his legs up, wrapped them around the gull's neck, and began to squeeze. The startled bird opened its mouth to squawk. Tom immediately opened his legs, and fell to the water some thirty feet below. He struck hard, and was stunned for a moment. He began to sink. But before he had a chance to worry about drowning, an enormous pike struck, swallowing him in one gulp—which was actually lucky for Tom, as it saved him from being slashed to bits by the pike's needle-sharp teeth.

Down the gullet Tom slid, until he was in the fish's stomach, which burned like fire.

Now he was sure that he had at last come to his final moments. But as he was waiting for his doom, he felt the great fish jerk and convulse. It was flung around, then smacked down, moving so violently that Tom had no idea what was happening at all—until he saw a smear of light. He began to shout and scream and thrash about himself.

"Well, well, what have we here?" cried a rough voice. "Something the fishie et is still alive. Let's have a look, shall we, missy? Always intersting to see what these beasties swallow down."

Tom shrank back as a flash of silver cut open the stomach wall. He covered his eyes to shield them from the bright light that flooded in. Then he felt himself once more plucked up.

"It's Tom!" screamed a familiar voice. "It's Tom! Oh, do put him down. Please, please be careful!"

A moment later Tom was standing on a table, and little Titania was gently pouring water over him to wash away the many revolting things that had covered him that day. "Poor Tom," she kept saying, and sometimes she would start to cry. "Poor, poor Tom."

"Not so poor," he said. "I'm still alive. But how did I get here?"

"That's what I'd like to know," said a deep voice.

"Who are you?" asked Tom, gazing up at the tall, bearded man.

"I'm Titania's father, Arthur Kring. We were out for an afternoon of fishing on Lake TTT and when we caught a fish we caught you as well. Thank goodness the captain here planned to grill the thing now. But how in heaven's name did you get inside that monster?"

After Tom told them of his adventures Titania said, "Daddy, we can't let Tom stay in that horrible lab anymore."

Her father agreed (he agreed with almost everything his daughter said), and so Tom was brought to live at the executive quarters of TTT.

He sent for Charger to come live with him, but the mouse had disappeared, and had not been seen since the afternoon Tom fell into the pot.

Though Tom mourned for his old friend, all in all his new home was very pleasant. He wanted for nothing at all, since Titania doted on his every wish. But in time he began to have a hankering to see his real parents, and asked over and over if he might visit them. Finally Titania agreed, and said that she herself would take him. So one morning the two set out for the little cottage where Tom had spent his earliest days. To Tom's surprise, he found his father in a state of gloom, and his mother in even greater despair.

"What is wrong, what is wrong?" he asked.

"We've been let go!" wailed his mother, throwing her apron over her face. "After all these years, we've been let go! They're going to replace us with those mechanical men Dr. Lyon invented. Oh, whatever will we do? Whatever will we do?"

"I shall talk to my father," said Titania decisively.

But now the little princess discovered the boundaries of her power, for Mr. Kring told her this was a matter of business, and in those things she must not interfere.

Titania was so vexed she stamped her foot, but it did her no good.

"I'm sorry, Tom," she said sadly. "I cannot help you."

"Perhaps you still can," said Tom. "There is a desk drawer in Dr. Lyons office that I would like to examine."

"Why?" asked Titania, wiping away her tears.

"I'm not sure. But he was always so careful to keep it locked that it makes me wonder what is in it. Can you help me check?"

"I'll be glad to."

They decided that Titania would visit the lab with Tom hidden in her pocket. While there, she would get Dr. Lyon to show her something on the far side of the lab. She would slip Tom out of her pocket, and he would make his way into the desk drawer to see what it contained.

"Why, Titania, what a pleasant surprise!" cried Dr. Lyon, when the little princess entered the lab the next day. "We've missed you around here." He scowled slightly at her, then added in mock seriousness, "I'm not sure we can forgive you for taking our little friend away from us."

"He's much safer where he is now, Dr. Lyon," said Titania. At the moment this was quite true, since he was clutched in her hand, which was in her pocket.

With her other hand, she pointed to the far side of the lab. "What's **that?**" she asked, feigning great interest.

Dr. Lyon, well aware that it was important to keep the boss's daughter happy, agreed to explain it to her. As he turned to lead the way, she deposited Tom onto the desk. Quickly, he slipped into the center drawer.

In his hand he had a tiny flashlight that Titania had had made for him. Shining it around him, Tom saw that the drawer was like a long, low chamber, one in which he could stand with his head just barely below the ceiling. To his right he saw an eraser big enough for him to sit on. Behind him were pencils as thick as his legs. Not far in front of him lay a file folder that would have made a nice tennis court for someone his size.

Tom made his way to the top of the folder.

"Spacesaver 3000, Mark I," read the label.

The words had a familiar ring, though Tom could not say why.

He lifted the edge, crawled under it, and began to read. Soon his tiny heart was pounding with rage, and excitement.

Suddenly he heard footsteps. Titania and Dr. Lyon were coming back. "Wait, wait," he heard Titania say. "I want you to explain **that** to me."

"In just a moment, my dear," said the doctor.

Stepping behind the desk, he slammed the drawer shut.

Tom was trapped inside! His excitement turned to fear. Had Dr. Lyon known he was in here? Was he trying to catch him? Even if he wasn't, Tom didn't want to be found inside the drawer—especially not after reading what was in that folder.

Clenching his tiny flashlight in his trembling hands, he made his way to the back of the drawer.

It was sealed tight. He should have expected that; there was no way that Dr. Lyon would have a cheaply-made desk. He was trapped.

Hours passed. Tom wondered if he would ever get out. Then he remembered that it was Friday. What if Dr. Lyon left for the weekend? Tom began to wonder if he would he die from lack of food or water before the drawer was opened again.

Then, to make things worse, his flashlight went out, leaving him in utter blackness.

It was impossible to know how much time had gone by before he heard a scratching at the back of the drawer. New fear clutched Tom's heart. Was something trying to get in here with him? *Scratch. Scratch, scratch.* Something was gnawing at the wood. The sound went on and on, until Tom thought he would go mad with terror.

Then it stopped, and he heard a new sound, at first terrifying, and then, when he recognized it, soothing. It was the sound of a mouse —and not just any mouse. It was his old friend, Charger.

A moment later Tom felt Charger's furry body rub against him. When he grasped his former steed by the tail it led him to the back of the drawer, where it had gnawed a hole just big enough for a mouse, or a boy the size of a thumb, to escape.

"Wait," murmured Tom. "Wait!"

He returned to the folder and with great effort rolled a piece of paper until it was no thicker than a pencil. He carried it to the hole and pushed it through ahead of him. Then he followed Charger through the hole.

The climb to the floor was treacherous, and Tom nearly fell more than once. When at last he was down, he embraced Charger. With the paper tucked underneath his arm, he went back to the dollhouse where he had once lived, which was still tucked into a corner of the lab, and called Titania.

A few minutes later she arrived, guards in tow.

Tom showed her the paper he had found in Dr. Lyons' drawer, her eyes narrowed in anger.

"Wait until I show this to father!" she said.

Her father was angry, too, not only at Dr. Lyon, but at the jury that awarded Tom half ownership of TTT in compensation for the company's unethical act of combining mouse genes with his own in order to make him come out so small. Dr. Lyons' plea that he was only trying to help humanity overcome its crowded condition fell on deaf ears.

It took several years, but the technicians at TTT finally managed to find a way to make Tom grow to a full two feet in height. At Titania's request, they also found a way to shrink her to almost the same size.

Soon after, the pair were wed in a pavilion in front of the very lake where Tom had been swallowed by the pike. His parents sat in the front row, weeping and smiling, and cheered when the happy couple kissed.

As for Tom and Titania Thumb, they ran TTT wisely and well, doing much good in the world and turning a tidy profit as they did.

It was a short life, but a happy one.

The Troddler

Anders hated the stone troll that stood at the corner near his house. Every time he walked past it, it reminded him that his father had been lost to the trolls: "Troll-taken," as the neighbors put it.

"Serves you right," he would say to the statue each afternoon as he came home from school. "If you'd stayed underground where you belong, you wouldn't have been turned into stone."

Yet some days he couldn't help staring at it, fascinated by the tragic look on the troll's face. Even so, on the afternoon that everything changed Anders passed the statue with no more than his daily insult and continued straight to his house, where he burst through the front door with his daily cry of, "I'm home!"

He paused, waiting for his mother's usual response of, "And I'm in the kitchen!"

He was greeted by nothing but silence. With a shrug, Anders ambled into the kitchen, expecting to find a plate of his mother's baking with a note tucked underneath to explain where she was.

The table was bare.

It was then that Anders noticed something else, something that sent a tremor of fear rippling through him. Faint, but unmistakable, he caught the cold, stony scent of troll.

His hand crept to the sprig of trollbane he wore around his neck. He didn't know if the plant really kept trolls away; some of his friends claimed the idea was mere fogwump, and his father had never told him either way. Even so, it made him feel better to know it was there.

Setting his schoolbooks on the table, Anders moved his other hand to the knife at his waist. Then he shook his head. What foolishness! No troll could be here now, not in the day. Wasn't the statue at the corner—not to mention the other three statues he passed on the way to school, each the remains of a once living troll who had been caught by the trollwatch and dragged into the light to be petrified—proof enough of that?

Yet even if no troll were here now, Anders' nose insisted one had been recently.

"Mother?" he called nervously. "Mother, where are you?"

No answer.

He dashed through the house, checking the living room and the dining room, then up the stairs to look through all four bedrooms. No sign of her—but neither was there any sign of a struggle, any hint that she might have been taken against her will.

Anders forced himself to stay calm. It was possible she had simply gone to the market, or across the way to visit old Gerda, who had been sick recently. But without leaving a note? That was not like her. His mother always left a note if she was going to be away when he got home, even if she was only going across the street.

Anders sat on the edge of his bed to think. Trolls could not go out in the daylight. So when could a troll have come into their home?

It had been dark when he left for school, of course, as it would be until the end of winterdim, which was still four months away. So there had been an hour after he left for school that trolls might have been out and around—though it was hard to imagine how one could have gotten past the trollwatch.

All right, what about his mother? It was unlikely she would have gone out before the weak winter light had straggled into the sky. *Had she been here when the troll came?* Anders felt a new surge of panic. He tried to fight it down by telling himself that since there was no sign of a struggle she could not be troll-taken. He repeated it out loud—"My mother has not been troll-taken!"—and his panic began to subside. But it still left the question: If not troll-taken, where was she?

And why the smell?

He was about to head for Gerda's cottage, to see if his mother might be visiting the old woman after all, when he heard a noise from across the hall.

"Who's there?" he cried.

Silence.

Slipping his knife from his belt, Anders tiptoed to the door. He paused, holding his breath, listening intently.

Silence…silence…then, from his mother's room, a whimper.

Anders bolted across the hall. The room—dark from the drawn curtains—was still empty. He turned to the closet. He had not looked inside it on his previous inspection of the room; it had never occurred to him that his mother might be in there. But that whimper had to have come from somewhere.

"Mother?"

No answer.

Gripping his knife more tightly, Anders yanked the door open—then cried out in astonishment and disgust. Crouched in the corner, gnawing on one of his mother's shoes, was a baby troll. The creature looked up at Anders with wide eyes, then took the shoe out of its mouth and began to scream, a terrible, high-pitched keening. At the same time Anders saw a blaze of light in his own hand—his knife, flashing a troll alert, just as it had been created to do. No wonder the little monster was screaming. Small as it was, it must sense that the knife had been made to cut troll flesh.

Anders hesitated. Much as he hated trolls, he couldn't bring himself to simply stab a baby one. But the thing's screeching was piercing his ears. He hesitated, then thrust the knife into its sheath.

Instantly the little troll stopped squalling. Anders pulled the knife partway from the sheath. The troll's voice rose again. Anders pushed the knife back. The shrieking subsided.

Clutching the haft of the knife, ready to draw it again if needed, Anders crouched to look at the creature more closely. *Thor's belt but it was ugly!* Anders wasn't sure which was worse: the huge, pointed ears; the squashed nose with its gaping nostrils; the blunt fingers and toes; or the cracked, stone-gray skin.

What was supposed to do now? His mother had taught him all sorts of manners and rules, but she had provided no advice for a situation like this. And her all purpose rule of, "When in doubt, simply be kind and honest" surely couldn't apply to trolls.

Could it?

How did one go about being kind to a troll anyway?

Anders sat on the corner of his mother's bed, trying to think. A troll had been in the house. His mother was missing. Now he had found a baby troll in the closet.

He felt a sudden surge of panic. Could the thing's parents be here as well?

No, he told himself. *That's not possible. There's no place a full grown troll could be hiding.*

But what did it all mean? And what should he do now?

Well, the last question was easy. He **should** just drag the little monster outside and let the lingering sun turn it to stone. But when he looked at the creature, he remembered the expression on the statue at the corner, and found he didn't have the heart to petrify it.

The other choice was to take it to the constable. Of course, if he didn't want to turn it to stone, he couldn't do that until after darkfall, which was still an hour away—longer by far than he wanted to wait with this creature.

Maybe he should just go for the constable by himself.

No. He couldn't leave a troll—even a baby one—alone in the house. It might be hiding in the closet now, but who knew what havoc it might wreak by the time he got back?

His stomach reminded him that he had been starving when he came home and he decided to get something to eat while he worked out the problem. "Stay there!" he ordered the baby, shutting the closet door.

Not that he expected the thing to understand him.

Closing his ears to the little troll's pathetic whimper, Anders headed for the kitchen, where he sliced himself some cheese and meat. He put them on a plate, then drew a mug of cider from one of the big taps in the wall. He had meant to eat downstairs, but kept worrying about what the troll baby might be doing and finally decided to go back upstairs with the meal.

After putting the plate on the corner of the bed, Anders opened the closet door. The little troll stared up at him with huge eyes, then farted. Anders cried out in disgust and backed up to the bed. He waited for the rotten cabbage odor to fade before he picked up his plate again.

The little troll watched solemnly as Anders began to eat. After a moment it lurched to its feet. So it was a troddler, a troll just learning to walk. Moving carefully, setting one blunt foot ahead of the other, the troddler wobbled toward him. Then it leaned against his leg and stared at the plate, its wide nostrils twitching. After a moment it made a sound that pretty clearly indicated hunger.

"Go away!" said Anders sharply.

The troddler reached up and made the same noise.

Anders sighed. Being kind to a troll, even one that was only a troddler, seemed like the height of stupidity. But "be kind" was the only advice his mother had given him for situations like this. So he broke off a piece of cheese and handed it to the little creature.

A wide grin split the infant's face, revealing seven or eight gray teeth that looked like small stones set in its jaw. The grin revealed something else, too: a piece of paper stuck to one of the creature's teeth—paper with writing on it.

The troddler was about to pop the cheese into its mouth when

Anders grabbed its hand. The baby began to squawk. That was all right with Anders; squawking forced the thing to keep its mouth open. Fighting an urge to vomit, Anders darted his fingers over the thick, gray tongue and into the gaping mini-cavern of the troddler's mouth. With a cry of triumph, he snatched out the bit of paper.

When he let go of its arm the baby instantly jammed the cheese into its mouth and began to chew, smacking noisily.

Ignoring the creature and its sounds, Anders hurried to the bathroom, where he placed the moist paper on the shelf, then carefully washed his hands to get rid of the thick, sticky troll-drool. Once he had dried them again, he picked up the paper. It was sticky, too. He considered trying to wash it off, but was afraid the ink would run more than it already had. Working carefully, he unfolded it and smoothed it against the mirror. He was able to make out some of the words, which were indeed in his mother's handwriting, but between the smears and the chew marks, it was frustratingly incomplete:

Dear And
      been called away rgent mission.
not sure   I will to return.
   much not told you.
 meant to, soon.   need to find out for
yourself   dare not write it all
   become dangerous   try to
follow snowflakes lead you to the red
stone. The red stone is the key. need only
   father's name for troll
    you will be frigh
much you think you know is fal
   Do not go for help, or all will be lost!
              ve,
        Moth

Anders shook his head in mystification. What could it possibly mean?

He took a deep breath. Well, the first thing it meant was that his mother had not gone against her will. That was good. But what were the things she had not told him—things she did not even dare write down? Why couldn't he go for help? And how in the world were snowflakes supposed to lead him to a red stone?

Hearing a sound, he turned toward the door. The troddler stood there, gazing at him with wide eyes. A string of orange spittle ran from one corner of its mouth and it was clutching the rest of the cheese in its stubby hand.

Anders was about to shout at the little creature for chewing up the note when it held the cheese out to him. The gesture was touching, and not at all what he would have expected from a troll. But even though it calmed his anger, the idea of eating something that had just been in a troll's hands was too much for him, and he pushed the cheese back.

"Gurk!" said the troddler happily. Then it popped the cheese into its own mouth.

Still clutching the soggy note, Anders returned to the bedroom. The troddler trailed behind him and stared with wide, eager eyes as Anders picked up his mug. Anders took a deep swallow of the cider. Then, against his better judgment, he passed the mug to the troddler. It gulped down the remainder of the amber liquid, then belched happily.

Anders stared at the piece of paper again, trying desperately to make sense of his mother's fragmented words. They indicated trouble, and urgency, but not panic. He was more mystified than ever.

"How did **you** get here?" he asked, glowering at the troddler. "And where's my mother?"

"Glurp?" it asked, not very helpfully.

Anders sighed and pushed himself to his feet to start another search—not for his mother, this time, but for more clues to where she might have gone.

He started by examining her room. He felt hesitant and shy, as if he were spying on her, and didn't go so far as to open the drawers in her dresser, telling himself he would do that later, if he absolutely had to. Finding nothing, he stepped into the hallway. The troddler came tottering after him. Anders started to shoo the creature back into the room, then decided it was better to keep it nearby.

He had finished with the upstairs and was searching the kitchen when he found his first clue: a small white flower lying beside the doorway. Anders stared at it for a moment, then felt his heart leap. The common name for the flower was "winterkiss." But he and his mother had always called the blossoms by his baby name for them: "snowflakes."

snowflakes lead you to the red stone...

The troddler reached for the blossom, but Anders held it back, which caused the thing to squall again. Fortunately it stopped when he tucked the blossom into the pouch he wore at his side. He straightened his shoulders, feeling a surge of confidence now that he had figured out the first clue. Then he realized he had lost sight of the troddler.

"Now where have you gone?" he muttered.

It took only a moment to find the baby; it was sniffing around the door to the cellar. Beside the door, tight against the frame, was another white blossom.

Anders felt a clench of fear. He had not checked the cellar on his first tour of the house. The scary stories his father had told him about it when he was little had left him with a permanent reluctance to enter it. His mother, he knew, felt the same way. It would never have occurred to him to think she had gone down there.

Now he had to think about it.

He pulled the door open.

Cool, dank air rolled out.

The stony scent of troll was stronger here, terrifyingly strong. He might have turned away—except he saw a small white blossom lying on the third step down.

Anders swallowed nervously. Everyone knew if a troll was going to enter your house, it would come through the cellar.

But his mother's note...

He shook himself and muttered ferociously, "If that's where she's gone, that's where I follow."

He went to the cupboard to fetch one of the torchsticks old Gerda made in return for the soup his mother so often took over. Returning to the cellarway, he whispered, "*Ignis*." At once the upper end of the stick began to glow. The troddler gasped in fear and pulled back, landing on its rump.

"It's all right," said Anders soothingly. But the troddler just looked at him with wide eyes and whimpered. Anders sighed and took the little creature's hand. Its skin was thick and bumpy, but pleasantly cool. The creature burped happily as Anders pulled it to its feet.

They started down the stairway, Anders leading the way, the troddler scooting along behind, sliding from step to step on its bottom. The torchstick glowed more brightly, automatically adjusting to the increased darkness.

Suddenly Anders stopped, cursing himself for six kinds of a fool. The troddler bumped into him from behind, but he scarcely noticed. The stairs were coated with dust. He should be looking for footprints!

Holding the torchstick ahead of him, he bent to study the next step. It was clear enough that something had disturbed the dust—disturbed it so much that he could not see a clear footprint. How many feet had passed over this stairway?

Extending the torchstick farther he could see, two steps down, a small footprint. That had to be his mother's! The surge of relief he felt was quickly replaced by terror. One step below it, near the edge of the stair, was another print, wide and blunt, too big for the narrow plank to hold completely.

The mark of a troll foot.

Anders shuddered. Part of him wanted to bolt back up the stairs and flee the house. Another part insisted he had to go on. His mother had told him to follow the snowflakes, and he could see another blossom lying right at the base of the stairs. He took a deep breath. Onward it was.

"All right," he said to the troddler. "Let's go."

When they were all the way down, Anders found a new problem: dust did not show on the moist, earthen surface of the cellar floor the way it had on the stairs. And he did not see another snowflake.

It was the troddler who provided the solution. It began sniffing, its wide nostrils growing even wider, then lunged forward as if it had caught a scent it wanted to follow.

For lack of a better idea, Anders let the little creature lead the way.

At the far side of the cellar an old carpet hung over a hole in the wall. The bottom of the hole was about a foot and a half above floor level. Oval shaped and four feet high, the hole led to a root cellar where the family could store vegetables for the winter. Except they never did, since that would have meant coming down here to fetch them.

Better to get them at market.

Anders drew aside the carpet. On the ledge you had to step over to enter the root cellar lay a white blossom.

He picked up the snowflake and climbed in.

The troddler scrambled after him.

The torchstick grew brighter in response to the deeper gloom. Anders, easily able to see the whole of the small room, felt a surge of relief at finding nothing awful, and at the same time a sharp stab of disappointment as he realized he had come to a dead end. Raising the torchstick, he turned in a slow circle, looking for anything that might indicate his mother—or anyone else—had been here. Nothing. But as he turned to leave, the troddler began making urgent noises. Then it scrambled forward to point at the back wall.

"Come on," said Anders, reaching for its hand. "We have to go."

The baby still resisted. Anders stepped closer to pull it away, then gasped. Caught between two stones was a piece of fabric—troll fabric, easily identified by the dull color and coarse weave. He stared at it in astonishment. How could a piece of cloth have gotten stuck between the stones?

He looked more carefully, then caught his breath. One of the stones had a distinct reddish tinge.

He took out the remains of his mother's note and examined it in the light of the torchstick:

> snowflakes lead you to the red stone.
> The red stone is the key. You need only

The rest of the sentence had been chewed up by the troddler. Nearly ready to scream with frustration, Anders pushed the stone.

Nothing happened.

He tried to twist it.

Nothing.

Feeling foolish, he blew on it, whispered to it, hit it, kicked it, struck it with the torchstick.

Nothing, nothing, and nothing.

Then the troddler waddled up to the wall. Anders was about to pull the little creature back when it smacked the stone with the flat of its palm. A sudden grinding sound made Anders back away in surprise. His surprise was even greater when the wall pulled apart to reveal a low, wide tunnel. Even without stepping forward, he could see the small white blossom that lay just on the other side.

Anders put his hand on the troddler's head. "I don't know how you did that," he said. "But if I had some more cheese I'd give it to you right now."

"Gurk!" said the troddler. It was clearly eager to enter the tunnel. But Anders hesitated. His mind was racing with questions: What did it mean that there was a tunnel under his home? Was this how the trolls had come for his father? If that was so, why had they waited so long to return? Most important, what was he going to do if he actually came upon a troll?

Well, he still had his knife. And he had the troddler. Maybe he could use it as a hostage.

He wondered if that would make any difference to a troll, if it would even care about the baby.

Finally unable to resist the mystery of the tunnel, and the sense that it might lead to his mother, Anders hoisted the torchstick and started forward.

After a few steps he murmured "*diminis*" and the torchstick went to half light.

No sense making his presence too obvious.

The tunnel continued for some distance without change: cold, dank walls; low ceiling; occasional puddles of slimy water. A few times he heard the squeaking of a rodent. At least, he hoped that's all it was…

The troddler stuck close to him, clutching the leg of his trousers. He found himself oddly glad to have it so near.

Finally the tunnel began to widen, then quickly grew so wide that Anders could no longer see the walls on either side. He hesitated, then murmured "*ignis*."

When the torchstick came to full light he saw that he had entered a large cavern—so large he could not see the opposite side. He heard a rumbling noise behind him and turned just in time to see the mouth of the tunnel sliding shut. With a cry of horror he rushed back. He was too late; the opening had become a solid rock wall. Frantic, he began searching for some way to open it again. But the stone was seamless, without even a hint of what might be the edge of a door. After several minutes of desperate searching he lay his head against the stone in despair, trying not to weep. He didn't even pull away when the troddler reached up to hold his hand.

A moment later he heard a deep chuckle. Icy fear clutching his heart, Anders turned and found himself staring straight into the belly of an adult troll. He fought back a scream even as the troddler screeched with delight and wrapped its arms around the big troll's leg.

Anders put his hand to the haft of his knife, which somehow helped him find his voice.

"Where is my mother?"

He didn't expect an answer—didn't really expect anything other than a blow to the head that would crush his skull. So he was astonished when the troll spoke. In a voice like stones rubbing together it said slowly, "I will take you to her."

"Is she all right?"

"Of course," rumbled the troll. Then it stooped to pick up the troddler. "I am glad you brought back little Kratz-kah. We were very worried about her. Follow me."

Ignoring Anders's volley of questions, the troll turned and walked away. The boy waited a moment, then scurried along behind. After a while he realized they were actually following a downhill path, marked on each side by a row of reddish rocks. Eventually they crossed a stone bridge that spanned a dark chasm. He could hear water running beneath it—far beneath it.

On the far side of the bridge the path leveled out, and Anders saw the first of the troll dwellings, crude cottages made of stone. They didn't seem to have roofs, which struck him as odd until he realized there wouldn't be much need for a roof underground. It wasn't as if the trolls needed to keep out the rain!

The dwellings became more numerous. Soon Anders realized he had entered a village. His nervousness increased. Was his mother a prisoner here? How could he possibly help her? What was going to happen to them?

Trolls peered from their windows. Troll babies sat in the front yards, sucking on rocks. Older troll children chased each other around the cottages with a slow, clumping gait, but stopped to stare as he went by. Two old troll women, gossiping across a stone fence, turned and smiled toothlessly at him.

Anders tried to question his guide, but the troll did not speak again. Yet even as his fear was growing, another part of his mind registered surprise that the village appeared so...normal.

At last they came to what was clearly the town square. It was dimly lit by hanging cages filled with large, glowing slugs. In the center of the square was a table. Seated at the table were six trolls—and his mother. When she saw Anders approaching she leaped to her feet, smiling in relief.

"Anders!" she cried, spreading her arms to welcome him. "I'm so glad you're here!"

He ran to her embrace. "What's happening?" he gasped. "Are you all right? Are we prisoners? I don't understand!"

She held him close. "No, we're not prisoners, darling. It may be some time before we can leave here, but that won't be because of the trolls. It's because we're not safe at home. Listen, Anders, I'm sorry I had to leave so quickly. Thank goodness you were able to follow the clues in my note. I'm sorry I couldn't be more clear, but the danger was too great."

Anders laughed. "That note was less clear than you expected. There was a troddler in the house, and she ate most of it."

He took the remains of her message from his pocket and handed it to her.

His mother examined the tattered paper with dismay. "But how did you manage to find your way here?"

"I worked out the clues from what was left."

"But the tunnel—" She looked at the note again, then at him. "How could you possibly open the tunnel without knowing you had to put your hand on the stone and say your father's name?"

Anders blinked at the idea. "Is that what you're supposed to do? I tried everything I could think of. Finally the troddler—" He paused, then corrected himself. "Finally Kratz-kah put her hand on it, and it just…opened."

Understanding dawned in his mother's face. "Of course! The tunnel will always open to a troll's touch. Thank goodness Kratz-Kah sneaked into the house. You might be in prison now if she hadn't."

Anders looked at her in shock.

"This morning we learned that the trollwatch has found out about your father and me," she said. "That's why I couldn't come back today, or come to school to get you. They might have been waiting for me."

"I don't understand," said Anders plaintively. "What do we have to do with the trolls?"

"Your mother has been helping us for years," said one of the trolls at the table. "Now it's time for us to help her."

"Actually, both your parents were helping, until your father was taken," said a male troll at the other end of the table. He had a pair of stones in his hands, and was rubbing them idly together.

"But it was trolls who took him!" said Anders angrily.

His mother shook her head. "That was the story we put out, to keep down suspicion." She closed her eyes for a moment, and it was clear the next words were hard for her to speak. "Anders, your father was killed by the trollwatch."

"What? Why?"

"For daring to help the trolls. They caught him one night, as he was coming back from a meeting." Tears welled up in her eyes, and the sorrow in her voice brought back all his own sense of loss. "We were lucky they couldn't identify him after the dogs were done with him," she whispered. "If they had figured out who he was, they would have come for us, too."

Anders felt his knees grow weak. "Why didn't you tell me all this before?" He gazed around at the trolls, creatures he had been taught to hate and fear. "You lied to me all these years."

"Your father and I didn't know what else to do. We didn't dare tell you the truth about the trolls when you were little. One slip at school, even one suspicious sentence, and the trollwatch could have taken your father and me away, and put you in an orphanage. It was safer not to let you know. The time was coming to tell you everything, but I didn't know when or how I was going to do it." She shook her head and smiled ruefully. "I did hope to do it more gently than this!"

"I still don't understand what you have to do with trolls!" he said, part baffled, part angry.

"Your mother is a great healer," said the troll sitting next to her. "Though we do not fall ill very often, and it is hard to injure us, our stony flesh is also slow to heal. Your mother knows how to help us, as did her mother, and her mother's mother before her. As, we hope, will you."

"That's why we have a troll tunnel leading to our cellar," said his mother gently. "Ever since the new government banned trolls and humans from mixing—"

"Because that way it was easier to make us work as slaves in their mines," growled one of the trolls.

His mother nodded. "Ever since the government decided to do that, I have been forced to do my healing in secret. Otherwise, I could be sent to prison." Her indignation flared. "Sent to prison for healing! Can you imagine?"

Anders looked around at the troll village. "How often do you come here?"

His mother shrugged. "Only when a troll needs me. Probably not more than once a month. Usually I came at night, while you were sleeping. But just after you left for school this morning I learned that the trollwatch was after me and I had to flee at once. If I had not, you would still have come home to an empty house, for I would have been in prison." She took a breath, then added bitterly, "Or, more likely, dead from an 'accident' arranged by the officials."

"It was I who brought the warning to your mother," said the troll next to her. She was bouncing the troddler on her knee. "I did not know Kratz-Kah here had followed me. We have been looking all over for her. Thank you for bringing her back." She wiped a tear from her eye. "I was terrified for her."

Kratz-Kah made a gravelly chuckling sound. The troll woman wiped a string of drool from the corner of the troddler's mouth. Kratz-Kah squirmed and held her stubby, stony arms out to Anders.

He hesitated, then reached out to take her.

She was heavier than he expected.

"So," he said to his mother, as Kratz-kah wrapped her arms about his neck. "How long will we need to live down here?"

"Until the trolls are free again."

Anders looked around at the faces of the creatures he had been taught to fear for so long. The creatures his father had died fighting for.

They began to smile at him. The smiles were ugly and lopsided, filled with misshapen teeth. But they were also warm and genuine.

"All right," he said, holding the troddler closer. "What do we do now?"

Old Glory

Donald Henderson
Civic Responsibility Class

Ms. Barnan
Sept. 15, 2040

Essay: The Day I Did My Duty
by
Donald B. Henderson

My great grandfather was the craziest man I ever met. Sometimes it was embarrassing even to have him be part of the family.

For example: you should have seen how he acted when Congress passed the S.O.S. law last June.

He actually **turned off** the holo set!

"Well, that's the end of life as we know it," he said as the image started to fade. Then he stared at the floor and started to mutter.

"Oh, Arthur, don't be ridiculous," said my mother. She switched the set back on and waited for the newsgeek to reappear in the center of the room.

"Ridiculous?" yelped Gran-Da. "You want to see ridiculous? I'll show you ridiculous!" He stood up and pointed to the big flag that hangs over our holo-set. "That's ridiculous! Thirteen stripes, sixty-two stars, and not a bit of meaning. After what they did today, it's all gone."

"That's not so, Grampa," said my father quietly. His voice was low and soft, the way it gets when he's really angry. "Now sit down and be quiet."

That was a relief. After Gran-Da came to live with us, I was always afraid he was going to get us into trouble. So I felt better whenever

83

Dad made him be quiet. Sometimes I wished Dad would just throw him out. I didn't really want him sleeping on the streets, like all the old men I walk past on the way to school. But I didn't want to make our Uncle angry, either.

Later that night, when I was going to bed, Gran-Da called me into his room.

"How you doing?" he asked.

I shrugged. "I'm okay."

Gran-Da smiled. "Are you afraid of me?"

I wanted to say no. Only that would have been a lie. So I just nodded my head.

"Afraid I'll talk dangerous?"

I nodded again. I didn't know what I would do if my friends were ever around when he started talking like he does sometimes. I knew what I **should** do, of course. But I didn't know if I could do it. I mean, he **was** my great grandfather, even if he was crazy and wicked.

He looked sad. "Are all the kids at your school like you?" he asked.

"What do you mean?"

"Scared little sheep, afraid to talk."

"I'm not afraid to talk," I said loudly. "I just don't talk nonsense, like…"

I broke off.

"Like me?" he asked, scratching at the little fringe of white hair that circled the back of his head. (I don't know why he never got his head fixed. All the other great grandfathers I know have full heads of hair, whatever color they want. Not mine.)

I looked away from him. Suddenly I realized what was wrong with his room. "Where's your flag?" I asked.

"I took it down."

I must have looked pretty funny. At least, the look on my face made him snort.

"How could you?" I asked in a whisper.

"It was easy," he said. "I just pulled out the tabs at the corners, and then—"

"Gran-Da!"

"Donald!" he replied. "When the government passed S.O.S., they took away the last thing that flag stood for. I don't want to look at it anymore."

He paused and stared at the floor for a while. I looked at the door, wondering if he would say anything if I just left.

Suddenly he looked up again. "Listen, Donald. I'm ninety years old. That's not that old, these days—I could probably last another thirty."

That was no news. It was one of the reasons my mother was so upset when he moved in. I felt sorry for her. Thirty years of Gran-Da was my idea of a real nightmare.

"The thing is," he continued, "I'm just a normal guy, not a hero. But sometimes there's something you have to do, no matter what it costs you."

I looked at him in horror. "You're not going to do anything crazy, are you?" I felt sick in my stomach. Didn't he understand he could get us **all** in trouble? If he wasn't careful, the Uncles might come and take us away. I glanced at the ceiling, half expecting it to open up so that a giant hand could reach down and snatch my great grandfather then and there.

"Why are you telling me this?" I asked at last.

"Maybe I'm hoping that if I scare you enough it will make you start to think." He shrugged. "Or maybe I just want to see what you'll do."

"Can I go now?"

"Yeah," he said bitterly. "Go on. Get out of here." I slipped out of his room and ran down the hall to my own room. I flopped onto my bed and lay there, staring up at my beautiful flag and trembling.

I thought about Gran-Da all that night. I thought about him in school the next morning, while we were saying the pledge, and the Lord's Prayer, and reciting the names of the presidents. I remembered what Gran-Da had said the first time he heard me recite the list—that there had been more presidents than we were naming, that some of them were being left out.

I wanted to talk to my teacher, but I was afraid.

The next morning was Saturday. When Gran-Da came to breakfast he had a red band tied around his head. He was wearing a vest with fringe on it, a blue shirt, and faded blue pants; he was carrying a lumpy plastic bag. He had a button on his vest that looked like an upside down Y with an extra stick coming out of it.

"What's that?" I asked, pointing to the button.

"A peace symbol," he said. He dropped the bag to the floor and settled into his chair.

"Really, Arthur," said my mother. "Don't you think this is carrying things a little too far?"

"S.O.S. was carrying things too far," said Gran-Da.

My father sighed. "Look, Grampa, I don't really agree with the law either. But it's not really a problem. If you don't break the rules,

S.O.S. won't have any effect on you."

I was amazed to hear him say that. Then I decided he must be trying to get Gran-Da to calm down. It didn't work. Gran-Da shook his head stubbornly, and suddenly I knew what he had in the bag.

My throat got thick with fear. I couldn't finish my breakfast.

After breakfast I followed Gran-Da out of the house. He was heading for the town square. I was pretty sure I knew what he was planning. My stomach was churning. What if the Uncles thought he had polluted our whole family?

I could only think of one way to save us. I slipped into a televid booth to call my Uncle. When I told him what was happening he looked stern and shocked.

"You won't hold this against the rest of us, will you?" I asked nervously.

He shook his head. "Of course not," he said. "You've done the right thing. We'll have to come and talk to all of you when this is over, of course. But I wouldn't worry about it much."

The screen went blank. I hurried back out to the street.

I felt embarrassed, and frightened. But I was also a little excited. Would the S.O.S. men really show up? My friends would think I was a real hero. I hurried toward the town square.

Gran-Da was already there. He had climbed onto the bandstand, of all places, and he was shouting about S.O.S.

People looked at him nervously. To my surprise, a few actually stopped to listen. I stood beneath a large tree, about a hundred feet away. I didn't want to get too close.

Suddenly Gran-Da reached into the bag and pulled out the flag he had taken off his wall the night before. Holding the upper edge, he rolled it over the side of the bandstand. A slight breeze made the stripes slide and shift.

I covered my face with my hands and wished the terrible scene would end. Where were the S.O.S. men?

"Friends!" cried Gran-Da. "When I was a boy, this piece of cloth used to stand for something. Yes, it did. In fact, it stood for a whole lot of things. Ideas. Like that a man should be free to say what he thinks, and worship where he wants, and get together with other folks if it pleases him."

More people were stopping to listen now. Someone started to boo.

"But that's all over," shouted Gran-Da. "Bit by bit, piece by piece, we've given away all the things this used to stand for. S.O.S. was the end of it. Now this poor old flag doesn't stand for anything at all.

"That being so, I think it's time I put it out of its misery."

I looked around. Where were the S.O.S. men? Why didn't they get here?

Now that people realized what Gran-Da was going to do, they started to back away. Some of them left. I could tell that others wanted to, wanted to get as far away from the terrible thing he was about to do as they possibly could. But they couldn't bring themselves to go. They wanted to see if he would really do it. Gran-Da raised the flag and lit a match.

"Goodbye, Old Glory," he said sadly. "It was a good idea while it lasted."

He touched the corner of the flag with the match. Nothing happened, of course, since like all flags it was made of flameproof material. You can't burn a flag even if you try.

Gran-Da knew that. He wasn't stupid—just crazy. A crazy, dangerous person—the kind who could ruin the wonderful country we've built.

Suddenly I saw the S.O.S. men. They looked beautiful in their blue pants, white shirts and red vests.

Gran-Da saw them, too. I know he did.

So it's not like it's my fault, really. He had a chance. Everyone knows that even though the law allows for instant executions, the Shoot On Sight men are supposed to give a guy a chance.

But Gran-Da didn't care. When his first match went out he lit another one. He held it to the corner of the fireproof flag and just stood there smiling at the three men.

So everyone could see that he was crazy.

The men lifted their laser rifles. The leader counted to three, and they fired in unison.

The light sliced right through the old man. He toppled over the edge of the bandstand. The flag curled around him as he fell. He was still holding it when he hit the ground.

My throat got thick. I could feel tears at the corners of my eyes. Crazy, I know. But he was my great grandfather after all. So I don't think it was too bad to feel a **little** sad about what had happened.

That doesn't mean I don't think I did the right thing by calling the S.O.S. guys. I mean, think about it. What would happen if other people started to think like Gran-Da—crazy things, like that everybody should be allowed to say whatever they wanted to?

What kind of a world would that be?

Just Like You

Just because I've tentacles,
And my skin is ocean blue,
Don't think I don't have feelings
Just the same as you.

Every time I fall in love
My knees are filled with bliss;
I pucker up my eyebrows
To give my girl a kiss.

The times we have a lover's spat
My liver's always broken;
Many times I've cried my ears off
Because harsh words were spoken.

When I am suspicious
My feet can smell a rat;
I try to eat nutritious,
Lots of sugar, salt and fat.

My nose runs and my feet smell—
I've heard that yours do, too.
I shine my ears with gobs of wax,
Just the same as you.

When scared, I feel my skin crawl,
The way you humans do.
Mine comes back when I call it
(I hope that yours does, too).

Though you're rarely eight feet tall,
I don't look down on you;
I know we're really much the same—
Even though you are not blue.

The World's

Worst

Fairy Godmother

by Bruce Coville

with illustrations by Katherine Coville

The World's
Worst Fairy Godmother

Chapter One:
Another Fine Mess

Maybelle Clodnowski stood at the edge of the swamp and took two frogs from her apron pocket.

"Here we go," she said, looking at them fondly. "This should suit you just fine."

Before Maybelle could put the frogs into the water she heard someone clear his throat behind her. It was a deep sound. A fierce sound. A definitely disapproving sound.

Maybelle turned around. Her eyes went wide. She swallowed once, then whispered, "Hello, boss."

Mr. Peters was as tall and slender as Maybelle was short and podgy. His nostrils flared and he raised his eyebrows so high Maybelle was afraid they might shoot right over the top of his forehead and keep on going.

"What," he asked in his deepest, crankiest, most boy-are-you-in-trouble-now voice, "What in heaven's name do you think you're doing?"

"Sending the young lovers off to a new life?" asked Maybelle, smiling hopefully.

Mr. Peters scowled.

"They're both happy," Maybelle added defensively.

"Happy?" roared Mr. Peters. "**Happy?!?** Maybelle, they're both **frogs!**"

"Well, they like the outdoors."

Mr. Peters made a rumbling sound deep in his chest. "Maybelle,

the Prince of Burundia and the Princess of Ghukistan were not raised to be frogs. They were raised to be rulers of a kingdom."

"Well, I know that, boss. But the poor things really didn't like the idea much, and I was trying—"

"You **were** trying, you **are** trying, and it looks very much as if you always will be trying!" roared Mr. Peters. He made a gesture with his hands, and the frogs disappeared. In their place, coughing and wheezing in a cloud of blue smoke, stood a handsome prince and an extremely beautiful princess. They both looked bewildered, and a little embarrassed.

"You two go on home," said Mr. Peters sharply. "As for you, Maybelle, I want you to meet me in my office tomorrow morning at nine sharp."

With another wave of his hand he disappeared in a cloud of white smoke.

The smell of daisies lingered behind him.

"His office?" asked the prince, stepping out of the swamp. He shook a minnow from his boot.

"Up there," said Maybelle, pointing toward the sky.

"Heaven?" asked the princess, her blue eyes wide.

"You could call it that," said Maybelle. "Though at the moment it doesn't quite feel that way." She sighed, then turned her eyes from the clouds back to the swamp. "I'm terribly sorry about the frog thing. I didn't mean for it to happen that way. When Princess Igrella kissed you, Prince Arbus, you were supposed to turn back into a human. Why Princess Igrella turned into a frog instead I'll never know."

She shook her wand in disgust, then tucked it into the belt that held her skirt close to her plump waist.

Princess Igrella patted Maybelle on the shoulder. "No need to apologize. I was pretty upset at first, but when I thought about life in court versus life in the swamp...well, somehow a lily pad began to seem a lot more comfortable than a throne. As far as I'm concerned, all that really mattered was that Prince Arbus and I could be together."

Maybelle smiled. "At least you're still both the same species. But maybe I can—"

Prince Arbus put his arm around Igrella's tiny waist. "We'll be fine, Maybelle," he said nobly. "One way or another. Please...feel free to go on to your next case."

"But maybe I should stay and—"

"We'll be fine," repeated the prince firmly, his voice a little desperate. "Thank you for your help."

"Oh, it was my pleasure," said Maybelle cheerfully. She glanced at the sky. "Certainly more of a pleasure than tomorrow morning is going to be."

The cloud directly above her grew dark and rumbled with thunder.

Maybelle rolled her eyes. "Such a fuss over one little mistake."

A bolt of lightning seared down beside her, charring a clump of ferns just inches from her right foot.

"All right, all right! So it wasn't a **little** mistake. So no one's perfect, all right? I'll see you in the morning."

Wrapping her cloak around her, she vanished in a cloud of pink smoke.

The smell of freshly baked muffins lingered behind her.

"I hope she'll be all right," whispered Princess Igrella.

"I'm sure Maybelle will be fine," said the prince. "It's her next client I'm worried about." He shook his head. "Really, she has to be the worst fairy godmother in the entire world."

As Prince Arbus guided Princess Igrella out of the swamp, a teardrop fell from far above him, landing on his head.

Chapter Two:
Maybelle's Last Chance

Maybelle hurried across heaven, leaping from cloud to cloud. The angels watched in amusement. The cherubs were in a state of high hysteria.

"Late again," she muttered, missing a cloud and falling several feet before her wings could catch her. "Late again. Oh, Mr. Peters is going to be mad, mad, mad."

Maybelle was nearly, but not totally, correct. Mr. Peters was not merely mad. He was furious.

"Maybelle, can't you do anything right?" he exploded, when she reached the spacious cloud where he had his office.

"Of course I can!" she said.

"All right, name one thing," he replied, crossing his arms. "One single thing that you've done right in the last one hundred and twenty years."

Maybelle paused. She started to speak, then shook her head. She made a face. She started to speak again, then sighed. Suddenly her eyes lit up. "How about that lovely gown I wove for Princess Aurora? The one I made of cobwebs and eiderdown and stitched together with moonbeams?"

"Beautiful," agreed Mr. Peters. "Until it started to rain and the gown dissolved—while she was wearing it!"

Maybelle hunched into herself. "So I made a little slip."

"You made a **very** little slip!" roared Mr. Peters. "That's why the princess was so embarrassed!" He shook his head and took a deep breath. "I'm sorry. I shouldn't lose my temper that way. I would have been promoted by now if I could break that habit. But really, Maybelle, you're the only one who does that to me. I never even raise my voice to anyone beside you. What am I going to do with you?"

Before Maybelle could answer, he said, "Never mind. I'll tell you what I'm going to do. I'm going to give you another chance. Your last chance."

Maybelle gulped. "**Last** chance?" she asked nervously.

Mr. Peters nodded. "This is it. Either you pull this one off, or you can trade in your wings and your wand for good."

"But Mr. Peters! You can't do that to me. The only thing I ever wanted to be is a fairy godmother! You can't—"

"Maybelle, you've had nearly two centuries to get this right! As far as I can tell you're no better at it now than when you started. I'm sorry, but I can't let this go on forever. I've already given you more chances than I should. I'm starting to get complaints from upstairs." He rolled his eyes, indicating the next level of clouds above them. In a whisper he said, "I had to pull strings just to get this job for you. So to make sure nothing goes wrong, you're going to have a supervisor."

"A supervisor?"

"To make sure nothing goes wrong."

"Jeepers, boss—what do you think I am? An amateur?"

"Yes. Now, your supervisor will be along simply to make sure things don't get too far out of hand. This is still your job; she'll step in only if you muff things. But if she **does** have to step in…" He scowled and made a gesture with his hands that indicated breaking something in half.

Maybelle clutched her wand. "You wouldn't!"

"Yes," said Mr. Peters. "I would."

Maybelle sighed. "Who is this supervisor?"

"Edna Prim."

Maybelle gasped. "Not **the** Edna Prim?"

Mr. Peters nodded.

"Fairy Godmother of the year for the last hundred and seventeen years running? **That** Edna Prim?"

"The same."

"She's my hero!"

As Maybelle spoke a tall, stern looking woman floated down to the cloud. Her dress billowed charmingly around her. "Good morning, Mr. Peters," she said. "I came as soon as I could."

"There it is!" cried Maybelle, rushing forward. "The Fairy Godmother of the Year Medallion! Oh, I am so impressed."

She clutched the medallion, pulling Edna's neck forward as she did. "It's beautiful," gasped Maybelle.

"Yes, it is, isn't it?" said Edna, yanking it back. She shook herself, looking something like a tall, thin cat that has just heard a joke of which it faintly disapproved.

"You understand the assignment, Edna?" said Mr. Peters.

Edna nodded. "It seems like a fairly simple case. I don't see how anyone could mess it up."

"You'd be surprised," said Mr. Peters darkly.

"Wait a minute," said Maybelle. "I don't understand. What **is** the assignment?"

"You'll see when we get there," said Mr. Peters. "In fact, if you're both ready, I think we should be leaving. Just follow me, ladies—"

With a wave of his hand, he disappeared.

Edna vanished a second later, leaving the scent of heavily starched laundry lingering in the air behind her.

"Wait for me!" cried Maybelle. Rushing forward, she leaped off the cloud and hurtled toward the earth far below.

She was halfway down before she actually remembered the spell for following the others.

Chapter Three:
Little Miss Perfect

Mr. Peters and Edna were waiting beside a small, tidy looking building that stood at the edge of a small, tidy looking town.

"For heaven's sake, Maybelle, make yourself invisible," snapped Mr. Peters when Maybelle floated down beside them.

Maybelle sighed. Then she muttered a few words as she made a circle over her head with her wand. She disappeared instantly—except for her left foot, which looked very strange standing there all by itself.

"Drat!" she muttered. Reaching down, she tapped her foot with her wand. The foot disappeared, too.

Edna rolled her eyes, but said nothing.

"All right," said Mr. Peters. "It's time to meet your next client, Maybelle. Let's slip inside."

Following Mr. Peters and Edna through a crack in the door, Maybelle found herself standing at the back of a school room. Standing at the front of the room was a very harried looking teacher.

About twenty children sat on hard wooden benches, working on slates. For about two minutes, everyone was very quiet. Then a boy near the front took a large spider from his pocket. It took Maybelle a moment to realize that the spider was made from black paper.

Using a string attached to one end, the boy dangled the spider over the shoulder of the girl in front of him.

The girl leaped to her feet. "Teacher! Teacher!" she shrieked.

The teacher sighed. "What is it, Maria?"

Maria, who by now had figured out that the spider was made of paper, straightened her shoulders and said with great dignity, "Gustav **tried** to scare me."

"Well, I think he succeeded," replied the teacher. "Gustav, you will stay after school today."

"Yes, Herr Bauer," replied Gustav with a sigh.

"Ah, I see," whispered Maybelle to Mr. Peters. "You want me to work with Gustav."

"No. Keep watching."

Two rows ahead of them a dark haired boy reached over and pinched a girl who had long braids. She immediately turned and punched him in the nose. He jumped to his feet, howling with anger. But before he could hit her back, the teacher snapped. "Friedrich! Heidi! What is this all about?"

"He pinched me!" cried Heidi.

"She **punched** me!" whined Friedrich.

"You did it first!"

"Did not!"

"Did too!"

"Did not!"

"Enough!" bellowed Herr Bauer. "If you twins can't get along, I'll have to separate you."

"Good!" cried both of them together.

"I will also have to inform your parents of that fact," said the teacher ominously.

The twins sank into their seats, muttering unhappily.

"Ah, it's **them**," said Maybelle. "Well, twins really ought to be able to get along. I think I can—"

"Keep watching," said Mr. Peters.

A boy in the third row began to smile. Taking something from his pocket, he poked the shoulder of the girl in front of him. When she turned, he held up a huge earthworm and mouthed the word "Watch."

Then he popped the worm into his mouth and swallowed it.

"TEACHER!" shrieked the girl. "Igor...ate a **worm!**"

"Me?" asked Igor, his face full of puzzled innocence.

"I saw you!" cried the girl.

"Do you have any evidence?" asked Igor.

"Of course not. You **swallowed** it!"

Herr Bauer had been watching this with one hand pressed to his forehead, as if he had a throbbing headache. Now he said, "All right, that's enough. Helga, calm down. Igor, save your lunch for recess."

"Oh, yuck!" cried Maybelle. "Are you going to give me that horrible Igor for a client?"

Mr. Peters shook his head.

"But Helga doesn't need—"

"It's not her, either."

"Oh, I've got it!" said Maybelle. "It's Herr Bauer! That makes sense. With a class like this, he needs some help."

"No, Maybelle. It's not the teacher."

"But...."

"Keep watching."

Now a girl who had been sitting quietly in the front row stood up.

She had blond hair and bright blue eyes. She was quite pretty, and her dress was so clean and perfect it looked as if it had just been made that morning.

Her posture was flawless.

Walking to the teacher's desk, she placed her paper on it as if delivering a gift from the gods. Then she stood beside the desk, something almost like a smirk on her face, as the teacher examined her work.

"Susan, this paper is wonderful—as usual."

"Thank you," replied Susan. "I tried my best—as usual!"

Three of the boys began to cough.

Susan flounced back to her bench.

"That's your client," said Mr. Peters.

"Susan?" asked Maybelle in astonishment. "But why? She's already just about perfect."

"Precisely."

"But all those other little monsters—"

"Are perfectly normal children, sometimes nice, sometimes disgusting. No, Susan is your case."

"But what's wrong with her?"

"Susan Pfenstermacher is a wonderful child. Unfortunately, she thinks she's perfect."

Maybelle's eyes went wide. "Uh-oh," she whispered.

"Precisely," said Mr. Peters.

Outside the school house a small red creature who had been peeking through the window did a little jig and chuckled with devilish glee.

"Wait till the boss hears about this!" he cried.

Then he scampered away from the school and went racing into the forest.

Chapter Four:
Little Stinkers

The creature who had been listening at the window was an imp named Zitzel. Once he had heard Maybelle's assignment he gave a wicked little chuckle and scurried away.

Zitzel was about two feet high. He was a hundred and forty-three years old—very young for an imp. He had red skin, tiny nubs of horns growing out of his forehead, and a long tail.

He loved mischief more than anything. On his way out of town he managed to startle three old ladies, frighten a cat, and make the glassblower sneeze at the worst possible moment. He was very pleased with himself.

When Zitzel entered the forest, he began to travel with more caution. The forest was scary—even for an imp. The trees were gnarled and twisty, with branches like the fingers of witches, and trunks that were sometimes as big around as a house.

Zitzel had not gone far when he spotted a woodcutter ahead of him, carrying a bundle of sticks on his back. The little imp wasn't sure what to do. The boss had told him not to let anyone see him. But it was already too late for that.

Well, he decided. *Since I've already been spotted, I might as well have some fun.*

Making a horrible face, Zitzel ran straight at the woodcutter, waving his arms, rolling his eyes, and shouting, "Ackety backety backety backety!" (He made up the words on the spot, in honor of the occasion.)

The poor man dropped his load of wood and ran screaming in the other direction.

Humming contentedly, Zitzel continued toward the cave that he shared with his boss. He couldn't wait to tell Zozmagog what he had learned about Maybelle.

Zitzel's destination lay deep in the forest, in the side of a rocky hill. Though the opening was small, the cave itself was large and roomy. A clear stream ran through the cave's back section. Near the center of the cave, on a large stone, sat a glass ball the size of a large pumpkin.

The ball flickered with red light. The light was dim, barely enough to let someone with good eyes make their way across the cave. But it cast eerie shadows that pleased the cave's occupants, who could see in the dark anyway.

In the back of the cave sat Zozmagog. He was muttering to himself in a cranky fashion. He was cranky for many reasons, some of them over a hundred years old, some of them things he still hadn't thought of yet. Right now he was especially cranky for three reasons. First, he was having problems with his tail again, and it made his bottom hurt. Second, he had just decided that he didn't like the fact that the sky was blue. Third, his assistant was taking too long to get back with the news he wanted.

Zozmagog sighed, a hot, steamy sigh it had taken him nearly thirty years to learn to do properly—another thing that made him cranky. He was thinking about going outside to turn a bird into a stone, which always made him feel better, when he heard a shout from the front of the cave.

"Boss! Boss! I got it! I got Maybelle's next assignment!"

Zozmagog's face lit up as if he had just been told he could have a thousand pounds of itching powder at half price. Hurrying to the front of the cave (the back was his private area) he said, "Good work, Zitzel! Who is it?"

The little imp who stood at the front of the cave was bouncing up and down with excitement. "It's no one you've ever heard of." He chuckled. "I guess after that frogifying stunt we pulled with the Prince of Burundia they're not going to trust Maybelle with any more royalty."

Zozmagog smiled at the memory, then quickly became very businesslike. "All right, tell me about this peasant."

"Her name is Susan Pfenstermacher. She lives in the village at the edge of the forest, just like your source told you she would."

Zozmagog nodded. "Good. Now what's her problem?"

"She's too good."

"What?"

"She's too good."

"That doesn't make any sense," said Zozmagog, giving Zitzel a noogie between his stubby horns.

"Ow! Cut that out, boss. Anyway, you'd understand if you saw her. She flounces around like she was you-know-who's gift to the world. I bet everyone who meets her wants to slap her."

Zozmagog's eyes lit up. "Aha—I think I've got the picture. Good work, Zitzel. Now, you weren't seen, were you?"

Zitzel looked uncomfortable.

"Zitzel…?"

The smaller imp still didn't answer. Zozmagog reached out and snatched his tail.

"No boss! No, don't!" cried Zitzel. But it was too late. Zozmagog began to twist.

"I asked if anybody saw you?"

"**Ow! Ow ow ow!** Yes, someone saw me. But only for a minute!"

Zozmagog let go of Zitzel's tail. "You idiot! I told you not to let yourself be seen! Who was it?"

"Just some woodcutter at the edge of the forest."

"Stay out of my sight!" snapped Zozmagog. "Stay out of everyone's sight while you're at it!"

Chuckling to himself, Zitzel scampered to the back of the cave. His tail didn't really hurt at all—he just yelled like that when Zozmagog twisted it because it seemed to make the boss happy. Zitzel had never been able to figure out why Zozmagog thought tails were sensitive; his own never hurt at all. The boss sure was weird for an imp. But he was great at thinking up new mischief, and that was what really counted.

Zozmagog stood outside the cave, tapping his chin with his finger and muttering to himself. "Ever since I put that hex on Maybelle's wand, she's made one mess after another. That frog episode was the worst of all. I'll bet this Susan Pfenstermacher kid is her last chance. If I can mess Maybelle up just this one last time it ought to end that wretched little fairy godmother's career forever! Ha! Aha! Ah ha ha ha ha ha!"

His laughter peeled the bark off a nearby sapling, startling a squirrel that happened to be bouncing past. The squirrel had an acorn in its mouth. Zozmagog turned the acorn into a brick, just because he was in such a good mood.

Still laughing, he turned and skipped back into the cave.

Chapter Five:
Maybelle's Plan

The next morning two women entered the little village of Grinder-snog. One was tall and thin, the other short and plump. Standing side by side, they looked like the letter "b."

From head to toe, they were dressed just like any of the village women. The short one, however, had a tendency to float a bit, and was having a hard time keeping her feet on the ground.

"Edna, do we really have to do this?" she asked, sounding slightly grumpy. "These shoes are killing me!"

"Tut tut. A little discomfort is a small price to pay for observing your client in a natural setting, Maybelle," said her tall companion in a prim voice. "After all, how can you help Susan without knowing more about her?"

"Easy! I just wiggle my wand a bit. Here a poof, there a poof, every-where a poof-poof. Presto change-o, you've got—"

"Instant disaster," said Edna darkly.

"Well, I miss my wings," said Maybelle.

"Tut tut. Wings are a minor part of our job. Ah, look—there's Susan's house. Let's watch."

The two women stood beneath a tree. Without ever actually seeming to disappear, Edna slowly became invisible. Maybelle turned invisible, too. But in her case, she vanished in a shower of sparks, and with a distinct popping sound.

"For heavens sake, Maybelle," whispered Edna sharply.

"Sorry," said Maybelle, who was just happy that she no longer was required to keep her feet on the ground.

They waited in silence, except for once when Maybelle sneezed.

After about ten minutes Susan came flouncing out of her house. Her golden hair was wrapped around her head in a braid from which not a single strand escaped. Her spotless white dress was perfectly pressed.

"Goodbye, mother!" she called in a voice that sounded like honey and sunshine. "I'll see you this afternoon. I love you!"

"Goodbye, dear," replied a tired looking woman. She was leaning against the doorframe, and her eyes were bleary with exhaustion. "You look lovely."

"Thank you, mother dearest!"

The truth was, Susan had been looking lovely more than an hour ago. However she had refused to leave for school until she thought she looked perfect.

Mornings were never easy at the Pfenstermacher house.

As Maybelle and Edna watched, Susan walked slowly along the cobbled streets of the little village—past the bakery, past the candle-maker's shop, past the house where Dr. Derek Dekter lived and worked. Though other children were on the way to school as well, Susan did not walk with them. And none of them called out to her to join them.

Near the church sat a blind beggar. He was holding a tin cup in front of him. Flouncing up to the beggar, Susan looked around. Waiting until the woman who was sweeping her front step on the other side of the street looked up, Susan pulled a coin from her pocket. "Oh, gracious!" she cried dramatically. "A poor, blind beggar. I must help the dear man!"

Then she threw the coin into the beggar's cup with such force that the clink could be heard up and down the street.

"There," she said loudly. "That's good." Looking upward,

she added piously, "After all, we must ever be mindful of those less fortunate than ourselves."

The woman across the street rolled her eyes. With a snort, she went back into the house and slammed the door.

For just an instant, Susan let her shoulders slump. Then she straightened her back so that her posture was once again perfect and continued toward the school.

"Why did that woman give Susan such a nasty look?" whispered Maybelle.

Edna sighed. "Really, Maybelle. Sometimes I think you're hopeless."

"But Susan did a good thing."

"Susan only gave that beggar some money to make herself look good."

"NO!" cried Maybelle in astonishment.

"Yes. Now come along. We need to have a little chat with Susan's mother."

Mrs. Pfenstermacher had already gone back into her house. This did not stop Edna, who simply marched up to the door and knocked firmly three times. She counted to six, then quickly stepped behind Maybelle, so that when the door opened Maybelle found herself facing Mrs. Pfenstermacher.

Looking past the frazzled woman, Maybelle could see that the house was considerably tidier than most places in heaven.

"Yes?" asked the woman.

"Uh…" said Maybelle, painfully aware that Edna would be listening to whatever she said. "Uh…"

Edna poked her from behind.

"Uh…it's about your daughter!"

Mrs. Pfenstermacher looked suspicious. "What about her?"

"Um, she's very…very…**nice!**"

Mrs. Pfenstermacher's eyes widened. "Do you really think so?" she asked, sounding quite surprised.

Maybelle felt as surprised as Mrs. Pfenstermacher looked. "Well, yes. I guess so." She paused, then asked, "Don't you?"

"Oh, of course!" said Mrs. Pfenstermacher quickly. "But something about Susan seems to—well, to upset people."

"In what way?" asked Maybelle.

Mrs. Pfenstermacher looked sad. "Well, she doesn't seem to have any friends. In fact, most of the time the other girls won't play with her at all." She paused. "They did have a game called 'Dead Girl' that they let her play last year. Susan always had to be the dead one." Mrs. Pfenstermacher sighed. "She said it was because she was the one most likely to become an angel."

"I see," said Maybelle.

A little tear trickled down Mrs. Pfenstermacher's cheek. "My own mother won't talk to her anymore. She says Susan makes her nervous." She put a hand to her mouth. "Goodness! I didn't mean to say all that!" Her shoulders slumped and she sighed heavily. "But I guess it's true. I wish someone could help me with her."

"Stay calm!" said Maybelle, lifting her forefinger as if she were about to holler **CHAAAARRRGE!** "Help is on the way."

Mrs. Pfenstermacher wiped at her nose. "What do you mean?" she sniffed.

Maybelle smiled slyly. "Let's just say that Susan has friends in high places."

Behind her, Edna groaned slightly.

"What are you talking about?" asked Mrs. Pfenstermacher suspiciously.

Maybelle put on her best mysterious look. "Remember, when everything seems darkest, help can come from out of the blue. Now, I have a suggestion. Susan needs to do more for others."

Mrs. Pfenstermacher snorted. "She's driving me crazy doing that now! She thinks it makes her more wonderful."

"Ah, but that's the problem," said Maybelle. "Her good deeds don't come from her heart. Now, does she have any relatives nearby?"

Mrs. Pfenstermacher hesitated. "Well, my mother lives just across the forest. But as I said, she doesn't talk to Susan any more."

"That's all right," said Maybelle. "Now, tomorrow is Saturday. Why don't you have Susan take a basket of fruit to her grandmother first thing in the morning?"

"What good will that do?"

"Just leave that to me," said Maybelle with a twinkle.

Mrs. Pfenstermacher scowled. "I heard that there are imps in the woods. One of the woodcutters saw one yesterday."

"Don't worry. I'll be there."

Mrs. Pfenstermacher's scowl grew deeper. "Just who are you, anyway?"

Maybelle stuck her hand behind her and wiggled her fingers. "Here," she said, bringing her hand around front again. "My credentials."

"Ribit!" said the frog she held in her hand.

"Ooops! Wrong credential. Just a second."

Putting her hand behind her again, she closed her eyes and concentrated very hard. "Ah!" she said, when she felt a piece of paper materialize in her hand. "Here you go."

She handed the paper to Mrs. Pfenstermacher.

"Half off while supplies last?" asked Mrs. Pfenstermacher, sounding puzzled.

"Sorry!" cried Maybelle. She reached behind her again, hoping desperately that Edna wouldn't feel it was time to step in yet. She concentrated harder than ever. "Here," she said, after a moment when she feared her heart might stop. "This is what I meant to give you."

Mrs. Pfenstermacher took the paper, which had a gold seal at the bottom, and read aloud: "Be it known that Maybelle Clodnowski is hereby appointed my special emissary to deal with difficult children." Her eyes widened. "It's signed by the king!"

Maybelle sighed in relief. "I was hoping it would be. So, will you send Susan out with that basket of fruit tomorrow?"

"Well…" said Mrs. Pfenstermacher nervously.

"It's the only way," said Maybelle. "Trust me on this. I'm an expert in helping people."

Mrs. Pfenstermacher looked at the letter again, and rubbed the gold seal with her finger. "Oh, all right," she said at last.

"Excellent!" cried Maybelle. "I promise you, you'll see a big change in Susan after tomorrow."

"That would be lovely," said Mrs. Pfenstermacher. "Now, if you'll excuse me, I think I need to go lie down."

As Mrs. Pfenstermacher closed the door, Edna grabbed Maybelle by the elbow and dragged her away from the house. Neither of them noticed the little red creature who scooted through the bushes behind them.

Rubbing his hands together with impish delight, Zitzel raced into the forest to tell his boss what he had learned.

Chapter Six:
Magic Apples

"Well what was **that** all about?" asked Edna sharply.

"I have a plan," said Maybelle.

"That's what I was afraid of. Well, you'd better tell me about it. What are you going to do?"

"Make a magic apple."

"A magic apple?" asked Edna in disbelief. She gave Maybelle a little push on the head, to get her feet back on the ground.

"Uh-huh," said Maybelle. "A **love** apple. I'm going to slip it into that basket of fruit Susan will be carrying."

Edna snorted. "Honestly, Maybelle, you are a simple thing."

"But Edna—love conquers all."

"What's that got to do with Susan?"

"She's lonely. She has no friends. That perfect stuff is all because she doesn't feel loved. But the best way to get love is to give it. So I'm going to make her a love apple."

Edna tightened her mouth. "Those things are dangerous, Maybelle. They can have awful side effects. And stop floating!"

"Fiddle-dee-dee," said Maybelle, as she struggled to get her feet back onto the ground. "What's wrong with love?"

"It makes people cuckoo! What would happen if **we** went around falling love?"

Maybelle made a face. "**We** can't."

"Oh yes we can. But we don't. And you know the reason why."

Maybelle sighed. "Of course. The Official Fairy Godmother Handbook, page twelve, paragraph six: 'Any Fairy Godmother who falls in love shall lose her powers, be stripped of her wings, and be doomed to live as a mortal.'"

"Right!"

"That's kind of rough, isn't it?"

Edna tightened her lips and let her eyes get all squinty. "It maintains order," she said in a cold voice.

"Oh, phooey," said Maybelle. "Anyway, this apple isn't for us, it's for Susan."

"Well how are you going to get her to eat it?"
"One bite is enough."
"Well how are you going to get her to take one bite?"
"I'll make it perfect."

"So?"

Maybelle smiled. "The apple will be perfect. Susan isn't. She won't be able to resist it!"

Edna began to smile, too. "Why, Maybelle," she said. "There may be hope for you yet!"

Out in the forest Zozmagog was pacing back and forth in front of his cave, muttering to himself.

Zitzel followed close on his heels. "So, what are you gonna do, boss?" he asked eagerly.

"Quiet! I'm thinking! And watch out for my tail, you twit!"

"Sorry," said Zitzel, hopping backward.

He walked farther behind Zozmagog for about three minutes, but then began moving closer and closer again. Suddenly Zozmagog stopped dead in his tracks. "I've got it!"

"Ooof!" said Zitzel, running into him. "Got what?"

Zozmagog turned around and gave his assistant a noogie. "Got what I'm going to do, you nitwit. Look, Maybelle's job is to humanize Susan, right?"

"Yeah."

"Well, we're going to do it for her."

Zitzel wrinkled his shiny red brow. "I don't get it."

"We'll make her cranky, nasty, and generally rotten."

Zitzel began to smile. "**Really** human. You're a genius, boss! How are we gonna do it?"

"With a 'perfect' apple. Now, where is that spell?"

"What spell?"

"I told you I was talking to myself!" said Zozmagog, giving Zitzel another noogie.

"Owww!" Zitzel rubbed his head. "Boy, you're awfully cranky for an imp, boss. We're supposed to be full of mischief. You know, merry pranks and all that?"

"Right," said Zozmagog. "I forgot. Jolly pranks. Ha ha ha ha ha. Have a laugh for me. Now where did I put—oh, never mind. Wait here."

He went back into the cave. Zitzel could hear a lot of scraping and thumping and muttering. After a few minutes Zozmagog emerged again, covered with dust and carrying a thick, leatherbound book. It looked very old. Plunking himself down beneath a huge oak tree, he opened the book and began to flip through its pages.

"Not that. Not that. Not that. Ah, here it is! Oh, wonderful! **Perfect**, you might say. We'll make this and slip it into that basket the kid will be taking to her grandmother. She'll never be able to resist it."

"But what is it?" asked Zitzel.

Zozmagog smiled, and now he did look like a merry prankster. "A **crab** apple. Now, get me these things: Two dead toads, a pickled lizard's tongue, a gallon of vinegar, a stack of—"

The list went on and on. When it was done, Zitzel rubbed his hands together gleefully. "This is going to be fun!" he cried.

Then he scampered off to the secret place where imps keep their supplies, while Zozmagog went back into the cave to gloat.

"One more prank," he sneered. "One more prank and that fairy godmother is done for good."

Then he laughed the laugh of the nasty.

While Zozmagog was in his cave, contemplating his revenge, Maybelle was rushing about gathering the ingredients she needed for **her** apple. Some of the things she had on hand already: the first sunbeam of a spring day, which she had been saving in a bottle for just such an occasion; the song of a meadowlark, a beautiful trill that she had caught in a handkerchief two summers earlier; the smell of bread just coming out of the oven, something that she carried with her always.

But the look of moonlight on still water, which was very hard to keep, she had to go out and fetch fresh. As she traveled she also managed to get a bit of a mother's smile, a gurgle from a baby that had just discovered its toes, and the laughter from a family picnic on a summer evening. She caught the sound of church bells, the whisper of wind on the grass, the smell of laundry just brought in from hanging in the fresh air. She gathered the feel of a mother's lap, the safety of a father's embrace, and something that hung in the air between two very old people who were sitting in rockers on their front porch.

When she was ready with all these things and more, Maybelle flew to a cloud and began her conjuration.

At the same time, far below her, Zozmagog began to work on **his** apple. Deep in his cave, he poured together his ingredients and chanted:

Handfuls of hatred,
Gallons of greed
One rotten apple
Will do my bad deed!

Up on her cloud, Maybelle delicately stirred together her ingredients, mixing them with sunshine and singing:

Handfuls of giving
Sent from above
This perfect apple
Will fill her with love.

She stirred and mixed and sang and fixed and finally she held up the apple, red and sparkling in the sunshine.

"There!" she cried triumphantly. "A perfect apple to do my good deed!"

"There!" cried Zozmagog, holding up his apple at the very same moment. "A rotten apple to do my bad deed!"

Then both of them began to laugh, Maybelle on her cloud and Zozmagog in his cave, one making a sound like wind chimes, the other a sound like stones grinding in the dark.

Clutching their apples, they hurried off to do their work.

Chapter Seven:
Into the Woods

Maybelle was hiding behind a very large tree, waiting for Susan to appear. Edna stood beside her, looking somewhat skeptical. They were three or four feet from the edge of the path.

"I can't stand all this waiting," said Maybelle fretfully.

"Oh, for heavens' sake, Maybelle! We haven't even been here for five minutes yet."

"Well, I get anxious. I want to—" She stopped. "What was that?" she asked in a low whisper.

Edna didn't need to answer. At that moment, Susan came flouncing into sight. She was carrying a basket of fruit, and singing to herself. As she got closer, Maybelle could hear the words:

I'm perfect, so perfect,
I'm as perfect as a perfect thing can be.

Suddenly Susan stopped. "Oh, what a glorious morning!" she cried. "What a divine day. A day almost as perfect as I am!"

Edna gave Maybelle a little shove. Somewhat to her surprise, Maybelle found herself on the path, directly in front of Susan.

"Oh!" cried the girl. "Who are you? Never mind. Pretend I didn't ask that. I'm not supposed to talk to strangers."

"I'm no stranger, I'm your fairy godmother."

Susan burst into laughter. "That's ridiculous! How could **I** have someone like **you** for a fairy godmother?"

Maybelle spread her hands and shrugged. "Heaven works in mysterious ways."

Susan blinked, then looked at Maybelle more carefully.

She was a pleasant looking little woman, though not very carefully put together, what with her apron being rumpled and the wisps of hair escaping all around the braid at the top of her head. Obviously she was crazy.

I'd better humor her, thought Susan, remembering some things her mother had told her. Out loud she said, "You poor dear. Here, sit down and rest."

Looking somewhat bewildered, Maybelle sat on the log that Susan gestured toward.

"Now," said Susan, sounding very solemn. "Tell me all about it. How did they start?"

"How did what start?" asked Maybelle.

"Why, the terrible troubles that have brought you to this sorry state?"

Maybelle blinked. "What do you know about my troubles?"

Susan shrugged. "Nothing, except that it's obvious you have them. When did they begin?"

Maybelle scrinched her face into its thinking position. "Well," she said at last, "I guess it was about a hundred and twenty years ago."

"Oh, my!" gasped Susan. "This is worse than I thought!"

Maybelle nodded. "I guess it is pretty bad when you think about it. It's been a long time."

Edna, who was now invisible, poked Maybelle in the side. Maybelle jumped and looked around, but didn't get the message.

"And what do you suppose caused these troubles?" asked Susan, her voice serious and sympathetic.

Maybelle shook her head. "I don't know." She sighed and lay down, resting her head in Susan's lap. "It's almost as if someone was out to get me."

"I see," said Susan, remembering an old man who used to wander around their town saying the same thing.

Edna poked Maybelle in the side again, then whispered in her ear, "The basket!"

Maybelle blinked. "I almost forgot!" she said.

"Forgot what?" asked Susan.

"Uh…uh…I almost forgot that I'm not here to talk about my troubles. I'm here to talk about yours."

As she spoke, Maybelle jumped up and put her hand in her apron pocket, where the perfect apple was waiting.

"How can we talk about my troubles?" said Susan primly. "I don't have any."

"You mean you're perfectly happy?" asked Maybelle.

"**Perfectly!**" said Susan, somewhat sharply.

"And there's nothing that bothers you?"

"Not a thing!"

"So everything is just the way you like it?"

"OF COURSE IT IS!" bellowed Susan.

"That's wonderful," said Maybelle softly. "I'm glad you're so happy."

"It's not fair," said Susan, her voice grumpy now. She crossed her arms and looked in the other direction.

"What's not fair?" asked Maybelle, slipping the magic apple into Susan's basket.

"I work very hard at being good."

Maybelle smiled. "That's nice, but it's not unfair."

"BUT NOBODY LIKES ME!" shouted Susan.

"Now **that's** not fair."

"I don't get it," said Susan bitterly. "I try to be nice. I try to be sweet. I try to be kind."

"Well, you certainly are trying," agreed Maybelle.

"But it doesn't do any good." Susan's shoulders slumped. "Maybe **I'm** no good." No sooner had the words left her mouth then her eyes shot open and she sat straight up. "That's ridiculous. I'm perfect!"

"Is that important?" asked Maybelle.

"Certainly. If I'm perfect, people will have to like me."

"Well, do people like you?"

"No!"

Maybelle smiled. "Does that tell you anything?"

"Yeah. They don't know a good thing when they see it!" Susan crossed her arms and plunked herself down on the log. "They're all rats anyway. I'm too good for them. But they think they're too good for me!"

"Maybe you're all wrong," said Maybelle gently. "I don't think anyone is too good for anyone else."

Susan looked surprised. "What do you mean?"

Maybelle sat down beside Susan. "Listen, dearie. People are more complicated than you think. Inside the roughest bully may beat a heart of gold; you just have to dig it out of him. People always seem to put up masks—as if they're afraid of what they are inside. Don't worry about not being perfect."

"Oh, but I am perfect," replied Susan primly.

"You're a little young for it, aren't you?"

"I started early."

Maybelle sighed. "You've got more inside you than you've even dreamed of, Susan. Why don't you start sharing it?"

"I always share!"

"No you don't."

"What don't I share?"

"Your laughter for one thing. I don't think you **can** laugh!"

"Of course I can.

"Prove it!" challenged Maybelle.

"Ha."

Maybelle made a face and rolled her eyes.

"Ha ha."

"Pathetic," said Maybelle sadly.

"Ha ha HA!"

Maybelle just shook her head.

"Teach me!" demanded Susan.

Maybelle sighed. "It can't be **taught**. It's already there. You just have to let it out."

Susan made a face that looked a little like she had just swallowed a frog. Then she rolled her eyes back in her head, as if she was looking to see what was there. "Hahahahahaha!"

"Stop trying so hard," said Maybelle. "You sound like a drum-roll."

Susan folded her hands in her lap. "Effort should always be rewarded."

"Well try harder at not trying. That should be an effort for you."

"Huh?"

"Laugh!"

"Ha?"

"Laugh!"

"Hoo?"

"Laugh!"

Standing up, Maybelle flung her arms wide, as if she was conducting a symphony. As she stepped backward, she tripped over a stump and tumbled to the ground.

Susan laughed—and laughed—and laughed.

"Now **that's** not funny!" snapped Maybelle.

"It sure looked funny," gasped Susan. Quickly she put her hand to her mouth. "But you're right. It wasn't nice to laugh. Oh, no!"

"Well, it wasn't all **that** bad."

"I know. But it wasn't perfect, either. And if I'm not perfect—"

"People won't like me," finished Maybelle. She sighed. "Listen, Susan. The sad truth is, if you **were** perfect, people would avoid you like the plague. They can't handle it. But you're not perfect, and I like you just fine."

"You do?" cried Susan in astonishment. "Really?"

"Really," said Maybelle.

Susan paused. "I like you, too," she said at last, as if she was trying out the words to see how they sounded.

"Really?" asked Maybelle. She seemed just as surprised as Susan had a moment early.

Susan scrinched up her face as if thinking real hard, then said, "Really!" Then, as if she had said too much, she added quickly, "But I should go see my grandmother now."

Grabbing her basket, which now had the love apple on top, Susan started down the path.

"Have a good time," called Maybelle.

As she stood and watched Susan go, she was so excited it was all she could do to keep from floating.

"This is going to be just...lovely!" she whispered to herself.

Chapter Eight:
The Old Switcheroo

Zozmagog was waiting impatiently (which was the only way he ever waited) at the edge of the same path where Maybelle had found Susan. Clutched in his hand was the crab apple.

Zitzel crouched in a bush on the other side of the path. It was his job to create a distraction when Susan finally came along. He was supposed to do this by being very quiet, and then making a sudden movement. The problem was, Zitzel hated being quiet, and wanted to move all the time.

"Will you stop wiggling, you little git!" hissed Zozmagog, after Zitzel had wiggled his bush for the fifteenth time in five minutes.

"Geez-o-pete, boss," whined Zitzel. "Gimme a break, will ya?"

Before Zozmagog could answer they heard Susan coming. An instant later she appeared, swinging her basket and singing, "She likes me, she likes me, she green and yellow likes me. She likes me, she—"

Suddenly the bush on her right rustled violently.

Susan stopped in her tracks. "What was that?" she said. "Oh, perhaps it is a dear little bunny. I want to see the fluffy thing."

Setting her basket on the path, she tiptoed over to the bush.

As Susan tiptoed toward the bush, Zitzel scooted back into the forest. At the same time, Zozmagog moved silently from the bush where **he** was hiding. He snatched an apple from the top of Susan's basket, and replaced it with the crab apple. Then he hurried back to his hiding place—completely unaware that the apple he had snatched was Maybelle's love apple.

Susan looked all around the bush without finding any sign of a rabbit, or of Zitzel, for that matter.

"Oh, poobity-pobble," she said softly. She went back to the path to get her basket. When she did, she noticed for the first time that the apple resting on the very top was remarkably beautiful.

In fact, it was just about...

"Perfect!" said Susan. She looked around. No one was watching, at least as far as she could tell. "It's so perfect, it's as if it was made for me," she said slowly. She paused and frowned, wondering if she was being wicked.

"Well, if it was made for me, then it would be wrong for me not to take it," she said. "Besides, Gramma would never want me to go hungry. She would **want** me to eat this apple, if I wanted it."

And with that she took the apple from the top of the basket. Though it already sparkled in a stray ray of sunlight that had made its way through the leaves above her, she polished it on her dress for good measure.

Then she took a big bite.

A strange expression crossed her face. Her eyes grew very wide, and then narrowed. With an cry of disgust, she flung the apple against the nearest tree, throwing it so hard that it splattered into mush when it hit.

"Phooey!" she cried. "Why am I taking a basket to my grand-mother anyway? I hate stupid baskets. And I hate grandmothers. And Granny hates me, for that matter. The skinny old bat. And who designed this stupid forest anyway? It has too many trees! It's ugly. **Uglyuglyugly!**"

With that, Susan stomped off through the woods, cursing at the top of her lungs and spitting at baby birds.

As soon as she was out of sight Zitzel came rolling from behind a tree. He was laughing so hard he couldn't stand up.

"Oh, boss," he gasped, "that was per…per…**perfect!**"

"Not bad, if I do say so myself," replied Zozmagog. He was still holding the apple he had taken from the basket. "In fact, I think that ought to finish Maybelle Clodnowski's career for good, Zitzel. At last—victory is ours!" Holding up the apple he had taken from the basket, he said, "Here's to apples!"

Then he took a big bite.

At once he began to choke.

"Boss!" cried Zitzel. "Boss, are you all right?"

Zozmagog was bent over double, unable to answer.

Zitzel raced behind him and began to pound him on the back. Suddenly Zozmagog swallowed the chunk of apple that had been lodged in his throat. As he straightened up his face began to twist itself into shapes and expressions that it had never worn before.

Without even looking at Zitzel, he began to run down the path. Ahead of him he saw Edna, who was just coming back onto the path after having a conversation with Maybelle.

When Zozmagog saw the tall fairy godmother he stopped in his tracks.

"You!" he cried. "You are the most beautiful thing I have ever seen."

Edna turned toward him, then gasped in astonishment and horror.

"Oh fair one, I think I love you!" cried Zozmagog. "No. Forget that. There's no 'think' about it. I love you. I adore you. I worship the ground you walk on! Will you be my snookie-wudgums?"

With that, he rushed toward her.

With a shriek, Edna turned and ran into the forest.

Zozmagog ran after her, shouting, "Kiss me, kiss me, kiss me, Snookie, or I think that I shall die."

Trailing after them came Zitzel, crying, "Boss! Boss! Come back!"

Chapter Nine:
The Inner Brat

Doctor Derek Dekter was crossing the town square when Susan Pfenstermacher's mother came me hurtling out of her house. "Oh, Dr. Dekter, Dr. Dekter!" she cried. "I'm so glad you were passing by. Can you help us?"

Doctor Dekter was a tall man, heavy set, dressed all in black. His white beard was neatly trimmed. In fact, everything about him was neat and precise. In a severe voice he said, "Whether I can help you, Frau Pfenstermacher, depends entirely upon what is wrong, which you have so far failed to tell me."

"It's Susan. She's changed all of a sudden."

Mr. Pfenstermacher came out of the house. His eyes were wild, his face desperate. "She's not cheerful and well-behaved like she always was, Dr. Dekter."

"She's gotten mean!" added Mrs. Pfenstermacher.

"Nasty!" agreed Mr. Pfenstermacher.

"Rotten!" cried Mrs. Pfenstermacher.

"And she's started making bad puns!" moaned Mr. Pfenstermacher.

"Will you inspect her, Dr. Dekter?" asked Mrs. Pfenstermacher desperately.

The doctor shook his head. "It sounds like a simple case of puberty to me. But if you insist—"

"Oh, thank you, Dr. Dekter!" cried Mr. Pfenstermacher. He grabbed the doctor by the hand and began dragging him toward the house.

Before they had gone three steps, Susan came leaping out the front door. She had the index finger of her right hand firmly planted in her nose.

"Dr. Dekter, Dr. Dekter, thank God you're here!" she cried. "My finger is stuck. It's stuck, I tell you, stuck, stuck, stuck and I'm going to die! Save me, doctor. SAVE ME!"

With her left hand she grabbed her right wrist and began to pull at it.

"Look at that!" she shrieked. "It will **never** come loose. And all I wanted to do was get out that potato that I stuck up there last night. Oh, God, I'm sinking fast. Help me, doctor. **Help me!**"

With that she threw herself to the ground and began to flop back and forth, screaming and making little choking noises. "Agh! Aaargh! Ack! Ack! Ack!" Gradually her voice grew softer and softer. Finally she was stretched out straight on the ground, flat and unmoving. She lay that way for about three seconds, then lifted her head and said, "Being stuck up was the death of me."

"All right, you've had your fun, Susan," said Dr. Dekter. "Stand up. I want to listen to your heart."

He took her by the wrist and tried to pull her to her feet.

"Watch it, frost fingers!" shouted Susan, yanking her hand free. She scrambled to her feet and began to dust herself off. As she did, Dr. Dekter removed his stethoscope from the black bag that he always carried with him. No sooner had he put the ends of it into his ears than Susan grabbed the other end and shrieked, "TESTING, TESTING, ONE TWO THREE! DOC, DOC, CAN YOU HEAR ME?"

Dr. Dekter staggered backward and pulled the tubes from his ears. "Susan, stand still. I want to check your throat. Stick out your tongue, please."

"Gladly!"

She grabbed the edges of her mouth and pulled it as wide as she could. Then she stuck her tongue out so far it looked as if it might come loose at the other end. But when Dr. Dekter bent forward to examine it, she snapped her mouth shut.

"Ah ah ah," she said. "Let's not get too personal. A girl's throat is private, you know."

"Susan, open your mouth!"

Susan clamped her mouth shut and shook her head.

"Susan, I want to take your temperature."

"Try it and you'll feel my temper, sir!"

"Now, Susan, don't you act like that."

"Can't help it, I've become a brat! I'm such a brat, I'm such a brat you won't believe."

"Susan, you are not a brat."

"Yes I am, and that is that."

"Will you stop making those stupid rhymes?" roared Dr. Dekter.

Susan turned around and wiggled her butt at him. Then she began to run in circles, shouting, "What's for supper? Booger stew! Some for me and some for you!"

When Dr. Dekter tried to grab her, his hat fell off.

"A rat!" cried Susan. Shrieking with joy, she jumped on the hat. Then she gasped in dismay. "Oh, dear! It's not a rat after all. It's Dr. Dekter's hat!" She picked it up and handed it to him. "Here's your hat, Doc. Stop by again sometime."

Then she went running into the house shrieking, "I hate bunnies! I hate bunnies!"

After she slammed the door, Susan's mother said desperately, "Can you correct her Dr. Dekter?"

"NO!"

"But what should we do?" asked Susan's father.

"If I were you," growled Dr. Dekter, trying to put his hat back in shape, "I would put her in a box and send her to Australia! Good day!"

With that he stomped away from the Pfenstermacher house.

The doctor hadn't gone more than fifty feet when he spotted a plump little woman sitting on the edge of the town fountain, sobbing hysterically and wiping her eyes with the edge of her apron.

"Well what's the matter with **you?**" he asked impatiently.

"Waaaaah!" replied Maybelle.

"Good heavens, woman, stop that horrible caterwauling and tell me what's wrong."

"I'm Susan's godmother."

The doctor rolled his eyes. "If I were you, I'd be crying too."

"You don't understand," sniffed Maybelle. "I'm her Fairy God-mother."

"What in heaven's name are you talking about?"

"Well you see," sniffed Maybelle, "for about a hundred and twenty years everything I do has been going wrong. So Mr. Peters, he's my boss, sent me to take care of Susan, because he figured I couldn't do too much to her, I guess. Only I did, because after I made the apple **this** happened, and now Edna will have to step in and then I'll lose my wings and I don't know what I'm going to...to...to do-o-o-o-o!"

She began to wail again.

"Come, come," said Dr. Dekter gruffly. "It can't be that bad. Now, let's start again. You say you're Susan's godmother?"

"Her **fairy** godmother," sniffed Maybelle.

"You mean, that was how she thought of you," said Dr. Dekter reasonably.

"No, that's what I am. And I made a love apple to help her." She held up an apple. "Here, I found it on the path. You can see where she took a bite out of it. But it didn't work. Somehow I created a m-m-m-monster!"

Before Dr. Dekter could answer, Edna shot into view. She was holding up the edge of her dress and running as fast as she could. "Help!" she cried. "Save me!"

Zozmagog was hot on her heels. "Wait for me, Dear Heart, morning sun, little dew drop. Wait for me!"

"Edna!" cried Maybelle in horror. "Oh, **now** what's happened? Here, take this," she said, thrusting the apple into Dr. Dekter's hand. Then she raced off after Edna and Zozmagog.

Dr. Dekter sat on the edge of the fountain, blinking in astonishment. Tossing the apple up and down, he went over everything that had happened from the time Mr. and Mrs. Pfenstermacher had grabbed him. He looked at the house. He looked down at where Maybelle had been sitting. He looked in the direction where everyone had run off.

Finally he shrugged and absentmindedly took a bite of the apple.

Instantly, his eyes grew wide.

"Wait!" he cried. "Little pudgy woman, come back! I think I love you!"

He paused. "Love her? How can I love her? I just met her! Besides, she's so short!"

He shook his head. "What does time matter? What does short matter? What does pudge matter? I LOVE HER!"

And with that, he raced off after Maybelle, Edna, and Zozmagog.

Chapter Ten:
Zozmagog's Secret

Edna Prim was running in circles around a big tree, and she had just about had it.

She had been horribly startled when the imp had spotted her in the forest and begun chasing her. But no mere imp was going to torment her like this. Stopping in her tracks, she turned around and drew herself to her full height. Holding up one hand, she snapped, "That will be about enough of **that!**"

It was a voice that could have stopped a bull elephant, much less a mere imp. Zozmagog stood stock still, staring at her in astonishment.

"Why are you chasing me?" demanded Edna.

"Because I love you," moaned Zozmagog. "You are the sun and the moon and the stars. You are—"

"Oh, angel feathers. Cut the baloney you little monster. Imps can't fall in love."

"I have," said Zozmagog. Then he tipped his head back and moaned hopelessly. "I'm in loo-o-o-ove with a wonderful woman."

"Oh, sit down," commanded Edna. "**Now!**"

Zozmagog sat. At that moment, Zitzel came on the scene. When he saw what was going on, he hid behind a tree to listen. After all, it was possible the boss was working on some master prank. If he interrupted now, it could mean noogies for a week.

"All right, describe this 'love' of yours," said Edna, pronouncing the word **love** as if it tasted like mustard mixed with vinegar.

Zozmagog made his thinking face. "Well, my insides are all jumbled up." He put his hand on his chest. "And I have a burning sensation right here. My stomach is in a knot. Yet I feel all bubbly inside."

Edna snorted. "That's not love, it's heartburn. You've been eating too much hot food."

Zozmagog threw back his head and howled mournfully.

"Stop that!" said Edna.

"Well it's not easy being an imp in love."

"Not easy? It's impossible! Magic can't create love out of nothing. And imps have no love. So that apple couldn't have affected you."

"But it did." He sprang to his feet. "Kiss me, or I shall die!"

"**What???**"

"Kiss me, you gorgeous tower of femininity!"

He rushed toward Edna. She sidestepped him, and he ran into the tree.

He was too much in love to notice. Spinning around, he began to chase her again, crying, "Kiss me, kiss me, kiss me!"

They made another three or four circuits of the tree when Edna stopped, turned around, and rapped him sharply on the nose with her wand.

"Owwww!" cried Zozmagog. "Ow! Ow! Ow! What did you do that for?"

Grabbing his nose, he turned away from her and bent over, sobbing and moaning as if he was in blazing agony. Actually, his nose didn't hurt that much. But he was hoping he might get some sympathy.

He was barking up the wrong Fairy Godmother. Reaching forward, Edna grabbed his tail. "Straighten up!" she ordered, giving his tail a stiff tug.

It broke off in her hand.

"Good heavens!" she shrieked, staring at the severed tail in horror. "What have I done?"

Zozmagog spun around. "Give me that!" he cried, snatching the tail back from her. If anything, he was even more horrified than she was. He stared at the tail for a moment, then threw himself to the ground and began to roll around, moaning and groaning. Finally he looked up and said, "If you tell Zitzel about this I'll never forgive you." He paused for a moment, then added. "Of course, I'll still **love** you. But I'll never forgive you."

"But how could it happen?" asked Edna, who was feeling horribly guilty. Suddenly her eyes widened. "Wait a minute. Look at me." She bent down, so that she was face to face with Zozmagog, who was desperately averting his eyes. "Look at me!" she said again, in a voice that gave no room for disobedience.

Zozmagog turned back, and looked her right in the eye. "All right," he said mournfully. "You've guessed it. I'm **not** an imp. When I was born my fairy godmother delivered me to the wrong place."

"Impossible!" snorted Edna.

"Just because you think something is impossible that doesn't mean it can't be true," said Zozmagog. "Anyway, the imps that got me were thrilled. They loved teaching me to be rotten."

Edna took a deep breath. "Then what you really are…"

"Is a love-struck cherub," moaned Zozmagog.

Edna reached up and snapped her fingers, then pulled a lace handkerchief from the air. She wet it with her tongue, then began to scrub at Zozmagog's forehead.

"Hey, watch it," he said, trying to squirm away from her.

"It's true!" cried Edna, after she had cleaned off several layers of grub and grime. "You *are* a cherub!"

"I told you," said Zozmagog. "Anyway, those imps made my life so miserable that I vowed I would get revenge on the woman who did this to me."

"And who was that?" asked Edna.

"Maybelle Clodnowski."

Edna let out a heavy sigh. "Suddenly it all makes sense." She sat down next to him and put her arm around his shoulder. "You poor little cherub," she said sadly.

Zitzel was still watching from the bushes. "I think I'm gonna puke," he muttered, holding his stomach.

Suddenly Edna stood up. "Well, I'll take care of this," she said decisively.

"Will you really?" asked Zozmagog.

Edna snorted again. "I haven't been fairy godmother of the year for a hundred and seventeen years in a row for nothing, buster."

Zozmagog sighed. "You're wonderful. I love you so much. What's your name?"

In the bushes, Zitzel was sticking his finger in his throat and pretending to vomit.

"You know, I never wanted to be bad," continued Zozmagog in a dreamy voice. "It was just the way they raised me. Naughtiness was the only thing I knew, until I met you." Turning toward her, looking her right in the eyes, he said sincerely, "I was so lonely. My heart hurt so much that I finally put a wall around it. But when I saw you today, somehow that wall just crumbled."

A little tear trickled down his cheek.

"You poor thing," said Edna. She reached forward to brush the tear away. As she did, she felt a strange fluttering in her chest. Her eyes widened. "Oh, no!" she whispered in horror. "Not that! I can't let **that** happen! Listen, you—"

"My name is Zozmagog."

"Listen, Zozmagog. I **need** a wall around my heart. It saves me from chaos. If that wall starts to crumble then my career as a fairy godmother is over. Please—don't knock on a door that I don't dare answer. Please." She took a deep breath. "I want to help you. You've been terribly wronged, and it is my duty to give you assistance. But that's all. A fairy godmother must **never** fall in love."

Zozmagog sighed as if his heart would break.

"Look," said Edna primly. "We'll find a cure for that apple. Then you'll be just fine."

"But I don't want to be cured!" cried Zozmagog. Suddenly he sat straight up, and his eyes went wide. "Wait a minute! Apples! What about that poor girl who got **my** apple? I feel awful about that."

Edna looked at him nervously. "What are you talking about?" she asked.

Quickly Zozmagog explained to her about the crab apple he had made.

"Well, that certainly does complicate things," said Edna disapprovingly. "But with your help, I'm sure I can fix the poor girl."

"It won't be easy," said Zozmagog. "The spell can only be broken one way. She has to tell someone she loves them."

Edna gasped. "But if she's so cranky and crabby—"

"Exactly," said Zozmagog glumly. "And that's not the worst of it."

"What else?" asked Edna sharply.

Zozmagog looked away, embarrassed.

"Zozmagog," said Edna, "what have you done?"

The cherub-in-disguise sighed. "Susan is contagious. Any other kid who comes into close contact with her is going to start acting in the same incredibly bratty way."

"Gracious, you **were** nasty, weren't you!" cried Edna. "I'll have to see to that spell, and quick! Come on!"

Grabbing Zozmagog by the hand, she pulled him to his feet.

Zozmagog started in the direction of the cave.

Zitzel was about to follow when he saw Susan coming in his direction.

"Hey, you!" she said, stepping up and giving him a noogie. "Yeah, you. The weird little red guy. Wanna help me cause some trouble?"

Zitzel began to smile.

Maybe things weren't so bad after all.

Chapter Eleven:
Susan's Rampage

"I'll tell you what I like," said Susan. "I like spittin'. I like cussin'. And I like fightin'."

"Hey, me too!" said Zitzel.

"Man, I can't believe all the time I wasted," growled Susan, as she whacked Zitzel on the head. "Years of perfect sweetness! Yetch! I never got out of my seat unless I was supposed to. I never took off my shoes until it was time for bed. Heck, I never even picked my nose in public! I tell you, it is time for this girl to cut loose."

"I agree," said Zitzel, rubbing his hands together. "What shall we do first?"

"Let's beat each other up!" cried Susan. With that she launched herself at Zitzel and began to pound him on the head.

"Ow! Ow! Ow!" he cried. "Stop that, will ya? I'm on your side."

"You're not on my side, you're underneath me!" shouted Susan as she pinned the little imp to the ground. She began flicking his ears, singing "Flickety, flickety, flickety, bop!" Then she grabbed them and pulled them out sideways. "Man!" she cried. "These are big enough to be wings!"

Before Zitzel could squirm his way free, Gustav happened along. Susan jumped up and grabbed him by the shoulders. "Hey Gustav!" she cried. "Let's fight!"

Gustav looked totally astonished. "Susan, is that you?" he asked.

"Sure is, you little slimeball," said Susan as she punched him on the shoulder.

Gustav stood stock still for a moment. Then his mouth began to twitch. His eyes got wide, and then very narrow. "I hate everything!" he shouted.

"All right!" cried Susan.

"Shut up!" replied Gustav. "You make me sick."

Susan laughed. "So what's new? I always made you sick, liver brain."

Then she hit him on the head.

Gustav began chasing her. They went barreling toward the town.

As they did, they met Maria. Susan stopped long enough to grab one of Maria's pigtails. "Hey, Maria!" she cried, running in circle and pulling Maria with her. "You must be built upside down, because your nose runs—and your feet smell!"

Maria gasped in astonishment. "Susan, what are you—"

She broke off in mid-sentence. Her eyes got wide, and then very narrow. Then she slapped Susan.

Susan slapped her back.

Soon the two girls were having a slap fight. Slap! Slap! Slappitty slap bop!

"Owwww!" cried Maria.

"Get over it, Toots!" shouted Susan

Maria didn't answer. Instead, she began to growl, and came racing at Susan.

The yelling and screaming had brought Heidi and Friedrich running from their house.

"Stop it, stop it!" cried Heidi.

"Aw, let them work it out themselves," said Friedrich, who thought the fight was very funny.

Gustav jumped on his back. "Hey, Friedrich!" he cried. "Wanna wrestle?"

Actually, Friedrich and Gustav wrestled all the time. But when Gustav grabbed him now, Friedrich's face began to twitch. His eyes got narrow, and then very wide. He wiggled free of Gustav's grasp. "Of course I don't want to wrestle with you little hooligans," he said, sounding almost exactly like Susan used to. "Fighting is not a proper activity for a young gentleman."

"Great bonging bells!" cried Zitzel. "He must have been so crabby to begin with that the spell drove him right through to the other side. He's been double crabbed, and he turned out nice!"

Before Zitzel could decide what to do, Gustav came charging over to fight with him instead.

"I'm ashamed to be seen with you," cried Friedrich. Then he went running off, shouting, "Mommy, Mommy! Teacher, teacher! The children are being naughty, the children are being naughty. Save me, Mommy, save me!"

At the same time Heidi grabbed Susan and pulled her away from Maria.

"Leave me alone, pukeface!" cried Susan, breathing hard in Heidi's face.

Heidi's eyes went wide, and then got very narrow. "I've had it with you, you disgusting little china doll!" she shouted, grabbing Susan's hair and starting to pull. "You've made me sick to my stomach for as long as I've known you."

Susan knocked her away and ran off chanting, "Naughty girls and little pink pigs, Heidi and Maria are wearing wigs."

The commotion brought out Igor, who was soon infected as well. Helga showed up a moment later—and a moment after that she was screaming and hitting too.

Soon there was a battle going on at the edge of town unlike anything anyone had ever seen. Every kid in town had been attracted by the shouts and screams. Within seconds of reaching the fight, each newcomer was infected by the spell. Children who had been rambunctious but basically decent all their lives were soon screeching, swearing, and swinging punches left and right.

It was about then that Edna and Zozmagog showed up.

"Oh no!" cried Edna. "We're not a moment too soon!"

"I'd say we're about ten minutes too late," said Zozmagog. "Zitzel, what are you doing here!"

Zitzel, who had risen briefly to the top of the writhing mass of brawling children shouted, "Hi, boss! Just like the old days, huh?"

"Edna, my darling, my dearest, you'd better do something quick!" said Zozmagog.

Edna took a deep breath. "Well, this won't cure them, but it will slow things down," she muttered. Raising her wand, she waved it at the crowd of kids and chanted, "Imminny, Bimminny, Arphaz ig Nantio!"

Nothing happened.

Astonished, Edna shook the wand and tried again. "Imminny, bimminy, Arphaz ig Nantio!"

Again, nothing happened—at least, nothing magic. But at that moment, the townspeople began to arrive. The first woman to show up saw Edna shaking her wand at the children and screamed, "A witch! A witch!"

"I told you there were demons in the forest!" shouted the wood-cutter who had spotted Zitzel two days earlier.

Edna blinked in astonishment, then drew herself to her full height. But before she could announce that she was a fairy god-mother, not a witch, Susan shouted, "Grown ups! Head for the hills!"

The kids all turned and blew raspberries at their parents. Then they scattered and ran. The grown ups went chasing after them, leaving Edna and Zozmagog standing alone at the edge of the village.

"What happened?" asked Zozmagog. "How come you couldn't stop the fight?"

"I've lost my powers!" cried Edna in despair.

Zozmagog gasped. "How can that be?"

"It means I've fallen in love," said Edna, through clenched teeth.

"Wonderful!" cried Zozmagog. "I mean, that's too bad. I mean, great! I mean…is it with me, pookie?"

"It must be!"

"Oh, joy! Oh, rapture! Oh, heavenly bliss! Oh, Edna, my little kumquat, my gleaming star in the firmament, perfection on wings. Divine Edna, at last my life is complete!"

"Oh, shut up! I have to think."

Chapter Twelve:
Farewell to Heaven

Maybelle and Dr. Dekter were walking through the forest, talking quietly.

"So you really **are** a fairy godmother?" asked Dr. Dekter.

He was having a hard time with the idea, since they had never taught him anything about this in medical school.

"I certainly am!" replied Maybelle. "The reason you fell in love with me was because you took a bite of that love apple I made to help Susan. I can't figure out what made Susan so crabby, though."

"But why aren't I in love with you now?" asked Dr. Dekter.

"Because the darn thing wore off!" said Maybelle in disgust. "I blew it—just like I've blown everything else I tried to do for the last hundred and twenty years. I am a total failure, the worst fairy godmother in the entire world!"

Dr. Dekter put his hand on her shoulder. "Now, now, Maybelle. It can't be all that bad."

"Oh no?" she cried. "How would you like to lose your wings and your wand?"

Dr. Dekter frowned. "Ah," he said sympathetically. "I see what you mean." He frowned. "What's that?"

In the distance, but coming toward them, they could hear a great shouting and commotion. As they reached the edge of the forest, a herd of children came thundering past them.

Following hot on heir heels was a mob of shouting parents.

"What was that all about?" cried Maybelle, when they had all gone past. She was about to turn and follow them when she noticed two figures sitting on the side of the road that led into the town.

"Look!" she cried. "There's Edna. Edna! Oh, Edna—I blew it again."

"I am well aware of that," said Edna sharply.

"You might as well step in and fix things," said Maybelle sorrowfully. "I'm bound to get kicked out after this mess."

Edna sighed. "Maybelle, I can't fix a thing. I've lost my powers."

Maybelle's eyes grew wide with astonishment. "What? **How?**"

"Guess," said Edna, her voice dripping with disgust.

Maybelle thought for a moment, then cried, "You're kidding! **You** fell in love?" She sounded astonished, delighted and horrified all at once.

"Yes, I did," said Edna. "And you needn't look so surprised."

"Who's the lucky man?"

Edna gestured to Zozmagog, who was sitting next to her.

Maybelle, who had been so focused on her own troubles that she hadn't really taken a look at Edna's companion, was now more astonished than ever. She looked at Zozmagog for a moment, then motioned frantically for Edna to come close so she could speak to her in private.

When Edna obliged, Maybelle stretched up and whispered into her ear, "Edna, do you—uh, do you know exactly what he is?"

"Yes, I know what he is!" said Edna sharply. "He's a cherub, believe it or not. And most of his troubles are due to you."

Maybelle rolled her eyes. "That figures. Aren't everyone's?"

"You delivered him to the wrong place when he was a baby," said Edna. "It ruined his life."

Maybelle turned pale. "Are you serious?"

"She most certainly is," said Zozmagog. "Look, here's proof. I've saved it all these years." Reaching into whatever place it is that imps and cherubs store their belongings, he pulled out a piece of cloth with a paper tag attached to it.

"What's that?" asked Edna.

"My diaper and address tag!" said Zozmagog.

Maybelle snatched it from him. "Let me see that!"

She studied the items carefully, then said, "I'm sorry, but I delivered him to exactly where this says. I remember that trip very well. It wasn't easy."

"Let **me** see," said Edna. She took the diaper and tag from Maybelle. "Well, it's misaddressed," she said sharply.

She blinked and looked at the tag again. Her eyes grew wide and the color drained from her cheeks, until she was even paler than Maybelle. "I can't believe it!" she wailed. "That's **my** handwriting! I'm the one who caused it!"

"There, there, dear," said Maybelle, reaching up to pat Edna on the shoulder. "None of us are perfect."

Zozmagog rushed to Edna's side. "Don't cry, dear heart. It's perfectly all right. After all, without that mistake, I might never have come to know you. I would have lived in the darkness forever, gone my entire life without ever walking in the sunshine."

"Holy Moses," said Maybelle. "He really does have a case on you."

Edna sighed. "He certainly does. But it's only because of that foolish love apple of yours."

Maybelle smiled. "Edna, I've got news for you. That love apple doesn't work."

"**What?**"

"Ask him," she said, gesturing toward Dr. Dekter.

"She's telling the truth," said the doctor. "I was crazy about Maybelle half an hour ago. But it wore off."

"It's the story of my life," muttered Maybelle.

Edna blinked. "But if the apple doesn't work—"

"Then this is for real!" cried Zozmagog. "Darling, how wonderful!"

"Oh, be quiet!" snapped Edna. "Don't you realize we won't be welcome anywhere now, Above or Below?" She sighed. "Oh, I will miss heaven."

"What's it like?" asked Zozmagog. "I never got to see it, you know."

"It's…it's…well, it's heavenly," said Edna.

"It sure is," said Maybelle. "We've got choirs of angels, and troops of clowns. Music, light, and laughter all day long. Nectar dripping right out of the vine. And the dancing! Oh, I do love dancing on those golden streets of ours."

She fluttered into the air and began to do a little polka.

"And the pearly gates," sighed Edna. "You can see them shining in the dark no matter where you are." She sniffed sadly. "I will miss it up there, Maybelle."

Zozmagog sighed. "I can't let you give up all that for me, my darling little pookie-kumquat."

"I don't have any choice," said Edna. "Besides, you should have been there to begin with, and it's my fault you're not." Straightening her shoulders, she said, "We'll just have to make a little bit of heaven here on earth."

"Boy," muttered Maybelle to Dr. Dekter. "She's as gone as he is."

"Yes," said the doctor. "And it's all very sweet. But you've got another problem right now."

"Like what?"

"Like a village full of angry parents!" he said, pointing toward the forest.

Even as he spoke, most of the population of the village came pouring out of the forest. The parents had the children firmly in tow, carrying them over their shoulders or pulling them along by their ears.

The children were screaming and squalling, kicking and shouting.

"Let me go!" screeched Susan. "LET ME GO!"

"Look!" cried the woman at the front of the crowd. "There she is!"

She was pointing at Edna.

"I saw her waving a wand over the children," continued the woman. "She's the witch who caused all this!"

"Witch?" said Edna in disbelief.

"And that other one with her is her helper!" shouted Susan's mother. "They came to my house yesterday and convinced me to send Susan into the woods. That's when she changed. They must have cast an evil spell on her!"

"Evil spell?" asked Maybelle in astonishment.

"There's only one way to break a witch's spell!" shouted one of the men. "Burn them!"

The villagers took up the cry. "Burn them! Burn the witches!"

Chapter Thirteen:
Out of the Blue

"Edna, do something!" cried Maybelle.

"I can't do anything," said Edna, and for the first time Maybelle heard fear in her voice. "I have no powers. You do something, Maybelle."

"But…" Maybelle took a deep breath. "Oh, all right. Here goes nothing." Lifting her wand, she waved it at the crowd and shouted, "**Zitzenspratz!**"

Immediately, everything went dark.

Edna sighed. "For heaven's sake, Maybelle, turn on the lights."

"Sorry. **Brechensprech!**"

Lightning crackled all around them. Horrendous bursts of thunder shook the sky.

"Maybelle," said Edna quietly. "That's very exciting, but it's not going to do anything to help. In fact it will probably make things worse."

"I know, I know!" said Maybelle desperately. Waving her wand, she shouted, "Cut!"

Instantly the thunder and lightning stopped. The light came back, and everyone could see again.

"Oh, lordy!" cried Zozmagog. "I know what the problem is!" Snatching Edna's wand, he handed it to Maybelle. "Here," he said. "Use this one!"

He was too late. Several of the men had raced forward and grabbed the two women.

"Leave them alone!" shouted Dr. Dekter.

"Stay out of this old man," shouted one of them. "Now, witch— prepare to meet your maker!"

"I already have," said Maybelle. "He's quite nice. And frankly, I don't think he would approve of this."

"Kindly take your hands off me," said Edna in frosty tones to the man who held her. "I am **not** a witch!"

"Then what are you?"

"A Fairy Godmother!"

The men burst into laughter. "And I suppose this is just a sweet little cherub," sneered one of them, gesturing at Zozmagog.

"As a matter of fact, that's exactly what he is," said Edna fiercely.

The men laughed harder than ever.

"This is **not** funny!" said Edna.

"I'll say it's not!" shouted one of the women, who was struggling to hold on to a screaming, shouting little girl. "What have you done to these children?"

"Bewitched them!" shouted another woman. "That's what they've done! Bewitched them!"

"Burn them!" cried the crowd. "Burn the witches!"

"No!" cried Susan.

"Susan!" hissed Mrs. Schwartz. "Be quiet."

"I won't be quiet!" shouted Susan.

"Take her away," said one of the men. "Take them all away. What we have to do now isn't for children's eyes."

Susan squirmed free of her mother's grasp and ran to stand in front of Maybelle. "Don't you touch her!" she cried. "They're telling the truth. She **is** a Fairy Godmother. She's **my** Fairy Godmother!"

"Susan!" cried Mr. Pfenstermacher. "Come away from there. That woman is dangerous! She might…might…turn you into a frog!"

"Hey," said Maybelle. "No fair bringing up old mistakes."

Several of the men began to advance on her, muttering menacingly as they came.

"I'm warning you," said Susan. "Don't touch this woman! She's the only person who has ever liked me. And I…I…I love her!"

An enormous crack of thunder sounded overhead.

Susan sighed and collapsed in a heap.

At the same time the children stopped squirming and struggling.

A sense of peace seemed to settle over the villagers.

"She did it!" cried Edna. "She broke the spell. Congratulations, Maybelle!"

Susan shook her head and pushed herself to a sitting position. "What happened?" she asked, sounding groggy.

The townspeople were all asking pretty much the same thing, shouting, "What happened? What's going on?"

"Make way, make way!" cried a stern voice. It was the blind beggar to whom Susan had given a coin the day before. "Be quiet," he said, pushing his way to the front of the crowd. "All of you."

He spoke softly now, but his voice held a strength and a power that immediately calmed the crowd. Their shouts grew softer, turning to mutters, then fading to silence.

The beggar turned to Susan. "Well done, young lady!" he said. "I didn't think you had it in you."

"Who are you?" asked Susan, staggering to her feet.

"My name is Mr. Peters," said the beggar, taking off his hat and pulling away his false beard.

"Well, I never!" said Maybelle in astonishment. "Look at that, Edna!"

"I decided to watch you up close this time, Maybelle," said Mr. Peters. "You made some awful blunders."

"Boy, you can say that again. Well, we might as well get it over with. Take my wings. Break my wand. Tarnish my halo!" She sighed. "There's nothing worse than a failed Fairy Godmother."

"But Maybelle, you're no failure. You said it yourself: Susan needed to learn to love. It was your open heart that brought out that love. That's the most important thing a Fairy Godmother could ever do. Failure? Maybelle—you're a smashing success!"

Maybelle blinked in astonishment. "Love, huh? Gee, that's pretty classy."

"It beats the heck out of magic apples," said Mr. Peters.

Edna, who was standing behind Maybelle, began to sniffle.

Maybelle turned around. "Why Edna," she said. "What's the matter?"

"I'm so embarrassed!" wailed the tall Fairy Godmother. "Mr. Peters has seen what I've done!"

"What have you done?" asked Maybelle, genuinely puzzled.

"I fell in love!"

"Oh, **that**," said Maybelle, waving her hand as if shaking something away. "You should never be embarrassed about loving someone."

Mr. Peters nodded. "Well put, Maybelle. She's right, Edna. You can't be embarrassed about loving someone."

"But the rules..." sniffed Edna.

"Are made to be broken," said Mr. Peters. "As in this case. The being you fell in love with is not a human but an immortal. Therefore, you can still live in the blue."

"Wonderful!" said Maybelle.

"What about Zozmagog?" asked Edna suspiciously.

Mr. Peters smiled. "He comes, too. But I'll warn you, he's going to have to earn his way."

"How can I do that?" asked Zozmagog.

"I want you and Edna to start a school to train Fairy Godmothers. You should be very useful, Zozmagog; you can teach the trainees about some of the dirty tricks they can expect to face from imps." He stooped to pick up Maybelle's wand. "Tricks like **sabotaged** magic wands."

"Why you little devil!" said Maybelle.

"Sorry about that, Maybelle," said Zozmagog, sounding embarrassed.

Zitzel rolled his eyes. "I think I'm going to be sick," he said. Then he spun in a circle three times and disappeared.

"Now," said Mr. Peters, "I think it's time we headed for home."

"Not yet," said Edna. "There's one more thing, and I want to do it now, before we go." Turning to Maybelle, Edna lifted the Fairy Godmother of the Year medallion from around her own neck. "Here, Maybelle," she said gently. "I think you should have this."

"The Fairy Godmother of the Year award! Oh, no, Edna. I couldn't—"

"Take it, Maybelle," said Mr. Peters gently. "You've earned it."

"Gosh," said Maybelle, as Edna placed the medallion around her neck."

"Oh, Maybelle!" cried Susan. "I'm so happy for you." She threw her arms around Maybelle and gave her a hug. "Only—will I ever see you again?"

Maybelle smiled gently. "I don't think so, dear. After all, you don't really need me anymore."

"But..."

"But there's one thing you need to know. I really do like you a lot. And I'll be watching over you."

Susan smiled.

"Come along, Maybelle," said Mr. Peters. "it's time for us to be going."

Maybelle gave Susan a kiss on her forehead. "That's for luck," she whispered. Then she went to stand with Mr. Peters, Edna, and Zozmagog.

Mr. Peters made a gesture, and all four of them disappeared in a little puff of white smoke. The smell of daisies and cinnamon lingered behind them, mingled with just a trace of beer and peppermint.

"Well," said Mr. Pfenstermacher, "that was the most amazing thing I've ever seen. Are you all right, Susan?"

"I never felt better in my life," said Susan, running to her parents and giving them each a hug.

"Me too!" cried Gustav.

"And me!" cried Helga and Igor and Friedrich.

"Well," said Mrs. Pfenstermacher, "I guess they really were what they claimed to be."

"Not exactly," said Dr. Dekter.

"What do you mean?" asked Susan.

Dr. Dekter smiled. "Maybelle told me she was the world's worst Fairy Godmother. But if you ask me, she was the world's best."

"Naturally," said Susan. "What other kind would I have?"

And she said it with such a charming laugh that no one wanted to slap her.

The Box

Once there was a boy who had a box.

The boy's name was Michael, and the box was very special because it had been given to him by an angel.

Michael knew it had been an angel because of the huge white wings he wore. So he took very good care of the box, because the angel had asked him to.

And he never, ever opened it.

When Michael's mother asked him where he had gotten the box, he said, "An angel gave it to me."

"That's nice, dear," she answered, and went back to stirring her cake mix.

Michael carried the box with him wherever he went. He took it to school. He took it out to play. He set it by his plate at mealtimes.

After all, he never knew when the angel would come back and ask for it.

The box was very beautiful. It was made of dark wood and carved with strange designs. The carvings were smooth and polished, and they seemed to glow whenever they caught the light. A pair of tiny golden hinges, and a miniature golden latch that Michael never touched, held the cover tight to the body of the box.

Michael loved the way it felt against his fingers.

Sometimes Michael's friends would tease him about the box.

"Hey, Michael," they would say. "How come you never come out to play without that box?"

"Because I am taking care of it for an angel," he would answer. And because this was true, the boys would leave him alone.

At night, before he went to bed, he would rub the box with a soft cloth to make it smooth and glossy.

Sometimes when he did this he could hear something moving inside the box.

He wondered how it was that something could stay alive in the box without any food or water.

But he did not open the box. The angel had asked him not to.

One night when he was lying in his bed, Michael heard a voice.

"Give me the box," it said.

Michael sat up.

"Who are you?" he asked.

"I am the angel," said the voice. "I have come for my box."

"You are not my angel," shouted Michael. He was beginning to grow frightened.

"Your angel has sent me. Give me the box."

"No. I can only give it to my angel."

"Give me the box!"

"No!" cried Michael.

There was a roar, and a rumble of thunder. A cold wind came shrieking though his bedroom.

"I must have that box!" sobbed the voice, as though its heart was breaking.

"No! No!" cried Michael, and he clutched the box tightly to his chest.

But the voice was gone.

Soon Michael's mother came in to comfort him, telling him he must have had a bad dream. After a time he stopped crying and went back to sleep.

But he knew the voice had been no dream.

After that night Michael was twice as careful with the box as he had been before. He grew to love it deeply. It reminded him of his angel.

As Michael grew older, the box became more of a problem for him.

His teachers began to object to him keeping it constantly at his side or on his desk. One particularly thick and unbending teacher even sent him to the principal. But when Michael told the principal he was taking care of the box for an angel, the principal told Mrs. Jenkins to leave him alone.

When Michael entered junior high he found that the other boys no longer believed him when he told them why he carried the box. He understood that. They had never seen the angel, as he had. Most of the children were so used to the box by now that they ignored it anyway.

But some of the boys began to tease Michael about it.

One day two boys grabbed the box and began a game of keep-away with it, throwing it back and forth above Michael's head, until one of them dropped it.

It landed with an ugly smack against the concrete.

Michael raced to the box and picked it up. One of the fine corners was smashed flat, and a piece of one of the carvings had broken off.

"I hate you," he started to scream. But the words choked in his throat, and the hate died within him.

Cradling the box in his arm, he carried it home. Then he cried for a little while.

The boys were very sorry for what they had done. But they never spoke to Michael after that, and secretly they hated him, because they had done something so mean to him, and he had not gotten mad.

For seven nights after the box was dropped Michael did not hear any noise inside it when he was cleaning it.

He was terrified.

What if everything was ruined? What could he tell the angel? He couldn't eat or sleep. He refused to go to school. He simply sat beside the box, loving it and caring for it.

On the eighth day he could hear the movements begin once more, louder and stronger than ever.

He sighed, and slept for eighteen hours.

When he entered high school Michael did not go out for sports, because he was not willing to leave the box alone. He certainly could not take it out onto a football field with him.

He began taking art classes instead. He wanted to learn to paint the face of his angel. He tried over and over again, but he could never get the pictures to come out the way he wanted them to.

Everyone else thought they were beautiful.

But they never satisfied Michael.

Whenever Michael went out with a girl she would ask him what he had in the box. When he told her he didn't know, she would not believe him. So then he would tell her the story of how the angel had given him the box. Then the girl would think he was fooling her. Sometimes a girl would try to open the box when he wasn't looking.

But Michael always knew, and whenever a girl did this, he would never ask her out again.

Finally Michael found a girl who believed him. When he told her that an angel had given him the box, and that he had to take care of it for him, she nodded her head as if this was the most sensible thing she had ever heard.

Michael showed her the pictures he had painted of his angel.

They fell in love, and after a time they were married.

Things were not so difficult for Michael now, because he had someone who loved him to share his problems with.

But it was still not easy to care for the box. When he tried to get a job people would ask him why he carried it, and usually they would laugh at him. More than once he was fired from his work because his boss would get sick of seeing the box and not being able to find out what was in it.

Finally Michael found work as a night custodian. He carried the box in a little knapsack on his back, and did his job so well that no one ever questioned him.

One night Michael was driving to work. It was raining, and very slippery. A car turned in front of him. There was an accident, and both Michael and the box flew out of the car.

When Michael woke up he was in the hospital. The first thing he asked for was his box. But it was not there.

Michael jumped out of bed, and it took three nurses and two doctors to wrestle him back into it. They gave him a shot to make him sleep.

That night, when the hospital was quiet, Michael snuck out of bed and got his clothes.

It was a long way to where he had had the accident, and he had to walk the whole distance. He searched for hours under the light of a bright, full moon, until finally he found the box. It was caked with mud, and another of the beautiful corners had been flattened in. But none of the carvings were broken, and when he held it to his ear, he could hear something moving inside.

When the nurse came in to check him in the morning, she found Michael sleeping peacefully, with a dirty box beside him on the bed. When she reached out to take it, his hand wrapped around the box and held it in a grip of steel. He did not even wake up.

Michael would have had a hard time paying the hospital bills. But one day a man came to their house and saw some of his paintings. He asked if he could buy one. Other people heard about them, and before long Michael was selling many paintings. He quit his night job, and began to make his living as an artist.

But he was never able to paint a picture of the angel that looked the way it should.

One night when Michael was almost thirty he heard the voice again.

"Give me the box!" it cried, in tones so strong and stern that Michael was afraid he would obey them.

But he closed his eyes, and in his mind he saw his angel again, with his face so strong and his eyes so full of love, and he paid no attention to the voice at all.

The next morning Michael went to his easel and began to paint. It was the most beautiful picture he had ever made.

But still it did not satisfy him.

The voice came after Michael seven times that year, but he was never tempted to answer it again.

Michael and his wife had two children, and they loved them very much. The children were always curious about the box their father carried, and one day, when Michael was napping, the oldest child tried to open it.

Michael woke and saw what was happening. For the first time in his memory he lost his temper.

He raised his hand to strike his son.

But in the face of his child he suddenly saw the face of the angel he had met only once, so long ago, and the anger died within him.

After that day the children left the box alone.

Time went on. The children grew up and went to their own homes. Michael and his wife grew old. The box suffered another accident or two. It was battered now, and even the careful polishing Michael gave it every night did not hide the fact that the carvings were growing thin from the pressure of his hands against them so many hours a day.

Once, when they were very old, Michael's wife said to him, "Do you really think the angel will come back for his box?"

"Hush, my darling," said Michael, putting his finger against her lips.

And she never knew if Michael believed the angel would come back or not.

After a time she grew sick, and died, and Michael was left alone.

Everybody in his town knew who he was, and when he could not hear they called him "Crazy Michael," and whirled their fingers around their ears, and whispered that he had carried that box from the time he was eight years old.

Of course, nobody really believed such a silly story.

But they all knew Michael was crazy.

Even so, in their hearts they wished they had a secret as enduring as the one that Crazy Michael carried.

One night, when Michael was almost ninety years old, the angel returned to him and asked for the box.

"Is it really you?" cried Michael. He struggled to his elbows to squint at the face above him. Then he could see that it was indeed the angel, who had not changed a bit in eighty years, while he had grown so old.

"At last," he said softly. "Where have you been all this time, Angel?"

"I have been working," said the angel. "And waiting." He knelt by Michael's bed. "Have you been faithful?"

"I have," whispered Michael.

"Give me the box, please."

Under the pillow, beside his head, the battered box lay waiting. Michael pulled it out and extended it to the angel.

"It is not as beautiful as when you first gave it to me," he said, lowering his head.

"That does not matter," said the angel.

He took the box from Michael's hands. Holding it carefully, he stared at it, as if he could see what was inside. Then he smiled.

"It is almost ready."

Michael smiled too. "What is it?" he asked. His face seemed to glow with happiness. "Tell me what it is at last."

"I cannot," whispered the angel sadly.

Michael's smile crumpled. "Then tell me this," he said after a moment. "Is it important?" His voice was desperate.

"It will change the world," replied the angel.

Michael leaned back against his pillow. "Then surely I will know what it is when this has come to pass," he said, smiling once again.

"No. You will not know," answered the angel.

"But if it is so important that it will change the world, then…"

"**You** have changed the world, Michael. How many people know that?"

The angel shimmered and began to disappear.

Michael stretched out his hand. "Wait!" he cried.

The angel reached down. He took Michael's withered hand and held it tightly in his own.

"You have done well," he whispered.

He kissed Michael softly on the forehead.

And then he was gone.

My Little Brother is a Monster

I. Basket Case

Thump!

We both heard it, even above the late March wind whipping around the house. Mom looked up from the strand of red yarn she was weaving through the warp of her big loom and said, "Go see what that was, would you, Jason?"

I sighed, but it was mostly for effect. Despite the open math book in front of me, I was doing more daydreaming than working. So it made sense for me to go, rather than for Mom to interrupt her weaving.

However, what I saw when I opened the front door convinced me she should be interrupted after all.

"Mom," I yelled over the wind. "You'd better come here. **Now!**"

She reached the front hall in time to see me carry in the big black basket. After the last few years she's gotten pretty good at taking whatever comes along right in stride, so when she saw the baby inside, she didn't wig out. She just said, "Oh, the poor little fellow."

"What makes you think it's a boy?" I asked.

"Mothers know these things," she replied, reaching down to chuck the baby under the chin.

While Mom fussed over the baby I took another look at the basket. It was woven from thick, dark twigs. After a moment, I spotted a piece of coarse paper tucked next to the baby. When I pulled it out and unfolded it, I found this note:

Tu Whoom I Mae Consarn,
Pleeze tayk carr of mie babie. I cannut doo it,
and I want mie litul dum pling tu hav a gud home.

153

Thiss is moor importun than yew kan gess.

Tank yu veree muck

It was signed with an X.

"Better take a look at this," I said.

Mom read the note, wiped away a tear, and picked up the baby. "I'm so sorry, Little Dumpling. But I'm glad your mother brought you here. We'll take care of you."

Little Dumpling puked on her shoulder.

"How do you know the note came from its mother?" I asked, as I went to fetch the paper towels. "Couldn't it have been the father?"

"Mothers know these things."

I was getting a little sick of that line; Mom had been using it a lot since she and Dad divorced three years ago.

Probably I should have seen it coming when we kept the baby with us that night. But we live way out in the country, so it made sense when Mom said it was too late to take him anywhere else.

I did get suspicious when she managed to get too busy to contact the authorities the next day.

By the third day I was certain: she wasn't planning on doing anything about the baby anytime soon.

To tell you the truth, I wasn't sure I wanted her too; I was starting to like the little guy myself. On the other hand, I was worried that we might get into trouble.

"Don't we have to go to the police?" I asked that night, as we were hauling my old crib up from the basement.

Mom shook her head. "I've been thinking about it, and the fact is the police will just take him to a foster home. But Little Dumpling's mother chose **us** to take care of him. So that's what we're going to do. Besides, it will be good for you to have a baby brother, and the way things look now, this is the only one you're likely to get."

Then she tried to tell me that sharing my room with him as a treat. What kind of a "treat" it really was I discovered two weeks later, on the night of the full moon.

I had gone to bed early, mostly because I had joined the baseball team, and we were practicing so hard that my body felt like someone had put me inside a giant can and given me a good shaking.

Little Dumpling was already sacked out in my old crib.

(Yes, we were still calling him Little Dumpling—L.D. for short. I think that was because naming him would have made it seem like he really was ours, and Mom was still half-expecting the real mother to show up and want him back.)

I peeked in the crib. L.D.'s eyes were scrinched shut, and he was clutching the green plastic rattle I had bought him out of my allowance. (All right, so I'm a sucker; babies do that kind of thing to people.)

"G'night, Bonzo," I whispered.

"Bonzo" was my private name for him. I got it from an old movie I saw on TV one night, something co-starring Ronald Reagan and a chimpanzee (Bonzo was the chimp).

Climbing into bed, I turned out the light on my nightstand. I listened to the soft rain pattering against my window, the April wind rustling through the new leaves on the oaks and maples that surround the old house we moved to after Dad left. I was asleep in seconds.

When I woke the moon was shining through the window, and Little Dumpling was making a weird noise. I got out of bed to see if he was all right.

When I looked in the crib, I nearly wet my pants.

The baby was covered with fur!

He opened his eyes and smiled at me.

Fangs!

I began backing toward the door. "Mom?" I called nervously.

My voice didn't seem to be working. I tried again. This time it worked better than I expected: "MOM! GET IN HERE!"

In seconds she was pounding through my door, pulling on her robe as she ran. "What is it, Jason? Did something happen to the baby?"

Ignoring the fact that it would have been nice if she had asked if *I* was all right, I gasped. "T-t-t-take a look at him!"

She ran to the crib. "What is it?" she asked again.

"What do you mean, 'What is it?' He's covered with fur!"

She looked at me like I had lost my mind. "Jason, are **you** all right?"

Now she asks.

"Of course **I'm** all right. Little Dumpling's the one who just turned into a monster!"

"Jason, come here," she said in that quiet-but-firm voice that signals she means business. Nervously, I joined her at the crib. L.D. was sleeping soundly, sucking his thumb and looking cute as the dickens. The only hair I could see was the brownish-black fuzz that covered his adorable little head.

I rubbed my eyes. "But…but…"

"You had a bad dream, sweetheart."

I shook my head. "I **wasn't** dreaming. It was real. He was covered with fur. And he had **fangs**."

Even as I said it, I realized how stupid I sounded. For a moment, I wondered if I **had** been dreaming. But it had really happened. I was as sure of that as I was that there was no way I could convince my mother of what I had seen.

"Try to get back to sleep, Honey," Mom said. "You'll feel better in the morning."

I considered arguing, but what would happen? She would be convinced I was nuts—might even insist I see a shrink. And then what? If I tried to convince a doctor that my baby brother was a monster, I might end up locked in a rubber room until they could "cure my delusions," as they say in the movies.

I climbed back into bed. But I didn't turn out my light.

I had no intention of going back to sleep.

II. *Something* in a Closet

In the end, sleep won. When I woke the next morning, I had a moment when I wondered if I actually had been dreaming. No; it had happened. The only thing I **couldn't** believe was that I had fallen back asleep afterwards.

I sighed. If I had known I was going to fall asleep anyway, I would have tried to do it earlier. I was exhausted.

Little Dumpling started making "pick me up" noises. We had gotten into a routine by that time: when I woke up each morning I would haul him out of the crib and take him to the kitchen, where Mom would be making breakfast. Then I would feed him. I got a kick out of it, because he was so sloppy when he ate, and liked to smear oatmeal all over himself.

I wasn't sure what to expect when I went to the edge of the crib that morning. But Little Dumpling was holding out his chubby arms and looking like his regular self.

"Up!" he commanded, in a cute baby voice.

I blinked. "When did **you** learn to talk?" I asked.

He smiled, showing a tooth. It was short and square—a baby tooth, not a fang. But baby teeth don't come in overnight, at least not according to my father, who used to love to tell how miserable I had made him while cutting *my* first tooth.

Maybe **this** would convince my mother something weird was going on. But did I actually want to carry this kid into the kitchen? What if that cute little tooth turned into a fang once I got him close to my neck?

"UP!" he repeated urgently.

"Jason!" called my mother. "Time for breakfast. Bring the baby into the kitchen, would you, honey?"

I sighed. "Come on, Bonzo," I said, reaching down to lift him. He snuggled against me, and I felt my heart melt.

Babies are dangerous that way.

"He talked this morning," I said, as Mom fastened L.D. into his high chair. (Actually, it was **my** high chair, from when I was a baby. I didn't want it, of course. Even so, it felt weird to have this kid using all my old stuff.)

"Don't be silly, Jason," said Mom, as she tied a bib around his neck. "He can't be more than six months old. Babies don't talk at that age."

"And he grew a tooth," I added, knowing that at least I could prove that much.

"Are you serious?" Before I could stop her, she poked a finger into L.D.'s mouth and ran it over his gums. I was terrified. If he bit her, would she turn into a monster, too? But after a second she turned to me and said, "What has gotten into you, Jason? There's no tooth here."

"But I saw it!"

"Jason..."

"Let me try," I said, sticking my finger into L.D.'s mouth.

He gummed me pretty hard. But there was no tooth to be found. I pulled my finger out in disgust.

L.D. smiled at me—a big, happy baby smile.

"Goo," he said, blowing a spit bubble.

It was cute. But it didn't melt my heart.

It sent cold shivers down my spine.

Tired and worried, I had a hard time concentrating in school that day. And I totally screwed up baseball practice, because my mind was on the baby instead of the ball. I wondered if Mom was safe, home alone with that little monster. But nothing happened that day (or night)—or the next—or the next. After several nearly sleepless nights I began to wonder if I had dreamed it after all.

Or maybe nothing was going to happen until the night of the next full moon...

That was it—it had to be! It was the moon that brought out the monster in our little foundling.

Of course, I thought, *just being a monster doesn't necessarily mean that he's a menace.*

You can probably see what the problem was. The longer we had him, the more I was getting to like him. All right, all right, I guess I even sort of loved him. I'm only saying that because I'm trying to tell you everything, straight out. It's not something I would admit if I didn't have to, but it ties into the way things worked out.

Anyway, I decided that next full moon I would sneak the video-camera into my bedroom and make a record of just what happened to Little Dumpling during the night.

Of course, that meant staying in the bedroom myself. I had planned to avoid that, but I figured better to get this over with. For one thing, Little Dumpling was growing pretty fast. Not fast enough to be wildly abnormal, but fast enough that Mom had commented on it.

I wanted to settle this before he got **too** big.

It was a weird month. About halfway through it, something began howling in the distance at night. Mom claimed it was a neighbor's dog. I wasn't so certain.

Even worse were the noises that started coming from my closet at night. I tried to tell Mom about them, but again, I could see that she thought I was crazy. I started checking the door in the morning, to if there were claw marks on the back of it or anything. I was never sure whether I wanted to find them or not. It would be proof that something weird was going on. But what would it mean if I **did** find them?

I wished Dad was still with us. I did call him a couple of times, but I found I wasn't able to tell him what was going on. He was nice, but I didn't feel connected to him, didn't feel like he could help me, save me, from what was happening.

By the time the next full moon came, I was a nervous wreck.

Things might have gone differently that night if Mom hadn't been asked out on a date. Usually I don't mind when she goes out, though I would rather she was seeing my father, trying to get things back together. But this time I did mind. When she asked me to keep an eye on Little Dumpling I panicked.

"You can't go out tonight!" I cried. "It's the full moon."

Mom got mad, which doesn't happen often. "Any more nonsense like that, Jason, and you can forget watching *Creature Feature* until you're forty. This is a special evening; Delbert got these tickets weeks ago. And L.D. will be asleep before we leave. I just want you here in case of emergency. You've got a whole list of people to call if anything actually comes up."

Right. Like Mrs. Ferguson down the road would be any help if L.D. actually turned into a fur-bearing fang-beast! Well, at least there wouldn't be anyone around to hassle me about using the video camera...

Under the circumstances, I didn't think it would be possible to fall asleep—which was why I was so astonished to find myself waking up some time later.

The full moon was shining through my window.

I blinked, trying to remember what I was supposed to be doing. The snorts coming from L.D.'s crib brought everything back to me. It was monster time!

I grabbed the camera and stood on the end of the bed, hoping the moon would provide enough light to show the transformation. Silently, for fear a sound might stop whatever was going on, I focused on Little Dumpling.

My mouth went dry. I could see fur sprouting all over his sleeping form. His ears were getting pointy. Even worse, he had to be a half a foot taller than when we had put him to bed!

I pressed the trigger on the camera. The slight whir woke Little Dumpling. He opened his eyes, blinked, then scrambled to his feet— a kid-sized monster in yellow ducky pajamas that were splitting at the seams. Grabbing the bars on the side of the crib he began to shake them. Then he threw back his head and howled. A cold shiver spasmed down my spine. It was time to get out of there.

Before I could move, I was distracted by another set of noises. These came not from the crib, but from the closet. Turning, I saw a sliver of light under the door. That was scary enough, given the fact that my closet **didn't have a light in it.** But when green smoke started curling under the door, I thought my heart was going to stop.

Before I could decide whether to run for it or stay and try to protect Little Dumpling, I heard something scratching at the window!

What was going on around here?

"Up!" pleaded a low voice. "Up! Up!"

It was L.D., standing in his crib and holding out his furry arms. I hesitated, then grabbed him, hoping he wouldn't sink his fangs into my neck.

"We have to get out of here, Bonzo," I said, as the closet door started to rattle.

"Out!" he agreed happily.

I began backing toward the hall. Before I had gone three feet the closet door burst open.

III . Mazrak and Keegel Farzym

I started to scream. That may not sound real brave and manly, but tell me what *you* would do if your closet door blew open and you saw a green-skinned, red-eyed, fang-mouthed monster inside; a monster bathed in green light and surrounded by billows of curling smoke; a monster who raised one enormous, muscle-bound arm, pointed it right at you, and said, "Give me that baby," in a voice that sounded like rocks being smashed together.

"NO!" cried Little Dumpling, throwing his arms around my neck. "NO NO NO!"

Now he decided to be frightened. For an instant I had hoped he might yell, "Daddy!" Then I could have let the two of them work things out and just gotten my butt out of there.

Actually, I would have gotten my butt out of there at that point anyway, if not for three things:

(1) my legs seemed to have stopped working

(2) the monster didn't seem to be able to move out of the closet; it was straining forward, as if pushing at some invisible barrier

(3) the **window** blew open and a blue monster with a long grey beard leaned through and growled, "If you want to live to see morning, follow me!"

I knew I wanted to live to see morning. I didn't know if following this guy was the best way to do that. Little Dumpling was no help; furry face buried against my shoulder he was whimpering, "No, no! Bad, bad, bad!" But whether he was referring to the first monster, the second monster, or life in general, I had no way of telling.

The monster in the closet turned to the monster in the window and growled, "Do not interfere, Keegel Farzym!" Then he turned back to me and bellowed, "Give...me...that...child!" At the same time he thrust his right arm into the room. The tearing sound that accompanied this action made me think he had actually ripped through the invisible force. His hand—enormous and green, with long fingers that ended in black, razor-sharp claws—stretched toward me.

When I turned to run my door slammed shut.

I grabbed the knob, turned, pulled. It wouldn't budge.

"No, no!" whimpered Little Dumpling, tightening his grip on my neck. "Bad, bad, **bad**!"

Another shredding sound. I turned. The closet-monster had managed to thrust its other arm into the room. Now it was leaning forward, stretching both arms toward us.

"Mazrak will break through in seconds!" cried the monster at the window. "If you don't want to die, come here **now!**"

The door still wouldn't budge. Mazrak was getting louder. Suddenly the window didn't seem like such a bad idea. Only heading for it meant I had to pass uncomfortably close to the closet.

Mazrak roared and lunged for me as I passed, but the invisible barrier held.

"Give me the baby," said Keegel Farzym.

I hesitated, until Little Dumpling turned and reached toward him. I decided to trust the kid's instincts—I figured he would know more about monsters than I did—and handed him over. The blue monster tucked Little Dumpling under his right arm. Holding the sill with his left hand, he swung sideways and growled, "Climb on my back!"

Another roar from the closet. More ripping. A claw brushed against my back. I yelped. All hesitation vanished. I scrambled onto Keegel Farzym's back, and he jumped.

As we hit the ground I heard a ferocious roar. Looking over my shoulder, I saw Mazrak's face in the window.

"Run!" I screamed. "He's coming!"

My shout was hardly necessary; Keegel Farzym was already barreling along at a good clip. But he was handicapped by the fact that he was carrying Little Dumpling in front of him, and had me clinging to his back. So when I saw Mazrak squeeze through the window and jump to the ground, I feared it wouldn't be long before he caught up with us.

I had an urge to kick Keegel Farzym in the side and shout "Giddy up!" But I didn't know if that would encourage him to run faster, or simply to turn around and kill me. I sank my fingers into his beard—the hairs were thick as my mother's yarn—and held on for dear life.

Soon I saw where we were heading: the cemetery.

Moments later we raced through the iron gate. The full moon caused the shadows of the tombstones to stretch ahead of us like open graves. Mazrak was only steps behind us. The sound of his voice was terrifying—though not as terrifying as knowing that if he caught up with us I would be the first thing he reached. I braced myself for the first swipe of his claws. But the gate, which had been rusted open for as long as I could remember, slammed shut behind us. I had a feeling Keegel Farzym did it, though I wasn't sure how.

Mazrak grabbed the iron bars. He howled with rage and shook them until they burst open again. But the tactic had bought us enough time to reach one of the mausoleums—the little buildings that stood on some of the family plots.

I was afraid we would be trapped if we went inside. But when we shot through the door, I saw no walls, only a thick, gray mist shot through with blue light. Keegel Farzym continued to run. It should have taken no more than a second to cross the floor, and I expected to slam into the far wall.

Ten seconds later we were still running, the mist was getting thicker, and I heard a waterfall off to our left.

"Where are we going?" I cried.

"To the Land of Always October," panted Keegel Farzym.

IV. The Woven Worlds

Several minutes after we had left the mist we entered a boggy, foresty place that looked like something out of the movies I get to watch on Saturday nights when my mother is in a good mood. We stopped underneath a large tree.

"I think we've lost him," panted Keegel Farzym. "With any luck, he won't have been able to enter that mausoleum, which will mean he'll have to go back through your closet to get home."

That was good news. If Mazrak was going home, wherever that was, it meant he wouldn't me waiting around to get my mother when she came back from her date. I had started to worry about that.

"Get down, would you please?" said the monster, squatting so that I could get off his back without having to jump. Once down, I leaned against the tree and looked around. Swampy forest stretched as far as I could see. Mist curled among the trees. A wolf—or something—howled in the distance.

I decided that I wanted to go home myself. I wondered what the odds of that were. "Are you going to kill us?" I asked.

Keegel Farzym laughed. It sounded like someone dropping rocks on a kettle drum. "If I had wanted you to die, I would have left you in your room."

That made sense.

I reached up for L.D. Keegel Farzym, who was about twice my height, handed the little monster down to me.

"Why did you bring us here?" I asked.

"Did you have someplace safer in mind?"

I thought of Mazrak and shivered. "Not really. But what's going on? Who are you? Why did you save us? **Did** you save us? Why was that other monster after us? What is this all about, anyway?"

He laughed at my barrage of questions. Then a serious look crossed his face. He ran a gnarled blue hand through his long gray beard. His broad nostrils flared, and he stuck out his jaw, causing his lower fangs to sparkle in the moonlight. "I am Keegel Farzym," he said at last, extending a blue hand.

I hesitated, then put out my own hand for him to shake. "My name is Jason. Pleased to meet you—I guess. I mean, **am** I pleased to meet you?"

All right, I was blithering. But it was the first time I ever talked to someone who was nine feet tall and blue. And I still didn't know whether he was on our side, or was simply an enemy of the other monster that had been after us.

"Most monsters would consider meeting me a great honor."

"Why?"

"I am the High Poet of Always October. I am also guardian of Dum Pling, who is a very important child."

"He is?" I asked in surprise. Then I narrowed my eyes and added, "How did you know we called him Little Dumpling?"

It was Keegel Farzym's turn to look surprised. "Dum Pling is his name," he said, making it two words, like a first name and a last name.

"You name your kids things like Dumb?" I asked in disgust.

"In the secret language of monsters, the word 'Bob' means 'the sound of a large dog puking.' However that does not make us think that when your people name someone Bob that that is what they are calling him. Here the word 'Dum' means 'Prince.' The baby's name, translated into your language, would be something along the lines of 'Prince Albert.'"

I glanced at Little Dumpling. He was squishing mud between his toes and eating a bug.

"Are you telling me this little monster is a **prince?**"

"If he lives, he will one day be king of the land where it is Always October."

"Where is that?"

"Here," rumbled Keegel Farzym, waving a huge, hairy arm around him.

I looked around. Until now, I had been too distracted to notice that the leaves were glowing with all the colors of autumn. Dead leaves rustled beneath my feet, and the smell of fall was thick around me.

I shivered. It had been May when we entered the cemetary.

"**This** is the land of Always October," said Keegel Farzym, "where twilight lasts for half a day, the moon is always full, and the sun is rarely seen. This is the home of the folk that you call monsters, the place that haunts your dreams at night, when you remember something frightening yet wonderful, a place you fear, but cannot bear to stay away from."

Little Dumpling looked up at the huge monster. A smile creased his furry little face.

I was still confused. "If Little Dumpling is the prince of the monsters, how did he end up sleeping in my old crib?"

"Ah," said Keegel Farzym. "Therein lies our problem. Come, we have a long way to go before we reach our destination. Walk with me, and I will speak to you of many things, of woven worlds, and infant kings."

Despite this promise, we traveled without speaking for several minutes. Keegel Farzym carried Little Dumpling. I walked beside them, except when I had to drop back because the path grew too narrow. The full moon shimmered on the murky water, and silvered the mist that twisted through the gnarled trunks of the great trees.

Weird cries echoed in the distance.

Twice we crossed paths that twisted into the darkness, looking both scary and irresistible.

We walked beneath a cliff. At the top loomed a mansion. A single light shone in its tower window.

"Who lives up there?" I asked.

"It depends," replied Keegel Farzym with a shrug.

It was the first question I had asked since we began walking. I had been waiting for him to start his story, but for some reason he seemed reluctant.

After another several minutes curiosity overcame caution and I said, "Are you going to tell me what's going on?"

A bat flew overhead. His hand moving faster than I could see, Keegel Farzym snatched it from the air and popped it into his mouth. He chewed for a minute, then spit out a bone, all the while staring into the distance. Finally he turned to me and said, "The Land of Always October is in danger."

"I'm sorry to hear that," I said sincerely. "But what does that have to do with me?"

"A great deal, if my theory is correct. With you, and every other human in your world. Not in the sense that it is your fault, but in the sense that you are in danger, too."

"What is **that** supposed to mean?"

Keegel Farzym sighed. "How long Always October has existed is a mystery; we know neither where it came from, nor how it came to be, though our poets and magicians have many theories. My own belief is that we are a reflection of your world—that we monsters are, in some strange way, a creation of you humans.

"Like all reflections, we show ourselves in reverse. This means that the worst of us are formed from the dark side of truly wonderful human beings, while the best of us are reflections of people who would be called monsters in your world no matter how they looked."

He spit out another bone. Little Dumpling snatched it before it hit the ground and began to chew on it.

"So. We have good monsters and bad monsters, just as you have good people and bad people, and things are pretty much in balance. But something is happening here that could disturb that balance, both in our world, and in yours."

I pulled the bone away from Little Dumpling, who growled but didn't bite, and hoisted him onto my shoulders. He looked at the moon and howled.

In the distance, something howled back.

"I'm not sure I understand what you're talking about," I said.

Keegel Farzym frowned—an awesome sight, given his face—and began to walk once more. I followed him, stepping around a steaming puddle.

"I lead a group that believes monsters and humans are part of the same family. We are opposed by a group of monsters who disagree. This group is seeking to unweave the Great Magic that binds our worlds together, to sever the threads that connect us." He paused and sucked his lower lip. "How can I explain this? It would be as if our worlds were getting a divorce."

The word made me shiver; my parents' divorce was the worst time of my life.

"How can you divorce a whole world?" I asked. "And why would they want to do that?"

Keegel Farzym lifted Little Dumpling from my shoulders and hoisted him into the air, a good twelve feet above the ground. Little Dumpling laughed and tried to grab the moon.

Keeping his eyes on the baby, Keegel Farzym said, "They say they do not want to be a reflection of anyone. They want to be totally independent. This may be possible; personally, I don't think it is. I believe we are all connected, and this Magic would be fatal for both worlds. We are woven of the same stuff, Jason, you and I, your world and mine. We are like the front and the back of a tapestry. Try to separate one side from the other, and you destroy the whole."

Lowering Little Dumpling, he tucked him into the crook of his arm and chucked him under the chin the way my mother liked to do. L.D. gurgled happily, and blew a spit bubble.

"Besides," said Keegel Farzym, gazing fondly at the baby, "Without humans, what would little monsters dream of to frighten them during the day?"

V. The Price

We came to a giant tree with a door in its trunk. Keegel Farzym told me to stand close to the tree. Then he walked around it in a wide circle, muttering to himself.

"You and the prince wait here," he said at last. "Do not cross this line. I must go and clear the way for us. Be careful. Speak to no one."

I took Little Dumpling's hand and nodded. Keegel Farzym opened the door, ducked his head, and disappeared into the tree.

I was alone in Monster Land. Well, I had Little Dumpling. But he was just a baby, and a monster to boot. So I felt pretty nervous. I got even more nervous when eyes began to appear in the darkness around us, glowing eyes that hung at all levels, as if the creatures they belonged to stood anywhere from a foot to twelve feet tall.

Then a flickering light, not an eye, began approaching us. Soon I could see that it came from a torch.

When the torchbearer finally came into sight I was overwhelmed by astonishment, and relief. It was my father! My father!

"Jason, thank goodness I found you!" he cried. "Come on—bring the baby and we'll go home."

Clutching Little Dumpling's hand, I started toward my father. I wondered how he had managed to track us here.

I had not taken more than three or four steps when the door in the tree opened and Keegel Farzym poked out his head. "Jason!" he roared. "What are you doing?"

"I'm getting out of here!" I said, picking up Little Dumpling and running toward my Dad.

"Jason, don't cross that line!" yelled Keegel Farzym.

I didn't slow down.

"Jason, that's **not** your father!"

Now I did slow down. It had to be my father, standing there beneath that tree.

It **had** to be.

But then, if it was him, why didn't he come and get me, instead of just standing there?

"Jason, hurry up," said Dad, his voice urgent.

I took a step forward.

"Jason, if you leave the circle, I can't protect you," cried Keegel Farzym.

I hesitated again.

"Hurry, Jason," said Dad. "I can't come and get you. He has that ring sealed against me."

"How do you know that?" I asked.

"I just do. Now hurry."

I took a step backward.

"Hurry!" he snarled.

I took another step back.

"Hurry, damn you!" As the words flew out, his face changed. Clothes splitting, he exploded into Mazrak, the monster who had been lurking in my closet.

Keegel Farzym grabbed me from behind and dragged me and Little Dumpling into the tree. He waited for me to stop crying before moving on.

We walked down a long spiral stair dimly lit by glowing fungus.

"Mazrak is the chief operative of the enemy," said Keegel Farzym. "He wants to keep the prince from returning to your world."

"Why?"

"Because as long as Dum Pling is in your world the Great Unraveling cannot work. The prince acts as a knot, tying our worlds together. That is why he was taken there to begin with. His mother is the wife of King Bork, who leads the faction that wants to split the worlds. She disagrees with this, and brought the Prince to your world to stop the Unraveling. It was a dangerous journey, and she undertook it to save both worlds. Alas, she acted hastily, and without our help."

Though he said nothing more, the tone of his voice made me think that Little Dumpling's mother had not made it back alive.

"Where are we going now?" I asked.

"You must speak to the Council of Poets," replied Keegel Farzym. "Then you must make a choice."

We entered a large chamber that was lit by flickering torches. Twisting roots—some fine as a hair, some thicker than my arm—thrust through the ceiling and the moist, earthen walls. Patches of toadstools dotted the floor. In the distance I could hear a waterfall.

"Pretty! Hello!" cried Little Dumpling when he saw the six monsters facing us. They sat in a half circle around a wooden table. At the center of the half circle was an empty chair, large and carved with strange designs.

While not one of the monsters looked like any of the others, they all had three things in common: they were large, they were strange and they were scary.

"Welcome back, Keegel Farzym," said the monster farthest to the right, who seemed to be a lady. "Congratulations on your safe return."

Keegel Farzym nodded to her. Then, after patting both me and Little Dumpling on the head, he walked around the table and took his place in the large chair at the center of the group. Looking me straight in the eyes he said, "Jason Burger, our worlds, the world of humans and the world of monsters, are in terrible danger. Are you willing to try to save them?"

"**Me?**" I squeaked. "What can I do? I'm just a kid."

"You can care for this child, who is our hope for the future."

I looked at Little Dumpling. He smiled up at me, showing his fangs.

"As long as he is in your world, then your world and ours will be bound together, and the Great Unraveling can be prevented. Should he be stolen and brought back here—or should he perish, perish the thought—then the end will begin. We do not know why his mother brought him to you. Was it choice? Accident? Fate? It does not matter. When the moment comes to decide what you will do for your world, the question is not, 'Why me?' It is simply 'Can I, **will** I, do it?'"

"Up," said Little Dumpling, holding out his arms.

"I never wanted a little brother," I said, even as I was hoisting him.

"Who does?" said the slimy green creature sitting at the far left of the group. It winked at me with an eye the size of a baseball.

"Little brothers can be a terrible annoyance," added the gaunt figure next to him. I could not see this monster's face, for it was hidden by the hood of its long black robe.

"True," said the lady monster at the other end of the table. "But then, so can first children. And what would happen if parents never bothered to have them, either?"

"All right, all right," I said. "I'll take care of him. I kind of like the little guy anyway. What do I have to do?"

"All that you would normally do," said Kargel Feezym, "plus this: You must take this amulet and place it about his neck."

He rummaged under his beard for a moment, then held out his hand. In the center of his huge blue palm rested a metal disk engraved with a strange design. It was attached to a golden chain. I stared at it.

"Will you take it?" he asked, after a time. "Will you place it about his neck?"

"Can't you do it?" I asked. My throat was dry, and my words came out in little more than a whisper.

Keegel Farzym shook his head. "It must be the hand of a human that places it about the baby's neck."

Setting Little Dumpling on the floor, I stepped forward and took the amulet from the hand of the High Poet of the Land of Always October. But as I moved to place it around the baby's neck Keegel Farzym said, "Wait! Before you do this, you must know one more thing. You must know what it will cost you."

I didn't like the sound of that.

"What do you mean?" I asked nervously.

"No magic comes without a price," said the shaggy, dark-eyed creature sitting at Keegel Farzym's right hand. "This, too, is part of the Weaving."

Keegel Farzym put his hand on my shoulder. It was heavy. "Dum Pling displays his true form in your world when the moon is full. Because he is but an infant, he cannot control this aspect of himself. Next full moon he will transform again. The energy this releases will reveal his location to the Unravelers, the monsters who wish to return him to **this** world. This amulet will collect that transforming energy as it builds throughout the month."

I was beginning to have a bad feeling about this. "And what happens to that energy when the full moon comes?" I asked.

"On that night you must take the amulet from Dum Pling and place it about your own neck."

"I think I can guess what will happen," I muttered.

Keegel Farzym nodded. "**You** will become a monster."

"Won't they find us anyway?" I asked. "For that matter, don't they know where we are already?"

"The answer to your first question is no; your human aura will mask and mingle with Dum Pling's monster energy, creating a mixture that is confused and less likely to be tracked. As to your second question—" He paused, then spread his arms. "We are doing our best to find Mazrak. If we can capture him, it is unlikely anyone else will come after you. On this I can make no promise; danger is part of the bargain. However I can offer a promise of help, and protection. Your closet, like most closets, and nearly all mirrors, can be a gate between your world and the land of Always October. We will guard that gate. We will watch over you. We will be nearby in case of trouble. "

I looked at them.

I stared at Little Dumpling.

I thought of how my life had unraveled when my mother and father divorced.

Lifting the chain, I dropped it over the baby's neck.

There isn't much more to tell—at least not yet. Once I had made my decision, Keegel Farzym took us down a long tunnel. We stepped into a pool of blue light, and next thing I knew we were walking out of my closet and into my room.

The big monster held Little Dumpling for a moment. A tear fell from his eye to the baby's forehead.

"Good night, little prince," he whispered sadly. "Good night and good bye, my grandson."

Turning, he stepped into my closet and disappeared.

I lifted Little Dumpling, who was now completely human in form, and placed him in the crib. I handed him his rattle, then tucked the blanket my mother had just finished weaving for him up to his chin. When he was asleep, I went to the window and stared into the darkness.

The world out there was stranger, more frightening, and far more interesting than I had ever guessed.

Suddenly it also seemed very fragile.

Returning to the crib, I pulled down the blanket and touched Little Dumpling's amulet. I would have to do some fast talking to convince my mother to leave it on him.

I would be doing a lot of fast talking over the next few years.

I lifted the amulet on two fingertips; it was light as a feather. Yet once a month, when I hung it around my own neck, it would carry the weight of the world—the weight of two worlds that were one.

I went back to the window, thrust my head into the night and began to howl at the moon.

I figured I might as well start practicing.

The Giant's Tooth

Edgar Twonky had no intention of getting eaten by a giant the morning he left for Cottleston Fair.

Sometimes these things just happen.

He was ambling along, humming tunelessly while he dreamed of what he might buy for Melisande with the money he hoped to make from his eggs that day, when an enormous hand swept down from the sky, scooped him up, and deposited him in a mouth the size of a cave.

The tongue on which he landed was coarse and soggy, like a bed of rain-soaked ferns. It flung him toward the back of the mouth, where a vast bulb of red flesh dangled above the gaping black hole that would, Edgar presumed, be the last thing he ever saw. With a leap, Edgar grabbed the dangling piece of flesh. It was moist and slick, and far too wide for him to put his arms around. Digging his fingers into the soft surface, he hung on for dear life.

"*Gunnnarrgh!*" said the giant, causing Edgar's fleshy perch to swing back and forth in a dizzying way.

When the giant's mouth was open, Edgar could see. When it closed, he found himself in a darkness deeper than any he had ever known.

"*Gunnarrrgh!*" repeated the giant.

Edgar's grip was loosening, and he was expecting to fall into the waiting hole at any second, when he heard a creaky voice call, "Over here! Hurry!"

Twisting toward the voice, he was astonished to see a flash of light—a torch!

"Hurry!" repeated the voice.

"*Gunnarrrgh!*" said the giant for a third time. Edgar flung himself

171

forward, landing on the giant's tongue once more. The great pad of flesh rippled alarmingly as the giant tried to swallow him. Digging his hands into its surface, which consisted of pulpy red fibers thick as his wrists and long as his arms, Edgar clung to the tongue like a barnacle to a ship's bottom.

"Come on, come on!" cried the voice behind the torch. "I can't hold this out here forever. It'll make him sneeze, which will almost certainly kill you!"

Reaching forward, Edgar grabbed another handful of tongue, and pulled himself along the rough surface. Fighting the motion of the tongue (which was accompanied by disgusting gagging sounds from the giant) he dragged himself hand over hand toward the beckoning torch, which was yards away. He had just reached a wart, wider than a tree stump, when the giant made a last, desperate attempt to swallow him. Edgar managed to get himself on the forward side of the wart—toward the teeth and away from the throat—and braced himself against it.

"*Gak gak gak!*" hacked the giant.

Edgar leaped forward, landing within a foot of the torch. A withered hand reached out to him. He grabbed it thankfully, and was pulled into the most astonishing room he had ever seen.

Well, it wasn't a room, exactly.

It was the inside of one of the giant's back teeth. But the flickering light of the torch showed that it had been hollowed out to make an area large enough to hold a table and two chairs. The back wall—back being the side toward the giant's throat—had a niche about six feet long and two feet wide carved into it. The ceiling was low—too low for him to stand at full height—And everything was too close together, giving the room a cramped feeling. That feeling was made worse by the clutter of items that covered both floor and table: cups, plates, knives, pitchforks, shovels, coils of rope, chunks of wood, and an old wagon wheel, among other things.

"Salvage," wheezed a voice behind him.

Edgar turned and received yet another surprise. His rescuer was a woman. Half a head shorter than Edgar, she had long stringy gray hair and eyes that burned with fever brightness. Her clothing, of which she had several layers, was an odd mix, some of it coarse homespun, some costly velvet. Nearly all of it was tattered and worn. It hung heavy on her body, as if it was slightly damp.

"By salvage," said the old woman, "I mean the stuff in the room, not you—though I suppose you might qualify as well. First time since I've been here that I've actually been able to save someone. Silly things all panic, and slide down his gullet before I can do a thing to help them. That was very good, the way you managed to grab on to something. Quick thinking. I like that in a man."

"Thank you," said Edgar nervously. He looked around. "How long have you lived here?"

The woman shrugged. "Hard to say. There's no way to keep track of the time, after all—no sunrise or sunset, no full moon or new, no summer or spring, winter or fall. It's all the same here in the giant's mouth." She stroked her hair. "I do know that I was young when I came here," she added, a slightly mournful note coloring her voice. "Young and pretty, some thought. And my hair was black as a raven's wing, or at least that's what the boys all said. Now come on, ducky. Sit down, sit down. I haven't had a visitor in…well, ever, actually."

"Then why two chairs?" asked Edgar.

"I live on hope," replied the woman as she thrust the torch into a bracket carved into the yellow wall. She returned to the table and cleared it with a sweep of her arm. "Sit," she said, gesturing to the seat opposite her. "Sit."

Edgar crossed to the table—it took only two steps to reach it—and joined her. He tried to pull the chair away from the table, but found that it was solidly joined to the floor. Only then did he realize that it had been carved from the tooth itself.

"It was something to do," said the woman with a shrug. She flipped her gray hair back over her shoulders and said, "My name is Meagan."

"And I'm Edgar."

"Good name," Meagan replied, nodding in approval.

Edgar smiled. "I seem to owe you my life."

Meagan arched an eyebrow. "I hadn't really thought about it that way. But now that you mention it, I suppose you do. Not that it's much of a life here in the giant's mouth."

"How do you live here, anyway?" asked Edgar, glancing around the room once more. "Where do you get your food?"

Meagan shrugged. "I scavenge."

"Scavenge what?"

"Anything that comes along that doesn't go down his gullet." She gestured toward a pickax that leaned against the enamel wall. "I've dug bits of meat out of his teeth that would feed a family of ten."

Edgar shuddered, and decided not to ask what she did for water. He was afraid he already knew the answer. He leaped ahead to the bigger, more important question.

"Have you ever tried to get out?"

"What do I look like?" she asked bitterly. "Of course I've tried to get out. I tried every way I could think of. Finally, when it became clear I wasn't going to make it, I gave up and accepted my fate." She narrowed her eyes. "You, you come in here and find me waiting to help you—you have no idea of what it was like for me when I first got here. No light, no one to explain, no one to talk to, weep with, hold. Just me, alone, in the dark, trying to find a way to survive. Just me in this hole, which back then was barely big enough to hold me, just big enough to keep from getting swallowed. I thought I would die of loneliness. I thought I would die of fear. More than once I considered just flinging myself down the big oaf's gullet. But that's not my way, Edgar. I cling to life—cling to it like a leech if I have to. So with every flash of light that came when the giant opened his mouth, I took stock of where I was. With every flash of light, I learned a little more. Many was the hour I spent huddled in this tooth, weeping to myself, wondering what was to become of me. But I didn't give up. I never gave up. I drank from pools of spit. I snatched passing food. And when I found my first tool, I began to dig, to make myself a home. Chip, chip, chip, I picked away at this tooth."

She paused, and actually chuckled. "He didn't like that, I can tell you. Oh, the roars of pain! I thought I would go deaf. And the shaking of his head. First time it nearly killed me. I would have had to give up, if I hadn't managed to grab a piece of leather harness that was tied to an ox he snatched up once. Used it to tie myself down. Then it didn't matter how he shook his head, I was safe."

She leaned across the table, fixing her glittering, half-mad eyes on Edgar. "Did I try to get out? Of course I tried to get out. But in the end, I made myself a home here. And I'm alive, while all the others he swallowed before and after are gone. But even so, it's lonely here, Edgar. At least, it was. Now you're here, that will be different."

"But I've got to get out!" cried Edgar.

"Well, be my guest," she said, gesturing toward the hole through which she had dragged him. "The door is open. Don't let me stop you."

"You don't understand," groaned Edgar. "I'm supposed to be married next week."

"That's very unfortunate," said Meagan sharply. "But it doesn't really change things. This is your new home—or, at least it is as long as I choose to share it with you." Her eyes glittered in the torchlight, and Edgar caught just a hint of menace in her tone. "After all," she continued, "*I* built this place. And it's barely large enough for one. You could throw me out, I suppose, and take the place for yourself. But you don't seem the type. Besides, after all the years I've survived living this way, I'm about as tough and nasty as they come. So I wouldn't advise you messing with me, Mr. Edgar. You might be surprised at what a woman can do."

Edgar, who had no intention of messing with this strange, repellent woman, put up his hands and said, "I'm not going to do anything to hurt you. After all, I owe you my life."

"Interesting point," said Meagan.

Night inside the giant's tooth came in two stages. The first was when the giant himself lay down to rest, which changed the floor into a wall, and the rear wall into the floor. Everything not locked in place—including Edgar—tumbled to the back of the tooth when this happened.

Meagan laughed, not unkindly. "Sorry," she said. "I should have warned you."

Stage two came when Meagan decided to put out the torch, which she only did after first checking to make sure that she had her flint and steel for relighting it tucked securely in her pocket. Prior to this she had gathered some soggy fabric and piled it in the carved niche he had noticed earlier. He understood now that this was her bed.

Edgar took his rest on the opposite side of a barrier she had erected between them, huddled on a collection of tattered pieces of damp cloth that she offered him—everything from a lace tablecloth to a single shirt sleeve. ("Almost managed to save that fellow," she muttered as she handed him that particular item).

As he lay in the dark, wrapped in misery, he thought of Melisande, wondering if he would ever find his way back to her, and what she would do if he did not. He had a horrible few moments when he imagined her giving up on him and marrying Martin Plellman, but beat the idea from his mind so fiercely that it was nearly ten minutes before it came creeping back.

After several hours he finally did drift into a fitful slumber—only to be jolted back into wakefulness by a deep rumble, something like a cross between a thunderstorm and an avalanche. It eventually tapered off to a high-pitched keening that Edgar thought for a moment must be the wail of a lost soul, and ended with three short peeps.

"What was that?" cried Edgar in horror.

"What was what?" asked Meagan groggily. It was clear from the sound of her voice that she had slept through the appalling sound.

Before Edgar could answer, it started again.

"That!" he cried, once the last of the peeps was over.

"You woke me up for that?" snarled Meagan incredulously. "It's just the giant, snoring. Forget it and go back to sleep."

The snoring started again. When it was over, Edgar wanted to ask Meagan how long it had taken her to learn to sleep through the horrible racket. But she was already snoring herself, and he dared not wake her again.

He was still wide awake, though completely exhausted, when Meagan lit the torch again. Only a few moments later the giant groaned and lurched to his feet, causing everything that had fallen to the wall the night before to return to the floor.

"I've been thinking," said Meagan, as she kicked the loose fabrics against the wall, "and I've decided that you're going to have to build a home of your own. This place really is too small for the two of us. Odds are good I'd end up killing you."

Though she sounded genuinely regretful, she was also firm on the point.

Edgar, who was still determined to think of this as a temporary situation, felt that digging out his own home would be a waste of time and energy. On the other hand, he was not the sort to impose—certainly not the type to force himself into the abode of a woman who did not want him there.

"Where do you suggest I make this home?" he asked, trying to keep both the snarl and the whine out of his voice.

"Well he has nearly thirty more teeth to choose from!" snapped Meagan. "However, I'd suggest you stick with the molars. They're roomier." Then, as if the idea of being pleasant was still new to her, she patted back her hair and said, "It might be nice if you built nearby. More neighborly, if you know what I mean. Best thing to do is start with a tooth that already has the beginnings of a hole. I'll help you look, if you want."

"Thank you," said Edgar. "I'd appreciate that."

And so, after a breakfast so gray that Edgar decided he didn't really want to know what it consisted of, they left Meagan's home to search for a tooth where he could live. Meagan carried the torch, and they both had picks and knives and coils of rope strapped about them. Before they left, Meagan anchored another rope to one of the chairs inside her tooth and tied it around them both.

Edgar understood why when they stepped down onto the giant's gums. A narrow trench between gumline and teeth provided a good foothold. Even so, the flesh was moist and slippery, and without the anchor rope it would have been all too easy to slide into the damp cavern of the giant's mouth. His tongue, pulsating beside them like a pink and fleshy whale, was a constant danger. Even worse, when they first started out they had to dodge into the gap between Meagan's tooth and the next one while the giant poked at their hiding spot with the tip of his tongue, as if he was trying to dislodge an irritating bit of food that had become stuck there.

It was a humbling thought for Edgar to realize that "an irritating bit of food" was, in fact, precisely what he had become.

"Does he ever use toothpicks?" he asked Meagan nervously.

"Too stupid," replied the woman. "Come on, he's done now. Let's go."

The tooth directly next to Meagan's was strong and solid, with no obvious place for Edgar to begin excavating a home. The one next to that, however—the farthest one back in the giant's mouth—had a hole twice the size of Edgar's fist. The odor of decay hung rank about it, but Meagan said that would disappear when Edgar had cut away the rot.

It had taken a while to find the hole, since they had had to crawl all over the tooth looking for it. Unlike the opening to Meagan's home, it was on the tooth's outer side, facing the cheek rather than the tongue. They had reached that side by crawling on their bellies through the same gap between the teeth where they had taken shelter earlier.

"Nice location," said Meagan when they found the opening. "Safer than mine, though not quite so convenient for snagging food. I suppose you might give yourself a door on the other side of the tooth as well, once you've dug through it. Need to be careful, though, not to weaken it too much."

Before Meagan would let him start to work she bound them both to the tooth with a combination of ropes and leather straps. When she had driven Edgar nearly mad with checking and rechecking to make sure they were secure, she nodded and said, "Dig in."

Edgar swung the pick, and knocked away a chunk of the yellowed enamel.

The outraged roar of pain that rose from deep within the giant nearly deafened him. At the same time, the giant slapped his hand against his cheek. The mushy cheek wall pressed Edgar and Meagan against the tooth. The torch went out with a sizzle.

"Meagan!" cried Edgar. "Are you all right?"

The question—and her answer—were lost in the giant's reverberating "*Owwwwwwwieeee!*"

Despite the horrifying darkness, the awful squishiness of the cheek pressed against him, and the fact that he could scarcely breath, Edgar almost felt sorry for the giant. Then he reminded himself that the only reason the creature was suffering this way was that it had tried to eat him.

"Now you see why I strapped us down," gasped Meagan after the bellowing died away. "I'm afraid you'll have to work in the dark for now. I won't be able to light the torch again out here."

Edgar located the hole by touch, then began chipping away at it. Without light the work was excruciatingly slow, since he could not take mighty swings with the pick. Instead he began tap-tap-tapping at the tooth, and in this way began to enlarge the hole. This method, although much slower, was clearly safer, since the giant merely moaned rather than howling in pain, and did not again slap his hand to his cheek. They did have one bad moment when he began digging at the back of his mouth with his fingertip, trying to dislodge whatever was bothering him. But Meagan had tied them down with slip knots, and as soon as she saw the light at the front of the giant's mouth, she knew what was coming and loosened the ropes so they could again take shelter in the gap between his teeth.

The giant's blunt and dirty fingertip prodded against their hiding place, but was far too wide to get at them. He did try his fingernail a couple of times. It came somewhat farther into the gap between the teeth, but by cowering back they were able to avoid it. Edgar longed to attack the probing nail with his pick, but Meagan held him back.

By the time they decided to rest, Edgar had managed to enlarge the hole to the point where he could get his head and shoulders into it. His arms ached, and he longed for some light. But he reminded himself that Meagan had done the same thing all on her own, with no company and no hope of light for relief, nothing but her own will to survive driving her on.

When they returned to the tooth where she made her home and she lit a fresh torch, he found himself looking at her with new respect

The outer coating of the tooth was hard, but brittle, and broke away fairly easily. After about four feet of this, the material changed to something dense and yellow, tougher to work with the pick.

It took five days—which is to say, five of the times between when they slept—to reach this inner material. Two days before that, the hole had been big enough that Edgar could crawl completely inside. Though it was big enough for him to fit in comfortably—if you consider being curled in a tight ball comfortable—Meagan did not make him move there immediately, as he had once feared she would. This pleased him, and not merely for the obvious reasons. They had grown more easy in their companionship as the work on Edgar's home had continued, and he had come to think of her not merely as someone sharing a disaster, but as a genuine, if somewhat irascible, friend.

Finally the time came when the excavation in the tooth was big enough for Edgar to take up his home in it. He moved his things— that is, the two or three items Meagan had given him, as well as a pitchfork (the single thing he had managed to snag on his own)—to his new abode.

After a day, he was surprised to find Meagan knocking at the edge of the hole he had made.

"I missed you," she growled. Then she showed him a bottle of wine she had recovered from a wagon the giant had swallowed two years earlier (she kept a calendar carved in her wall) and which she had been saving for a special event.

He invited her in and they had a small party, sitting in the darkness and discussing what he should do next to make his tooth more homey.

The following day, they ran a rope from Meagan's home, through the gap between it and the next tooth, and then along the outer wall of the teeth to Edgar's door, which made it easier for them to visit each other whenever they wanted.

While he continued work on his new dwelling, Meagan taught him how to snatch things from the tide of food and rubble that poured down the giant's throat three times a day. When she "went fishing," as she called it, she first secured a safety rope about her waist, anchoring the other end of the rope to one of the chairs inside the tooth. Normally she pulled things in with the help of a long pole that had a hook on one end. But if something particularly good came rushing past that was too far out on the tongue for her to snag simply by leaning for it, she would fling her whole body onto the surface of the tongue, then use the rope to haul herself back.

Once they saw an old man go past, but he was all the way in the center of the mouth, and they were not able to reach him despite their best efforts.

His cry of despair as he disappeared down the giant's gullet echoed in Edgar's dreams for many nights afterward.

Once Edgar was truly settled he began to explore the giant's mouth in search of a way out. Though he did not tell Meagan this was what he was doing, he suspected she was able to guess. Not that it made any difference. He could find no way of escape. His greatest hope had been to climb out of the giant's mouth while he was sleeping. But the moist walls of his lips were too slick to climb easily. Twice he tried using the pickax to help him make the climb, but both times this caused the giant to rub his mouth, with results that were nearly fatal. (The second time he barely made it back to Meagan's tooth, where she set his broken bones, but gave him no symathy for the pain that kept him awake for seven nights running.)

It was like being at the bottom of a well; easy enough to fall in, impossible to climb out.

Despite his misadventures at the front of the giant's mouth, Edgar continued his explorations, until he had at last made a complete circuit of the giant's mouth. He carried a torch with him, which he lit and waved it to Meagan when he reached the far side.

When he returned from that trip, he was burning with a new idea. "If we strung a rope directly across the center of his mouth, we might have better luck snagging things as they went by," he said.

"The giant would rip it out," replied Meagan.

"Well, what if we didn't make it permanent? We could put in a couple of hooks or pegs or something, one on each side of his mouth, and run the rope between them when we wanted to use it."

"Might work," said Meagan dubiously. "We'd have to put the pegs in the upper teeth, though; if we try it with the lower ones he's sure to snap it with his tongue right away."

The next day Edgar again made his way to the far side of the giant's mouth. As he traveled, he tucked a rope into the narrow trench that ran along the edge of the teeth.

He made the trip without incident, except for one frightening moment when he was at the front of the mouth and the giant happened to make a clucking sound. Then the violent forward movement of his whale-like tongue almost flattened Edgar.

After some searching, he found an upper tooth with a small hole, into which he pounded a peg. Then he waved his torch to Meagan, to let her know that he was going to take up the slack on the rope.

Once they had the rope tight he swung himself onto it. Then, moving hand over hand, he inched his way toward the center of the giant's mouth.

His ambition was rewarded when the giant tossed a cart full of melons into his mouth. Though it went directly down the center, Edgar was able to retrieve not only a pair of the melons, but one of the wagon wheels, which he thought would look nice in his new home.

When he returned to the other side, Meagan grudgingly admitted that the rope had been a good idea. Just how good an idea it became clear as the weeks rolled on and they were able to retrieve more and more items from the flow that rolled down the giant's throat three times a day.

The most unexpected of these items was a young man named Charles, who Edgar snatched from certain doom by hanging upside down from the rope and reaching out to him.

When he escorted Charles home with him, Meagan muttered about things getting too crowded in the giant's mouth. But when Edgar said that Charles could live with him until they were able to excavate another tooth for him, she settled down.

Charles turned out to be clever with his hands, and it was not long before they were hard at work at making a home for him in the tooth between the two they had already hollowed out.

Many hands making lighter work, the home took less time to construct then Edgar's had, and soon they were turning their energies to new and better ways to salvage things.

During Edgar's second year in the giant's mouth they rescued Farley. His arrival upset Meagan even more than Charles's had, and she began muttering that she didn't like having so many men around. On the other hand, she seemed to find Farley attractive, and once it became clear that he returned the compliment, she stopped fussing. They built his home in the tooth above hers—the first in an upper tooth—and soon the two of them were visiting each other several times a day to consult on various ideas and projects.

Their masterpiece was a system of buckets for collecting fresh water whenever the giant took a drink. This freed them from reliance on the giant's saliva, which was a great relief to everyone. Even better was when they could save some of the occasional flood of beer. Such a catch was always a signal for a party—which helped make up for the dangerous (not to mention putrid) belches that the giant inevitably unleashed an hour or so later.

Next to be pulled to safety, about six months later, were a pair of sisters named Babette and Cleo, and their dimwitted brother Herbert. The time had come to begin building homes in the teeth on the other side of the mouth. Babette and Cleo chose to live together. Herbert took the tooth above them.

Once their homes were complete, Edgar began thinking about doing some bridgework.

Before too many more years had passed a thriving community had risen in the giant's mouth. The people got on well enough, though there were occasional conflicts—as there always will be when you have people locked together in a crowded space.

To the surprise of no one save Edgar, he turned out to be the one who usually solved these conflicts, and eventually he was elected mayor of Giant's Mouth Township. They gave him a jewelled scepter which they had managed to retrieve one afternoon when the giant swallowed a king. (They had tried to save the king, too, of course, but his grip was weak and flabby, and he had not been able to hold on when Herbert reached out to him.) Many was the night Edgar sat in his tooth and looked out the window he had carved on the tongue-ward side, feeling warm and cozy at the sight of the lights twinkling on the other side of the giant's mouth.

In this way the years rolled on.

And then, one afternoon while he was setting a rope, Edgar was suddenly yanked from the giant's mouth.

It happened because the giant, who was in a foul mood that day, became particularly irritated by the feeling of things moving in his mouth. Edgar was stringing a rope across the roof of his mouth in order to do some salvage work when the giant reached in and began to scratch at the roof of his mouth. Though the rope was less to him than a silk thread would be to a human, it caught on his fingernail. When he pulled his hand out, one end of the rope came free—and with it, still clinging to the end, came Edgar.

As he hurtled out of the giant's mouth, two things caused him to blink. The first was the unexpected brightness of the sun, which he had not seen except at a distance, for so many years. The second was the horrifying distance that separated him from the ground.

Knowing he could not keep his grip on the saliva-slick rope, Edgar made a desperate leap, and landed on the giant's collar. The giant swatted at him, as one would at an annoying insect, but Edgar quickly scrambled under the giant's collar, where he held as still as he could, scarcely breathing.

All through the long, hot day he stayed there, peering sideways at the world below, longing for it, thinking of how he had missed it.

Finally night darkened the sky, bringing with it the stars that he had not seen in so many years. Their beauty made him weep.

The giant lay down to sleep.

Edgar climbed out onto his chest. He stood, staring out at the rising moon, the river on whose water it was reflected, the dark ridge of the distant mountains, and the road that led back to his village, back to Melisande.

He wondered if she had waited for him, or if she had married Martin Plellman after all.

The giant's clothing was so coarsely woven that the threads were almost like the rungs of a ladder. Now that he was lying down, it was only a few hundred feet to the ground.

Edgar took a deep breath of the clean, clear air, and released it with a sigh.

Then he began to climb the giant's shirt, not down, but up, onto the giant's chin, where the stubble grew so thick it was like a grove of small pine trees. Across the loose and pendulous lip Edgar climbed.

Then he lowered himself back into the moist cavern of the giant's mouth, where his home and friends lay waiting.

Ragged John

Tattered clothes all fluttering,
Worn out voice still muttering,
Ragged John comes knocking
At all the doors in town.

And when a door swings open
Then you can hear the hope in
The thin, cracked voice that wonders
If you've seen his unicorn.

And we all know John is crazy
And his mind has gone all hazy
And the only thing we really wish
Is that he just would let us be.

But John he keeps on questing
And the poor man knows no resting
For there's something hurt inside him.
And the pain won't go away.

I've heard when John was younger
He was taken with a hunger
To see that white-horned wonder
They call the unicorn.

But when that star-horned, moon-maned dancer
Finally called, John could not answer;
Fear held him like a prisoner,
And he watched it walk away.

So now empty-eyed John hobbles
Across the village cobbles
And the only fear he feels is
That it will never come again.

Oh, when I see old Ragged John
Go staggering by and wandering on,
I know there's nothing sadder
Than a heart that feared its dreams.

If a unicorn should call to you
Some moon-mad night all washed in dew,
Then here's the prayer to whisper:
"Grant me the heart to follow."

Saying No to Nick

Nick Foster used to be my best friend, and boy, let me tell you, I miss him.

It's not like we had a fight or anything.

It's just that I died.

Well, I didn't **just** die. The process was pretty painful and horrible—horrible for me, of course, but even worse, I think, for Nick. After all, the two of us had been best friends since kindergarten.

It seems so weird not to be able to talk to him now. I miss him every day. Of course, the fact that "What Do I Miss?" is one of the games we play most often here in The Waiting Room doesn't help any.

I don't suppose "The Waiting Room" is the real name for where I am. But it's what most of us call it, since it's been made clear to us that this is just a temporary stop.

But a stop before what? "Ah, that's the mystery, isn't it?" says Big Bill, every time I ask that question. It's not like Bill is in charge or anything. He's just another one of the people who's here, waiting.

Some of the people claim we're waiting to be sent back for another life. Others are bracing to be plunged into the inferno. A few are completely certain they're heading for heaven any minute now. (But I have to tell you, a lot of **them** are so self-satisfied I can't imagine God would want them around for long). Most of us are just mystified. Well, mystified and slightly nervous. I'm getting calmer about it, though, because it seems like whoever runs this place must basically be nice.

Okay, What Do **I** Miss?

Peanut butter. Summer vacation. Comic books. Coca Cola. Eighth grade, believe it or not. Those cross country practices when Nick and I used to run side by side for an hour at a time, sweat pouring down our faces. I even miss sweating. It's one of those things that makes you know you're alive.

Truth is, I didn't realize how much I loved my body until I didn't have it any more. It's amazing how much some people are bothered by the things our bodies do—burping, farting, sweating, stinking—not to mention all the sex stuff, which I hadn't even had a chance to get to yet. But every single one of those things means you're still breathing.

Still in the world.

Still part of life.

What do I miss?

My parents.

My dog.

Myhousemybedmyroom.

Nick.

Here's how Nick Foster and I became friends: It was the first day of kindergarten and we both had Mr. Fielding for a teacher. This was Very Cool, since there are almost no male kindergarten teachers. Even so, I was feeling scared about the whole thing. I guess Nick was, too, since when I went to hide behind the Big Blocks I found him there ahead of me.

His eyes got wide when he saw me. "Shhh!" he hissed, putting a finger to his lips.

I nodded, and scooched in beside him. We lay side by side on the floor, watching the class and not saying a thing, until Felicia Edmonds noticed us and cried, "Teacher! Teacher! Two boys are hiding behind the blocks!"

"Tattlepot!" cried Nick.

Tattlepot. I love that word. It was something they said in Nick's family. The Fosters had a lot of special words like that, so close to what most people said that you couldn't miss their meaning, but somehow changed to make them special to the family. Once I asked Nick's mother where they came from. "Nicky invented most of them," she told me. Then she smiled and added, "I call them 'Nickisms.'"

After that, I did, too.

Anyway, Felicia burst into tears, and Nick became my hero. (This position was solidified two weeks later when Felicia announced on the playground that she was going to marry me, and Nick clonked her on the head and said, "Jeremy is never getting married!")

The only year in elementary school Nick and I weren't together was third grade, when Nick fell behind in reading and they put him in a different class. If you don't count dying, getting into the *Rockets and Flags* reading book was the only time I can remember going someplace before Nick. It felt great in the beginning, but after a month or so I didn't really like it. Nick always took the lead, and somehow it just felt wrong for me to be in that book ahead of him. So third grade was a miserable year for both of us.

Of course, Nick worked like crazy to get caught up and by the next year we were in the same class again—except now he was one reading group ahead of me.

Typical.

We were in seventh grade when Nick got really interested in religion. Actually, what he got interested in first was Stacy Prendergast and her shining red hair. Since Stacy was all wrapped up in her church's youth group, Nick decided to join it so he could be near her. This meant that I joined, too, of course. That's the way we did things.

The youth group was all right. We did do a lot of praying, which kind of annoyed me at the time. But who knows—it might be one reason I'm here in The Waiting Room, and not someplace a lot worse! I should add that we had a lot of fun in the group. Despite that, I was just as happy when Nick decided he wasn't in love with Stacy anymore and we could drop out. But as it turned out, even though Nick was no longer in love with Stacy, he had fallen in love with God.

Which was how we ended up doing the baptism.

Nick had always liked ceremonies—we had buried more animals in his backyard than I could count, some of them pets that had passed away, others just animals we found along the roadside. Nick always said a few words over the grave. I think that was his favorite part. He was good with words—it was one of the things that made it so hard for me to say "No" when he got an idea. His mother used to claim Nick was going to be either a politician or a minister. Then she would shudder in mock horror at either idea.

Anyway, we were lying in my backyard one night last July, looking at the stars—which you can see a lot of in Arizona—when Nick said, "I think we should do a baptism ceremony, Jeremy."

"**What?**" I asked.

"A baptism. It's a way of cleansing ourselves. Starting over."

"What do we need a cleansing for?"

Nick laughed. "Are you telling me you've led a life without sin?"

I couldn't claim that, of course—though I hadn't thought much about it until we started going to that church group. I tried a new objection. "Don't we need a priest for something like that?"

"Nah. Priests just get in the way. They put a layer between you and God."

I didn't want to admit to Nick that if there really was a god, having a layer between me and him, her, or it didn't seem like such a bad idea.

"We'll do it at my house," continued Nick, already certain I would go along. "We can use the swimming pool."

"The pool?" I asked in astonishment.

"If we're gonna do this, we're gonna do it mountaintop."

Mountaintop was another Nickism, of course. It meant doing something all out, all the way.

"Total immersion is what it's called," he continued. "Come over after your folks have left for work tomorrow. We'll have the house to ourselves."

I liked going to Nick's. His parents make a lot of money, and he's got a pretty big house—not to mention a pool, which in July in Arizona is like having a little piece of heaven. But I still wasn't taking this baptism thing all that seriously. I thought it was just some kind of a goof. But as Nick kept talking, I realized he was dead serious. "This is going to help us get pure again," he said, still gazing up at the stars. "It will take us back to our state of original grace."

"What are you talking about?" I asked.

"It's going to wash away our transgressions. And don't tell me you don't have any, Jeremy. I saw you looking at Mary Sue Betts at the mall yesterday. Lust in your heart is a sin in itself. And we never told Mrs. Parker about that window we broke. Don't you want to get free of that stuff?"

Actually, I didn't want to get free of Mary Sue Betts at all, and I figured the best way to undo the sin of not telling Mrs. Parker we were the ones who had broken her window was to just go tell her. But somehow I couldn't bring myself to say any of that to Nick.

"So what are **your** sins?" I asked, by way of changing the subject.

"That's my business," said Nick, frowning just a little. "Come on, Jeremy. This is important. And I can't do it alone."

So the next day I showed up at Nick's house, ready for the baptism. He had written the whole ceremony out, and I have to admit it was pretty good. I think he had gone to three or four churches and looked in their hymnals, then grabbed some stuff from the web, plus mixed in stuff from his own brain. He had tucked the "script" inside a plastic binder sheet, so we could take it into the water with us.

"Are you sure it's not sacrilegious for us to do this?" I asked, after I'd read what he'd written. "I mean, it's not like we're priests or ministers or anything."

"I don't think God cares about that," said Nick. "Come on, let's get out of our clothes."

"What?"

"We've got to be naked to do this. It's like being born. And you don't get born with clothes on. Mountaintop, Jeremy, just like I said. Look, I've got sheets we can wrap around us when we go outside. But once we go into the pool, it's birthday suit city."

"Are you kidding?" I just about shrieked. It wasn't like we hadn't gone skinny dipping before. But we'd never done it in broad daylight.

"No, I'm not kidding. Come on, let's get going."

He assumed, of course, that I wouldn't refuse. I never had before. Why should this time be any different?

We got undressed and wrapped the sheets around us, then went out to the pool.

The sun was hot, the sky a perfect, clear blue. I remember that really well—partly because I miss it, partly because it was the last thing I ever saw.

We looked around to make sure no one could see us. There's a fence around the pool, of course, but we wanted to make sure no one was peeking over it or anything; not likely, but it would have been kind of embarrassing. Once we were sure we were clear, we dropped the sheets and walked down the steps into the shallow end of the pool.

"Who goes first?" I asked.

"Me," said Nick, "Because it was my idea. What we do is, I lie back in the water—you'll have to support me with one arm—and you follow the stuff on the script. It will tell you when to lower me into the water."

"How can I hold the script and lower you into the water at the same time?"

"We'll stand near the edge of the pool. That way you can set the script down when its time to dunk me."

Which is what we did. I held out my right arm, and cradled Nick's head. Then I read aloud what was on the script. When I got to the part that said, "It is time for you to be washed free of your sins," I lowered my arm to let his head into the water. Only he was kind of floating, so I had to push him down to get him completely under. I wasn't sure how long I was supposed to keep him that way, so I held my breath myself, and when it started to get a little uncomfortable I let him back up. He gasped for breath and shook his head, spattering water in all directions.

"That was great!" he cried. "Okay, now it's your turn."

We switched places, and I let myself lie back in the water until my head was cradled in the crook of Nick's arm. The sky was achingly blue, but I had to close my eyes against the sun, which was so bright that it hurt. Nick began to speak, though I think he was reciting from memory rather than reading from the script.

"We come to the water to be washed free of our sins, so that we may become as little children again, pure in the eyes of God, closer to the heart of the universe. Do you, Jeremy, come to this of your own free will?"

"Yes," I said.

I don't think that was a lie, really. I think I could have backed out, even then. But I had never said no to Nick before, and this didn't seem like the time to start.

"Then it is time for you to be washed free of your sins," he intoned as he pushed me under.

It wasn't Nick's fault that I panicked. I don't even know why I did. I could swim well enough. And we had rough-housed in the pool plenty of times. Maybe I was just spooked by all that god stuff. Whatever the reason, I began to thrash and fight to get up.

Did Nick try to hold me down? I honestly can't remember. What I do remember is that somehow I got a big mouthful of water and began gasping for breath. I was terrified, felt as if my heart was trying to beat its way out of my chest.

It wasn't Nick's fault. It surely wasn't his fault that I had a weakness in my heart that no one—not me, not my parents, not my doctor—even knew was there.

Not his fault that my heart blew a valve.

Not his fault that I went limp and died there in the pool, in his arms.

Not his fault at all.

You've probably read about what happened next: the tunnel, the white light, the people waiting to greet you. I experienced all that, and it was beautiful. But there was one thing more to my death experience. Somewhere far behind me I could hear Nick sobbing, "No! No, no! Jeremy, come back! Jeremy! **Jeremy!**"

But it was too late for that. For once, I couldn't do what Nick said.

It took me a while to get used to The Waiting Room. It helped that there were people here to welcome me. They couldn't tell me much, but they helped me be not afraid.

We don't have bodies here, though if you really concentrate on someone you can usually tell what they used to look like. And we don't get hungry, of course, though we do get what some of us call, "hungry for being hungry," which is this kind of aching memory/longing for having a body, for feeling the need to eat, and being able to do it.

I don't know how long I'd been here before I figured out how to "Drop In." That's what most of us in The Waiting Room call it when you go back to the physical world to check on things. It was a woman named Kwanisha who taught me. She said she'd learned how because she wanted to see her kids so badly.

"That's half the trick, honey," she said. "You got to **want** to see someone so bad you can just let that need pull you back."

A lot of people advised me not to do it. They think Dropping In adds time to your stay in the Waiting Room, somehow makes it harder to Move On. But no one knows, really. It's not like there's a set of rules posted on the walls.

Besides, I was in no hurry to Move On.

The first time I Dropped In only lasted a few minutes. I saw my parents. They looked terrible. I think my mom had lost twenty pounds. Even so, I could tell that they were going to be all right. I don't know how I knew; it was just something about the way they were holding on to each other. I didn't have time for much more than a look before I found myself back in The Waiting Room.

A while later I tried again. This time I went to see Nick. Only he didn't look like Nick. He was in school, sitting at the back of the room, his shoulders slumped, just staring off into space. I was somewhere above him, sort of near the ceiling, I guess. I tried to get closer, but suddenly I felt as if I were falling—or maybe floating away. Everything went white and next thing I knew, I was back here in the Waiting Room.

That was pretty frustrating. But Dropping In turned out to be like cross country running—the more I practiced, the longer I could keep going.

I would look in on my parents, which was hard, because their sorrow was so real it almost choked me—which was weird, since I don't have anything to choke. Even so, it was only sorrow, and I had the sense they going to get over it. It was Nick that I started to worry about. I could tell he was being turned inside out by guilt, which is much, much worse than mere sorrow.

It was kind of sad when you thought about it. The whole reason he had come up with the baptism was to get rid of guilt—and now he had more of it than ever. But after a while I figured out that it wasn't only guilt that was eating at him.

It was shame.

The whispering was what tipped me off, the kids whispering when Nick walked by. After a while I figured out how to listen in and I was shocked at what I heard. Nick had killed me, they were saying—killed me because we were boyfriends.

I was so furious and baffled when I heard them that it took me a while to figure out the obvious: Nick had called 911, of course, and when the Rescue Squad got to his place, they found my naked body. Nick was probably still naked, too. Someone on the squad had talked, naturally—probably someone who had a kid in our school. The baptism script might have been enough to convince the police of what had really happened, but it had no power against the mighty tongue of Rumor.

So the story going around was that Nick had killed me because he was jealous, or because I had wanted to break it off, or because we got in a fight because I was jealous, or because I had threatened to tell what we had been doing, or any of a hundred other stupid versions of the same idea. It made me sick. Not out of shame—you start to let go of that here in the Waiting Room—but just because it was so stupid, and so vicious, and because it was clear so many kids were getting malicious pleasure out of repeating it. But the main reason it made me sick was that I could tell it was making Nick sick, too.

Even so I didn't realize he was in danger until the afternoon I Dropped In to check on him and found him standing at the edge of the pool, staring into the blue ripples. He was naked again, almost as if he was thinking about repeating our "baptism." As I watched he knelt and dipped his hand into the water. Then he gripped the edge of the pool and lowered his head. His shoulders began to shake.

He stayed that way for a long time.

I wanted to talk to him, but didn't know how. I had no voice, no body, no way to say, "It's not your fault, Nick. I'm not angry. I forgive you. I miss you." So I was mute in the face of my friend's guilt and grief.

I checked on him every day after that, and every day I would find him standing at the edge of the pool, staring into the water as if he could still see me there, as if by looking hard enough he could bring me back, make it all go away.

How much of what was eating at him was guilt, how much shame at the rumors, I had no way of knowing. I only knew that it was getting worse.

"I'm worried about my friend," I told Kwanisha.

"That's the rough part about Dropping In, honey," she replied.

"You can see what's going on, but not much you can do to help. I worry and worry about those children of mine. Sometimes I want to knock 'em upside the head and say, 'What were you thinkin' about? Don't **do** that!' But not a thing I can do to change what they do." She sighed. "Maybe I shouldn't have taught you how to go back after all."

"No!" I said, quick, sharp, and hard. "It's good you taught me. I needed to go back."

So there he is, my friend Nick, standing at the edge of his family's pool—not at the shallow end, but the deep end. He's naked, just the way we were the day of the "baptism." It's a cloudy afternoon. Might even rain, which is unusual around here.

Where am I? I don't know. Where am I any time I come back like this? Somewhere nearby. Watching. Worrying. Hurting.

Nick goes into the house.

I follow.

He goes out to the garage and takes some rope from his father's work bench.

Then he picks up a concrete block.

I feel sick.

I can't watch this.

I have to.

I follow him back to the pool's edge, where he puts the block down and sits down next to it. He's crying. "I'm sorry, Jeremy," he sobs. "I'm so sorry."

"Nick!" I want to shout. "It's all right! Don't do this!"

He can't hear me, of course. Slowly, carefully, he ties the rope around his waist. I recognize the knot. It's one we both struggled to learn the year we were in scouts together. Nick learned it first, of course. Then he taught me.

"Nick, DON'T!" No words, of course. No sound, even though I'm shouting it with every fiber of my being.

He stands the concrete block on end, loops the rope through it, ties another knot. Ties it close, ties it tight.

"Nick, NO!"

He stands up, picks up the block, holds it over the water.

I fling myself at him, crying, "No, no, no!"

And then I'm inside him.

Jeremy?

I feel the question, feel his shock, feel his fear and astonishment and hope. Feel his heart pounding…pounding as hard as mine did the

day I died, but strong still, steady, not about to burst, despite the fact
that it has been broken.

I can feel that, too.

And I feel one more thing. Nick **did** love me, and not just as
a friend. He never touched me, not that way. Never hinted, never
whispered a word of his desire. But it's there inside his pounding
heart, or wherever such things are stored. He loved me, and never
dared say it, and I died in his arms with him feeling it, and all the
rumors that had no truth in reality had a rending, slicing truth in
his own heart.

My first feeling is to break away, to get out of him, go as fast and as
far as I can. I'm hit with a wave of disgust, and then disgust at myself
for being disgusted.

Jeremy? he thinks again, frightened and eager all at once.

I want to hide. But where do you hide when you're inside someone?

Here, I think. *It's me, Nick.*

He starts to cry. *I'm so sorry. I am so, so sorry. But I'm going to make
up for it. I'm going to make up for what I did.*

He holds the block out over the water.

NO! The word comes out of me. The word IS me. It vibrates
through him.

I have to! he thinks.

NO! NO NO NONONONO!

It's like a wrestling match for a while, Nick willing his arms to drop
the block into the pool, me fighting him, trying to control his body,
and all the while thinking, *It's all right, Nick. It's all right!*

It's not!

You were my hero, I tell him. *Heroes don't quit.*

*I'm so tired, Jeremy. And I hurt so much. And I'm so ashamed. I
hate myself.*

I don't hate you, I think back. And then I realize it's not enough, so
I give him the harder words, the words I could never have spoken, or
even thought, before I died, words it's hard to repeat even now, even
though they're true.

I love you, Nick.

And that stops him.

He puts the block down, then collapses next to it, clutching it as
if for some rough comfort, as if he needs something, anything to hold
on to.

He begins to sob.

He's still sobbing when his parents come home, come out to get him.

Which is when I leave.

So now I know. You can't fix someone else's broken heart. Only time can do that. And you can't take on someone else's guilt. All you can do is love them, and let time take care of the rest.

I'm going now. Someone—I don't know who—has called me. My stay in The Waiting Room is over.

I suppose I'll never see Nick again. But I'm glad I could be there for him that one last time.

Glad I could tell him I loved him, even if it wasn't the way he wanted.

Glad I could finally tell him "No."

Good-bye, Nick.

I love you.

clean as a Whistle

Jamie Carhart was, quite possibly, the messiest kid in Minnesota. The messiest kid in her town, no doubt. The county? She pretty well had that sewed up, too. And her mother was convinced that, were there a statewide competition, Jamie would easily be in the top ten, and might indeed take first place.

Not that Mrs. Carhart was amused by this fact.

"This room is a sty!" she would say, at least once a day, standing in the doorway of Jamie's room and sighing. Then she would poke her foot at the mess that threatened to creep out into the rest of the house, sigh again as if the whole thing was far too much for her to cope with, and wander off.

So it was a shock for Jamie to come home from school on the afternoon of April 17th and find her room totally, perfectly, absolutely neat, clean and tidy.

"Aaaaaah!" she cried, standing in her doorway. "Aaaaaah! What happened? Who did this?"

Jamie didn't really expect an answer. Her parents both worked, and wouldn't be home for another two hours.

For a horrible moment she wondered if her grandmother had come to visit. Gramma Hattie was perfectly capable of sneaking into a kid's room and cleaning it while that kid wasn't looking. Heaven alone knew where **she** might have put things. Even Jamie's mother found Gramma Hattie hard to cope with.

But Gramma Hattie lived in Utah (which in Jamie's opinion was a good place for her) and now that Jamie thought of it, she was off on a trip to Europe. Besides, if she had done this she would have pounced by now, crowing at her victory over disorder.

So it wasn't her.

Jamie hesitated, wondering if she dared go in.

"Anyone here?" she asked timidly.

No answer.

"***Anyone?***"

Silence, though she did notice that the cat was on her bed. This did not please her. Actually, she always longed to have the cat in her room. But Mr. Bumpo normally refused to come through her door. Jamie's mother claimed this was because the cat was too neat and couldn't stand the mess. Jamie denied this, usually quite angrily. So she wasn't amused to find Mr. Bumpo here now that the room was so clean; his gently purring presence seemed to confirm her mother's horrible theory.

Jamie looked around nervously as she entered the room. After a moment she dropped her books on her bed. She waited, half expecting someone to come dashing in and pick them up.

"What is going on here?" she asked the cat, scratching its orange and black head.

Mr. Bumpo closed his eyes and purred louder.

When Mrs. Carhart arrived home and came up to say hello to Jamie, she grabbed the edges of the doorway and staggered as if she had been hit between the eyes with a two by four.

"What," she asked in astonishment, "got into you?"

"What are you talking about?" asked Jamie sourly. She was sitting at her desk, working on a small clay project. She had generated a minor mess with the work, and managed to create a tad of clutter here and there. But overall the room was still so clean as to be unrecognizable.

"I mean this room," said her mother. She squeezed her eyes shut then opened them again, as if to make sure that she wasn't hallucinating. "It's so...so...***tidy!***"

Jamie looked at her suspiciously. "Didn't you hire someone to come in here and clean it?" she asked. She was still fairly angry about the invasion of her privacy (and not about to admit that she was delighted to find her clayworking tools, which had been missing for some six months now).

Her mother snorted. "The day we can afford a housekeeper, he or she takes on some of **my** work first."

"Then who did this to me?" asked Jamie.

Her mother looked at her oddly. "You are the strangest child," she said at last. "But thanks anyway."

Before Jamie could reply, Mrs. Carhart turned and left. Jamie growled and stabbed a long metal tool through the little clay man she had been making. She knew what her mother was thinking. She was thinking that she, Jamie, had cleaned up the room but was too embarrassed to admit it. She was also thinking that if she pushed the issue Jamie would never do it again. Which meant that when Jamie claimed she had nothing to do with this...this *catastrophe*, her mother would simply think that she was playing an odd game, and the more she tried to convince her otherwise, the more Mrs. Carhart would be convinced that she was right in her assumption. Jamie groaned. It was hopeless.

Of course, the other possibility was that her mother was lying, and really had hired someone to clean the room. Jamie considered the idea. "Unlikely," she said out loud.

But what other explanation was there? Some demented prowler who broke into people's houses to clean rooms when no one was at home? Jamie glanced around nervously, then shook her head.

Dinner that night was interesting. Mrs. Carhart had clearly warned Mr. Carhart that he was not to make a big deal over the clean room, for fear that Jamie would never do it again.

By the time the meal was over, Jamie wanted to scream.

By the time the night was over, she **did** scream. "I just want you to know that I am **not** responsible for this!" she bellowed, standing at the top of the stairs. "I had nothing to do with it!"

She heard her father chuckle.

Furious, she went back into her room, slamming the door behind her. When she undressed for bed she tore off her clothes and scattered them about the room. Once she was in her nightgown she went to the door, opened it a crack, and yelled "Good night!"

Then she slammed it shut, and climbed between the sheets.

When Jamie got home from school the next afternoon, yesterday's clothes (which she had studiously avoided touching that morning) had disappeared from her floor. Her clay working tools were lined up in an orderly fashion on her desk. The bits of clay that she had left around had been gathered together and rolled into a ball.

The cat was curled up in the middle of her bed, sleeping peacefully.

"Did you do this?" she asked, looking at him suspiciously. She was perfectly aware of what a stupid question it was. On the other hand, when things got this weird, stupid questions began to make sense.

Mr. Bumpo blinked at her, but said nothing. She reached out to stroke him and realized that his fur, which normally had a number of tangles and knots, was perfectly groomed.

"This is creepy," she said. "And I don't like it." She tossed her backpack on the bed and began to search the room for some clue or sign as to who might have done this. Under her bed she found only that the rapidly-breeding colony of dust-bunnies had become extinct. She checked her closet next, where she saw something she had not laid eyes on in over three years: the floor. When she looked in her dresser, she found that every item of clothing had been neatly folded. This was even worse than it had been the day before!

What she did not find was any sign of who had done this terrible thing to her.

She sat on the edge of her bed for a long time, stroking Mr. Bumpo and listening to him purr. Finally she decided to go back to her clayworking. Remembering a sketch for a new project she had made during math class, she overturned her pack and emptied it on the bed. Out tumbled a mixture of books, crumpled papers, pens and pencils in various stages of usefulness, candy wrappers, rubber bands, sparkly rocks she had picked up on the way to and from school, three crayons stuck together with a piece of used chewing gum, and a moldy sandwich.

Jamie dug her way through the mound of stuff until she found the sketch. She carried it to her desk and smoothed it out, then picked up the ball of clay and began to work. After about a half an hour, she decided to go get a snack.

When she got up from her desk and turned around, she let out a yelp of astonishment.

Her bed was perfectly clean! The mess she had dumped onto it had been organized and tidied into meek submission. The crumpled papers had vanished, the pencils lined up in a tidy row, the crayons unstuck, the gum that held them together mysteriously gone. Even the backpack's straps had been neatly folded beneath it.

"What is going on here?" she cried.

The only answer was a yawn from Mr. Bumpo.

Goosebumps skittering over her arms, Jamie wondered if she should run for her life. But nothing about what was happening was threatening. It was just **weird**.

She stared at her bed for a while, then made a decision. Stomping over to it, she snatched up the neat piles and tossed them into the air. Mr. Bumpo yowled in alarm, bolted from the bed, and ran out of the room. Jamie stirred the mess around a bit more, rumpled the bedcovers for good measure, then went back to her desk and picked up her tools. She pretended to work. What she was really doing was trying to look over her shoulder while bending her neck as little as possible.

For several minutes nothing happened, except that her neck got sore. In a way, she was glad nothing happened; part of her had been afraid of what she might see. Eventually the pain in her neck got to be too much, and she was forced to straighten her head. When she turned her head back, she saw a brown blur out of the corner of her eye.

"Gotcha!" she cried, leaping to her feet.

But whatever it was had disappeared.

Jamie stood still for a moment, wondering what had happened. *Under the bed!* she thought suddenly.

Dropping to her knees she crept to the bed and lifted the edge of the spread. All she saw was clean floor, and a ripple of movement at the other side of the spread. Whatever had been there had escaped.

"The little stinker is fast," Jamie muttered, getting to her feet. She stared at the bed, which was still a mess, and made a decision. Leaving the room, she headed for the kitchen.

When Jamie returned to her room the bed had been remade and the things from her pack were in perfect order. This did not surprise her.

She went to the far side of the bed, the side from which whatever-it-was had disappeared. She opened the bottle of molasses she had taken from the kitchen, then poured a thick line of the sticky goo the length of the bed, about a foot from the edge. Replacing the lid, she once again messed up everything on top of the bed. Then she returned to her desk.

It wasn't long before she heard a tiny voice cry, "What have you done, what have you done?"

Turning, she saw a man-like creature about a foot and a half tall. He was jumping up and down beside her bed. Covered with brown fur, he looked like a tiny, pot-bellied version of Bigfoot. The main differences were a long tail and a generally more human face.

"Wretched girl," cried the creature, shaking a hazelnut-sized fist at her. "What's the matter wi' you?"

"What's the matter with **you**?" she replied. "Sneaking into a person's room and cleaning it up when you're not invited is perverted."

"I was too invited," snapped the creature. Sitting down, he flicked his tail out of the way and began licking molasses from the bottom of his right foot.

"What a liar you are!" said Jamie.

"What a Messy Carruthers you are!" replied the creature. "And you don't know everything, miss. I was sent here by one of your blood. That counts as invitation if she is close enough—which she is."

Jamie scowled, then her eyes opened wide. "My grandmother!" she exclaimed. "**She** sent you, didn't she?"

"That she did, and I can see why, too. Really this place is quite pathetic. I don't understand why you wouldn't welcome having someone clean it up. I should think you'd be grateful."

"This is my room, and I liked the way it was," said Jamie.

This was not entirely true. Jamie did sometimes wish that the place was clean. But she felt that she couldn't admit that without losing the argument altogether. Besides, she mostly did like it this way; and she most certainly did **not** like having someone clean it without her permission. She felt as if she had been robbed or something. "What are you, anyway?" she asked, by way of changing the topic.

The creature rolled his eyes, as if he couldn't believe her stupidity. "I'm a brownie," he said. "As any fool can plainly see."

"Brownies don't exist."

"Rude!" cried the creature. "Rude, rude, rude! Your grandmother warned me about that. `She's a rude girl,' she said. And she was right."

"I think it was rude of my grandmother to talk about me like that in front of a complete stranger," replied Jamie.

"I'm not a complete stranger. I've been the MacDougal family brownie for nearly three hundred years."

"That shows what you know!" said Jamie. "I'm not a MacDougal, I'm a Carhart."

"Aye, and what was your mother's name before she was married?"

"Chase," said Jamie smugly.

"And her mother's name?"

Jamie's sense of certainty began to fade. "I don't have the slightest idea," she said irritably.

"Rude, and irreverent as well! No sense of family, have you girl? Well I'll tell you what you should have known all along. Your grandmother's maiden name was MacDougal—Harriet Hortense MacDougal, to be precise."

"What has that got to do with me?" asked Jamie.

"Everything," said the brownie. Having finished licking the molasses from his feet, he scooted over to her desk. Moving so fast she barely had time to flinch, he climbed the desk leg and positioned himself in front of her, which made them face to face (though his face was barely the size of her fist). "The last of your family in the old country died last year, leaving me without a family to tend to. Your grandmother, bless her heart, came to close up the house. There she found me, moaning and mournful. 'Why brownie,' she says (she being smart enough to know what I am, unlike some I could mention) 'Why brownie, whatever is the matter with you?'

"'My family is all gone,' I told her, 'And now I've naught to care for, so I shall soon fade away.'

"Well, right off your grandmother says, 'Oh, the family is not all gone. I've a daughter in the states, and **she** has a daughter who could more than use your services.'"

"Thanks, Gramma," muttered Jamie.

"I wasn't much interested in coming to this barbarian wilderness," said the brownie, ignoring the interruption. "But things being what they were, I didn't have much choice. So here I am, much to your good fortune."

Jamie wondered for a moment why Gramma Hattie had sent the brownie to her, instead of to her mother. It didn't take her long to figure out the answer. Jamie's mother would have been as happy to have someone clean her house as Jamie was annoyed by having her room invaded. Gramma Hattie would never have wanted to do anything that pleasant.

"What will it take to get you to leave me alone?" she asked.

The brownie began to laugh. "What a silly girl you are!" he cried. "You won't ever be alone again!"

Great, thought Jamie, rolling her eyes: *My grandmother has sent me an eighteen-inch-high stalker.* Aloud, she asked, "Are you saying I don't have any choice in this?"

"It's a family matter," replied the brownie. "No one gets to choose when it comes to things like that."

"But I don't want you here!"

The brownie's lower lip began to quiver and his homely little face puckered into what Jamie's mother called "a booper."

"You really don't want me?" he asked, sniffing just a bit.

Jamie felt her annoyance begin to melt, until she realized what the brownie was trying to do to her. (It wasn't hard to figure it out, since she tried the same thing on her parents often enough.) "Oh, stop it," she snapped.

Instantly the brownie's expression changed. Crossing his arms, he sat down on her desk and said, "I'm staying, and that's final."

"You're going, and I mean it," replied Jamie. But she realized even as she said it that she had no way to make the threat stick. The smug look on the brownie's face told her that he was well aware of this.

Now what was she going to do? Totally frustrated, she said, "I'm going to tell my mother about you." She hated talking like that; it made her feel like a little kid. But she couldn't think of anything else.

It didn't make any difference. "She won't believe you," said the brownie, looking even smugger.

"Wouldn't you like to go to work for her?" pleaded Jamie. "She'd be more than happy to have you."

The brownie looked wistful. "I would be delighted," he replied. "But the oldest female in the family has assigned me to you. I have no choice in the matter."

For a day or two, Jamie thought she might be able to live with the situation—though with the brownie taking up residence in her closet she made it a point to do her dressing and undressing in the bathroom.

The worst thing was the way her mother smiled whenever she passed the room. Jamie ground her teeth, but said nothing.

By the third day she was getting used to having the room neat and clean. And though she hated to admit it, it was easier to get things done when she didn't have to spend half an hour looking for whatever she needed to start. But just when she was beginning to think that things might work out, the brownie did something unforgiveable.

It began to nag.

"Can't you do anything for yourself?" it asked petulantly when she tossed her books on the bed one afternoon after she arrived home from school. "Am I expected to take care of **everything** around here?"

Jamie looked at him in astonishment. "I didn't ask you to come here!" she exploded. "And I certainly didn't ask you to be messing around with my stuff all the time!"

"I am not messing," said the brownie primly. "I am **un**messing."

"I don't care!" she screamed. "I want you to go away. I don't like having you here all the time. I don't like knowing you're in my closet. I don't like having my room look the way you and my grandmother think it should look instead of the way I think it should look."

"Messy Carruthers," muttered the brownie.

"Nosey Parker!" snapped Jamie, accidentally using one of her grandmother's favorite phrases.

She stomped to her desk. The brownie disappeared into the closet. A heavy silence descended on the room, broken only when Jamie crumpled a sketch she didn't like and tossed it onto the floor.

"You pick that up right now!" called the brownie.

Not only did she not pick up the paper, she crumpled another and threw it on the floor just to spite the creature.

That was the beginning of what Jamie later thought of as "The Great Slob War."

Immediately the brownie came dashing from the closet, snatched up the offending papers, and tossed them in the wastebasket. Muttering angrily, he stomped back to the closet (not very effective for someone only a foot and a half tall) and slammed the door behind him.

Jamie immediately wadded up another paper and threw it on the floor. The brownie dashed out to pick it up. Seized by inspiration, she overturned her wastebasket and shook it out. As the brownie began scurrying around to pick up the papers she plunked the wastebasket down and sat on it. "Now where will you put the papers?" she asked triumphantly.

Her sense of victory dissolved when the brownie gathered the trash in a pile and began to race around it. With a sudden snap the pile vanished into nothingness. Wiping his hands, he gave her the smuggest look yet. Then he returned to the closet, slamming the door behind him.

"How did you do that?" cried Jamie. When he didn't answer, she threw the wastebasket at the door and began to plan her next attack.

She smeared clay on the wall.

She emptied the contents of her dresser onto her floor, tossing out socks, underwear, blouses, and jeans with wild abandon. She tracked all over them with muddy boots, then crushed cracker crumbs on top. The brownie simply waited until she left for school. By the time she got home, everything had been cleaned, folded, and replaced, neater than before.

Furious, she opened her pencil sharpener and sprinkled its contents all over her bed, topped them off with pancake syrup, a tangled mass of string, and the collection of paper punch holes she had been saving all year.

The brownie, equally furious, managed to lick and pluck every one of the shavings from the thick weave of the spread with his tiny fingers. The entire time that he was doing this he muttered and cursed, telling Jamie in no uncertain terms what he thought of her, what a disgrace she was to her family, and to what a bad end she was likely to come. Jamie tipped back her chair on two legs, lounging un-repentently.

"You missed one," she said when the brownie had finished and was heading back to the closet. He raced back to the bed, but after an intense examination discovered that she had been lying.

"What a wicked girl!" he cried. "Trying to fool a poor brownie that way."

"You're not a poor brownie!" she screamed. "You're a menace!" Suddenly days of frustration began to bubble within her. "I can't stand it!" she cried. "I can't take any more of this. I want you to leave me alone!"

"I can't leave you alone!" shouted the brownie, jumping up and down and waving his tiny fists in the air. "We are bound to each other by ancient ties, by words and deeds, by promises written in blood spilled on your family's land."

"Get out!" cried Jamie. In a frenzy, she snatched up an old pillow that had come from her grandmother's house, and began smacking it against the bed. The pillow burst open, exploding in a cloud of feathers "Get out, get out, get out!"

Shrieking with rage, the brownie began trying to pick up the feathers. But the faster he moved the more he sent them drifting away from him. When Jamie saw what was happening, she began waving her arms to keep the feathers afloat. The brownie leapt and turned, trying to pluck the feathers out of the air. He moved faster and faster, wild, frenzied. Finally he began racing in a circle. He went faster still, until he was little more than a blur to Jamie's eyes. Then, with a sudden **Snap!** he vanished, just as the papers had the day before.

Jamie blinked, then began to laugh. She had done it. She had gotten rid of him!

And that should have been that.

But a strange thing happened. As the days went on, she began to miss the little creature. Infuriating as he had been, he had also been rather cute. Moreover, the condition of her room began to irritate her.

A week after the brownie vanished she was rooting around in the disarray on her floor, trying to find her clayworking tools, which had been missing for three days. Forty-five minutes of searching had so far failed to turn them up.

"Sometimes I actually wish that brownie had stayed around," she muttered.

From the closet a tiny voice said, "A-hoo."

She stood up. "Is that you, brownie?"

"A-hoo," repeated the voice; it sounded pathetically weak.

Feeling slightly nervous—ever since this started she had not been entirely comfortable with her closet—Jamie went to the door and asked, "Are you in there?"

"A-hoo," said the voice a third time. It seemed to come from the upper shelf.

"Brownie, is that you?"

No answer at all this time.

She ran to her desk. Kicking aside the intervening clutter, she dragged the chair back to the closet. By standing on it, she could reach the upper shelf.

"Brownie?" she called. "Are you there?"

"A-hoo."

The voice was coming from a shoebox. She pulled it from the shelf and looked in. The brownie lay inside. He looked wan and thin, and after a moment she realized to her horror that she could see right through him.

"I thought you had left," she said, her voice thick with guilt.

"I had no place to go." His voice seemed to come from a far off place. "I am bound to you, and to this house. All I could do was wait to fade away."

An icy fear clenched her heart. "Are you going to die?"

"A-hoo," said the brownie. Then he closed his eyes and turned his head away.

She scrambled from the chair and placed the shoebox on her bed. *I've killed him!* she thought in horror. Reaching into the box, she lifted his tiny form. It was no heavier than the feathers he had been chasing when he had disappeared. She could see her fingers right through his body.

"Don't die," she pleaded. "Don't. Stay with me, brownie. We can work something out."

The brownie's eyelids fluttered.

"I mean it!" said Jamie. "I was actually starting to miss you."

"A-hoo," said the brownie. Opening his eyes, he gazed at her uncomprehendingly. "Oh, it's you," he said at last. Then he lifted his head and looked at her room. He moaned tragically and closed his eyes again.

"I'll clean it up," she said hastily. "Only just don't die. Promise?"

The brownie coughed and seemed to flicker, as if he was going to vanish altogether. "A-hoo," he said again.

"Watch!" said Jamie. Placing his tiny form gently on the bed, she began a whirlwind cleaning campaign, moving almost as fast as the brownie himself when he was in a cleaning frenzy. Along the way she found her clay working tools, the pendant her nice grandmother had sent her, two dollars and forty seven cents in change, and the missing homework that had cost her an *F* the day before. She kept glancing at the brownie while she worked, and was encouraged to see that he seemed to be getting a little more solid. When she was entirely done she turned around and said, "There! See?"

To her enormous annoyance, the brownie had turned the shoebox over and was sitting on the end of it, looking as solid as a brick and smiling broadly. "Well done!" he said.

"I thought you were dying!" she said angrily.

"I wasn't dying, I was fading. And if you wanted me to live, why are so angry that I'm alive?"

"Because you were faking!" she snarled.

"I never!" cried the brownie, sounding genuinely offended. "Another few minutes and I would have been gone for good, faded away like a summer breeze, like the last coals in the fire, like dew in the noonday sun, like—"

"All right, all right," said Jamie. "I get the picture." She paused. Though she still wasn't sure she believed him, she asked, "What happens when you fade?"

The brownie shivered, and the look of terror on his face was so convincing that she began to suspect that he was telling the truth. "I'm just **gone**," he said.

Jamie shivered too. "Do you really have nowhere else to go?" she asked.

The brownie shook his head. "'Tis you to whom I'm bound, and you with whom I must stay until the day I fade away—or the day you become the oldest female in the family and assign me to someone else of your line."

Jamie sighed. She looked at the pendant, the tools, the change lying on her desk. "If I let you stay will you behave?"

The brownie wrapped his tail around his knees. "I am what I am," he said.

"And so am I," she replied.

The brownie looked startled, as if this had not occurred to him before. "Can you help a little?" he asked plaintively.

"If I do will you stop nagging me?"

The brownie considered this for a moment. "Will you let me keep the closet as neat as I want?"

"Can I have my desk as messy as I want?" replied Jamie.

The brownie glanced at the desk, shuddered, then nodded.

"It's a deal," said Jamie.

And so it was. They did not, it should be noted, exactly live happily ever after. The truth is, they annoyed each other a great deal over the years. However, they also learned to laugh together and had enormous good times when they weren't fighting.

That's the way it goes with family things.

With His Head Tucked Underneath His Arm

Fifteen kings ruled the continent of Losfar, and each one hated the others. Old, fat and foolish, they thought nothing of sending the children of their subjects off on war after war after war, so that the best and the bravest were gone to dust before they ever really lived.

The young men left behind fell into two groups: those who escaped the war for reasons of the body—the weak, the crippled, and the maimed—and those who avoided the wars for reasons of the mind: those too frightened, too smart, or simply too loving to be caught in the trap the kings laid for them.

This last category was smallest of all, and a dangerous one to be in. Questioning the wars outright was against the law, and standing up to declare they were wrong was a quick route to the dungeons that lay beneath the palace. So it was only through deceit that those who opposed the wars could avoid going off to kill people they had never met and had nothing against.

One such was a cobbler's son named Brion, who had avoided the wars by walking on a crutch and pretending that he was crippled. Yet he chafed under the role he played, for he was not the sort to live a lie.

"Why do I have to pretend?" he would ask his friend Mikel, an older man who was one of the few who knew his secret. "Why must I lie, when I am right, and they are wrong?"

But Mikel had no answer. And since much as Brion hated the lie, he hated even more the idea of killing some stranger for the sake of a war he did not believe in, he continued to pretend.

One afternoon when Brion was limping through the market place on his crutch, he saw an officer of the king's army beating a woman because she had fallen in his path. The sight angered him so much that without thinking he stepped in to help the woman.

"Leave her alone!" he cried, grabbing the officer's arm.

The man pushed Brion away, and raised his hand to strike the woman again.

"Help!" she wailed. "He's killing me!"

Brion hesitated for but a moment. Though he knew it would reveal his lie, he sprang to his feet and felled the man with a single blow.

In an instant he was surrounded by soldiers.

Within an hour he found himself chained to a dungeon wall, with no one for company save the occasional passing rat, and no music save the trickle of the water that dripped endlessly down the cold stones.

As the days went by Brion began to wonder if he had been forgotten and would simply be left in his cell to rot. But late one afternoon he heard the clink of keys in the lock. Two uniformed men came into his cell, unlocked his chains, and dragged him to his feet. Gripping his arms in their mailed gloves, they hustled him to the throne room, to face the king.

"Is it true that you refuse to fight for me?" asked the king angrily.

At the moment, Brion's main fight was with the lump of fear lodged in his throat. But he stood as straight as he was able and said, "It is true. I cannot kill a man I have never met for the sake of a war I do not believe in."

The king's jowly face grew scarlet with rage. "Let the court see the treason of this speech. Let it be recorded, so that all will understand why this rebellious youth is being put to death."

Three days later Brion was marched to the public square. His weeping mother stood at the front of the crowd, shaking with sorrow as the guards escorted her son up the steps to die. Pushed to his knees, Brion laid his head on the block. He heard his father's voice cry out. But the words were lost to him, because the executioner's axe had fallen.

The crowd roared as Brion's severed head tumbled into the waiting basket.

Body and head were buried in a shallow grave far outside the city, in a corner of the boneyard reserved for traitors.

Brion was about as mad as a dead man can be, which may explain why three nights later he climbed out of the ground. Reaching back, he plucked his head from the grave, gave it a shake to rid it of loose dirt, then tucked it under his arm and started for the city.

It was the quietest part of the night when he reached the palace. Most of the guards were nodding at their posts, but even the few who were still alert did not see him enter.

The dead have their ways.

Slowly, Brion climbed the stairs to the king's bedchamber. When he entered the room he stood in silence. But his presence alone was enough to trouble the king, and after a moment the fat old man sat up suddenly, crying, "Who dares disturb my sleep?"

"I dare," said Brion, "because I know you for what you really are: a murderer and thief, not fit to be a king. You have been stealing your subjects' lives, and I have come to set things right."

Then he crossed the room and stood in a shaft of moonlight that flowed through the window next to the king's bed. When the king saw the body of the young man he had ordered killed just three days earlier standing next to him, saw the severed head with its still raw wound, he began to scream.

"Silence!" ordered Brion, raising his head to hold it before the king's face. "Silence, if you wish to see the morning!"

Trembling beneath his blankets, the king pleaded with Brion to spare his life. "I will do anything you ask," he whimpered. "Anything at all."

Brion's head smiled. Then it told the king what it wanted him to do.

The next day the king's advisors were astonished to hear the king announce that the war was over, and that he was calling the armies back from the field.

"Why, your majesty?" they asked. They were deeply disturbed, for they loved their game of war, and were sad to see it end.

But the king would say nothing of his reasons.

Now life in the kingdom began to change slowly for the better. The youths who returned from the war began to take a useful part in the life of their homeland. With strong young hands to till the fields, the farms grew more productive. Some of those who returned from the wars were artists and poets; some were builders and thinkers. New ideas came forward, new designs, new ways of doing things. As time went on the kingdom grew stronger, happier and more prosperous than any of those surrounding it.

And in all this time Brion never left the king to himself. Though the guard was doubled, and doubled again, somehow they always slept when Brion walked the halls, as he did every night when he came to visit the king's bedchamber. And there, with his head tucked underneath his arm, he would instruct the king on what to do next.

When morning came, Brion would be gone. But the smell of death would linger in the room. The servants began to whisper that the king was ailing, and would not live much longer. But live he did, and for the next three years he continued to do as Brion told him.

In that time the kingdom grew so prosperous that the other kings on Losfar became jealous. They began to plot together, and soon decided to attack the rebellious kingdom that had left the wars.

"After all," said King Fulgram, "the only reason they have so much is that they have not been spending it to defend themselves, as have we. Therefore, a share of it should be ours."

"A **large** share," said King Nichard with a smile.

When Brion heard that the armies of Losfar were marching on his homeland, he did not know what to do. He certainly did not want a war. But neither did he want to let the outsiders tear down all that had been built. And he knew he could not let them murder his people.

"Send a message of peace to the enemy camp," he told the king, a few nights before the enemy was expected to arrive.

The king sneered, but, as always, did as he was told.

The messenger was murdered, his body sent back as a warning of what was to come.

Panic swept the kingdom.

That night, when Brion stood by the king's bedside, the old man began to gloat over the coming war. "See what you have brought us to," he taunted. "We are no better off, and in fact far worse, than when you started. Before, we fought on **their** soil, and it was **their** homes that were destroyed. In two days time the enemy will be upon us, and this time it is **our** city that will burn."

Brion said nothing, for he did not know what to do.

That night when he was walking back to his grave Brion met another traveler on the road. Brion recognized him as the murdered messenger by the stray bits of moonlight that flowed through the holes in his chest (for the king had described the man's wounds with savage delight).

The messenger turned from his path to walk with Brian. For a time the two men traveled in silence.

Brion felt a great sorrow, for he blamed himself for the messenger's death. Finally he began to speak, and told the man everything that had happened since his own beheading.

"Don't feel bad," replied the messenger. "After all, your heart was in the right place—which is more than I can say for your head," he added, gesturing to the grisly object Brion carried beneath his arm. It was sadly battered now, for dead flesh does not heal, and in three years it had suffered many small wounds and bruises.

Brion's head began to laugh, and before long the two dead men were staggering along the road, leaning on each other as they told bad jokes about death and dying.

After a time they paused. Standing together, they stared into the deep and starry sky.

"I am so tired," said Brion at last. "How I wish that I could be done with this. How I wish that I could rest."

"You cannot," said the messenger. "You must finish what you have started."

Brion sighed, for he knew that his new friend was right. "And what of you?" he asked. "Why do you walk this night?"

"I was too angry to rest," said the messenger. "I wish that those fools could know how sweet life is. But perhaps only the dead can know that."

"More's the pity," said Brion. And with that he left the messenger and returned to his grave.

But the messenger's words stayed with him, and the next night when he rose, he knew what to do. Finding the grave of the messenger, he called him forth, saying, "I have one last message for you to deliver."

Then he told him his plan. Smiling, the messenger agreed to help. And so the two men went from grave to grave, calling the dead with these words:

"Awake, arise! Your children are in danger, your parents may perish, your childhood homes will burn. All that you loved in life is at peril. Awake, arise, and walk with us."

Not every soul gave back an answer. Some were too long dead, or too tired, or too far away in the next world. Some had never cared about these things in life. But for many, Brion's call was all that was needed to stir them from their place of rest. The earth began to open, and up from their graves rose the young and the old, the long dead and the newly buried. And each that rose took up the message, and went to gather others, so that two became four, and four became eight, and eight became a multitude, shaking the earth from their dead and rotted limbs, for the sake of all that they had loved in life.

When the army of the dead had gathered at the gate of the graveyard, Brion stood before them. Taking his head from beneath his arm, he held it high and told them all that had happened.

He told them what he wanted of them.

Then he turned and headed for the camp of the enemy.

Behind him marched the army of the dead. Some moaned as they traveled, remembering the sweetness and the sorrow of the living world. Some were no more than skeletons, their bones stripped clean by their years in the earth. Others, more recently dead, left bits and pieces of themselves along the way.

Soon they reached the camp of the enemy, which was all too close to the city. Following Brion's lead, they entered the camp. It was easy enough to pass the sentries. The dead **do** have their ways. Then, by ones and twos, they entered the tents of the living, where they began to sing to them of death's embrace.

"Look on me, look on me," they whispered in the ears of the sleeping men. "As I am, soon you shall be."

When the soldiers roused from their dreams of killing and dying to find themselves looking into the faces of those already dead, fear crept into their hearts.

But the dead meant them no harm. They had come only to speak to them, slowly and softly, of what it was to be dead; how it felt to be buried in the earth; what it is like to have worms burrow through your body.

"This will come to you soon enough," they whispered, extending their cold hands to stroke the faces of the living.

Some of the dead women held out their arms. When the men cried out and cowered from their touch, they whispered, "If you fear my embrace, then fear the grave as well. Go home, go home, and there do good. Choose life, choose life, and leave this place in peace."

One by one, the terrified men slipped from their tents and fled across the hills to their homes, until the invading army had vanished like a ghost in the night.

Then the army of the dead returned to the cemetery. They laughed as they went, and were well pleased, and chuckled at their victory. For though they had spoken nothing but the truth, they had not told all that there was to tell. The departing men would know that in good time; there was no need for them to learn all the secrets of the world beyond too soon.

As dawn drew near, Brion stood at the edge of his grave and stared into it with longing. At last the time had come to discover what came next, the secrets and surprises he had denied himself for three long years.

Tenderly he placed his head in the grave. Crawling in beside it, he laid himself down and died.

Wizard's Boy

I. The Currents of Magic

"Hey Aaron!" jeered a tall, dirt-smeared boy. "Got any magic to show us today?"

"Careful!" cautioned his companion. "The little wizard might turn you into a toad."

The tall boy made a fake display of terror, holding his hands in front of himself. Then he and his companion collapsed against each other, laughing helplessly.

Keeping his eyes on the under-ripe peaches he had been picking through, Aaron pretended to ignore the boys. But their teasing comments burned inside him. When he finally finished the marketing and returned to the cottage he shared with the wizard Bellenmore, he went to stand in front of the old man and demanded, as he had so many times before, "When will I be ready?"

The wizard glanced up from the lizard he had just lifted from its cage. Peering through wire-rimmed spectacles, he scowled at the skinny youngster he had taken in so many years ago. Though he was very fond of Aaron, the boy's impatience was beginning to annoy him.

"**When?**" asked Aaron again.

"I don't have the slightest idea!"

"But Bellenmore—"

"Aaron!" The old man's voice was sharp. "We have gone over this time and again. High Magic is not a toy, not something you play with. Nor is it possible to use until something in you can reach out and touch it. You can't will yourself to be ready for it, any more than you can will yourself to be…oh, taller, for heaven's sake. Some people are ready very young. Some are never ready. It's different for everyone."

"You don't want to teach me!" cried Aaron. "You want to keep the power for yourself." A wrenching sob rose in his chest. Rather than release it, he turned and fled the cottage.

Bellenmore dropped the lizard into its cage, which was pleasantly furnished, and went to the door. Silently he watched the boy leave the clearing where the cottage nestled. Once Aaron had disappeared into the forest, the wizard shook his head sadly, causing his long white hair to ripple over his shoulders. Why were youngsters always so eager for something that was really so very painful?

Well, the boy would get over it. He always did.

He sighed and returned to the lizard, which looked up at him from its favorite rock and said in peeved tones, "I wish you wouldn't drop me like that. I think I sprained my tail."

After Bellenmore apologized, the lizard added, "Don't worry about the boy. If I remember correctly, you were much the same at that age."

The wizard snorted, then pretended that he hadn't heard.

Aaron stumbled blindly through the forest. The air was cold, and a sharp breeze rustled the blood red leaves. He ran until his breath burned in his lungs. Finally, when he could go no further, he stopped and pressed his forehead against an old oak that had a trunk so thick he could barely reach halfway around it.

He stood there, panting and gasping, for several minutes. When he finally felt a little calmer he began to walk toward the ravine.

He now regretted his sharp words, which came more from frustration than anything else. He didn't really believe Bellenmore was trying to keep anything to himself. But it was so hard to wait—especially with the boys in the village constantly tormenting him about it.

Aaron sighed. He had to admit that the jeers and teasing were partly his own fault. When he saw the other boys with their fathers, on the days that he went to town to do the marketing, he was jealous—so jealous he had begun to create stories about his life with the old wizard who had adopted him, wild tales about the great magics Bellenmore was teaching him. Carried away with his own words, he had boasted of how he would soon be a powerful magician himself, while the town boys remained mere apprentices and hired hands.

Naturally, the boys had asked him to show them some magic. Equally naturally, once they found he couldn't, they never let him forget it.

It wouldn't have been quite so painful if Aaron had been able to work even some minor spell. But no matter how he tried, the magic (both High and Low) refused to come to him. The real problem wasn't that Bellenmore was unwilling to teach him. It was just that the teaching did no good. No matter how Aaron tried, he could not touch the currents of magic.

He walked on, his eyes on the ground, so consumed in his misery he failed to notice the enormous creature that flew overhead.

He did notice, however, the heavy, four-toed footprint sunk deep into the soft ground at the edge of the next stream he came to. He bent to examine it, then wrinkled his brow in concern. It looked like a troll print. "Don't be ridiculous," he told himself, speaking aloud for courage. "There hasn't been a troll sighting in this area since before I was born!" He took some pride in knowing that the reason for this was that Bellenmore had driven the creatures away.

Aaron glanced around, looking for more footprints. But the leaves that covered the forest floor would not take an impression.

He stood at the edge of the stream, uncertain what to do next. It might be best to go straight back to the cottage to report this to Bellenmore. He shook his head. It was too soon for that; neither his anger nor his chagrin at his own foolishness had cooled enough for him to feel comfortable going back. Besides, it was only one footprint.

Using stepping stones so familiar to him he didn't even need to look at them, Aaron crossed the stream.

The sun was sinking lower in the sky. The breeze seemed to be picking up. An eerie cry in the distance made him shiver. Again he thought about turning back. Bellenmore was quick to forgive. It would be no problem to return now.

But the cry wasn't the sound of a troll—he knew enough about them to know **that.** Besides, he had made up his mind to go to the ravine, and he didn't want to give up on the idea. Walking its edge helped to calm the storms that raged within him.

Bellenmore won't be worried. And I'm no coward, ready to run home because of a weird noise.

Still, as he walked he found himself glancing around more often than was his habit.

Aaron had another reason to continue on to the ravine. He had a special spot beside it that he used for practicing. This was where he sat to try to find the quiet place inside himself—the place where Bellenmore claimed the Magic dwelt. Once or twice he actually thought he had caught a touch, for the briefest instant, of some deep power running through him. But it always vanished as soon as he became aware of it. Usually, there was nothing.

He sighed. Maybe Bellenmore was right after all.

The magician was still on Aaron's mind when he reached the ravine. He did love the old man. How could he not? Bellenmore had taken him in after his parents' deaths, reared him like a son. And if the magician's temper was a bit quick, his tongue a trifle sharp, all in all he treated Aaron very well. Aaron knew that many a boy in town would gladly trade places with him, despite all the teasing they gave him.

He reached the ravine and stood gazing pensively into its depths. At the base of its rocky, brush-cluttered banks ran a swiftly moving stream. The water caught the last of the sun's light, making it look like flowing blood.

Aaron took several deep breaths. But even as he began to feel a deeper calm the silence was shattered by an ear-splitting screech. The boy spun, aware as he did of the sound of giant wings beating above him. He looked up, then screamed and threw up his hands to protect himself. A hideous creature swooped toward him. Leather-skinned and twice the height of man, it had a wingspread like a house. Its knife-like talons stretched for his throat. Its oddly human face leered with malevolent glee as it hissed, "Come to me!"

"Get back!" cried Aaron, stumbling backward himself. His foot crossed the edge of the ravine. Losing his balance he went over, bouncing down the steep, rocky slope.

II. The Grangli

Save for the dim light flickering through the windows in the side of the hill, the world seemed made of blackness. Peering through those windows, an intruder would have seen Bellenmore the Magician pacing back and forth, pulling at his white beard and muttering great imprecations to the walls and furniture.

A green flame crackled on the hearth, holding a cauldron of thick stew at a simmer. Above the fire, on the mantel, a row of gargoyle-festooned mugs winked and smiled hideously, occasionally bursting out in a chorus of bawdy song.

The latch of the door rattled.

Bellenmore sprang for it and snatched the door open, then fell back with a cry of dismay as Aaron stumbled in. Twigs and grass clung to the boy's clothing. His face was covered with cuts and dark bruises. A smear of blood had dried on his right cheek.

More disturbing than all of this were his eyes, which were wide and haunted.

Bellenmore seized the boy by his arms and drew him toward the fire. "What happened, Aaron? Are you all right?"

As the boy gazed at Bellenmore the tumult in his eyes began to quiet. He swallowed twice, then whispered, "The Grangli is flying."

Bellenmore dropped his hands. He turned this way and that, as if searching for support, and finally looked back to Aaron. "I'm glad you're safe," he whispered. "Let me tend to those wounds. Then you can tell me what happened. No, on second thought, you should eat first."

He led the boy to the hearth and settled him onto a stool. Then he ladled up a plate of the stew and drew a mug of cider from the barrel in the corner. He thrust plate and mug into Aaron's trembling hands.

The boy took them gratefully.

As Aaron ate, Bellenmore washed his wounds. Then he worked at healing the boy, both with herbs and potions that were natural, and with spells that would speed their action.

When the healing and the feeding were finished, Bellenmore asked for the story. He paced the floor as the boy spoke of what he had seen, and how only his fall into a narrow ravine had saved him from the monstrous creature.

"The Grangli," muttered Bellenmore in astonishment, once Aaron had finished. "But that can only mean that Dark Anne has returned."

"Brilliant," muttered the lizard.

Far across the wood a wizened woman sat in a cave lit only by the flames that crackled beneath the enormous black cauldron she was stirring. Serpents hissed and crawled about her bare feet. More snakes clung to the stalactites that thrust like giant fangs from the cave's damp ceiling.

Peering into the cauldron's depths, the woman was able to observe the action in Bellenmore's cottage.

A wicked gleam lit her face. "So they know I'm back," she chuckled. "And they fear what I may do. Well, let them fear, the fools. My power now is greater than Bellenmore would ever dare to dream. And it has just begun to grow." She cackled wildly. "The Grangli flies, and oh, what woe we now shall work on the lands that Bellenmore is bound to protect!"

She snapped her fingers. An instant later the Grangli stood before her, its wings furled in front of it, its head surrounded by the weaving, hissing serpents that hung from the ceiling.

"How did you fare, my pretty one? Did you bring Dark Anne her due?"

The Grangli uttered a strangled cry and produced, from some unknowable place beneath its wings, the torn carcass of a sheep.

Dark Anne was pleased. The animal would provide both dinner and...ingredients.

Bellenmore was leaning over an oaken stand, paging through the large, leather-bound book that rested on its surface. He turned the yellowed leaves cautiously, for they were fragile with age.

Aaron stood at the magician's side, feeling frustrated because he couldn't do anything to help. "How could it happen?" he asked, when he saw Bellenmore pause. "How could she have escaped so quickly?"

The wizard scowled. "I don't know. When last we clashed, and I mastered her so narrowly, I used a spell that should have bound her for lifetimes yet to come. But now the Grangli flies again, and it is obvious Dark Anne has returned. She must have found new power someplace. But where? That's the riddle, Aaron. Her dealings with the dark side have gone on so long already it hardly seems there was anywhere left for her to turn."

The lizard climbed to the top of its cage. Poking its head over the edge it said, "Perhaps she found the Black Stone of Borea." Then it unrolled its tongue, caught a passing fly, and dropped back to the stone on which it had been lounging.

Bellenmore shuddered. "That would have given her the power to escape all right."

"What's the Black Stone of Borea?" asked Aaron.

Bellenmore twisted his fingers in his beard. "An object of enormous power," he said at last.

"Of course, it's not really a stone," pointed out the lizard.

"Well it is now," said Bellenmore.

Aaron, who was used to this kind of conversation between the wizard and the lizard, knew very well how long it could go on. Raising his voice, he said, rather sharply, "Please! Just tell me what it is!"

Bellenmore sighed. "The Black Stone of Borea was once the heart of the greatest wizard who ever lived. There is a long and very strange story about his death and how his heart came to be turned to stone— and an even stranger story about how it came to be lodged at the College of Wizards."

"Where it caused all sorts of mischief," said the lizard, its tongue flickering in and out.

"Though the stone itself is neither good nor evil," continued Bellenmore, "its ability to gather power, to call it forth from unexpected places, to focus it, made it an enormous temptation not only to those of evil intent, but to many of higher purpose who wanted to use its power to twist the world to their vision of goodness."

"Always a dangerous proposition," pointed out the lizard.

Bellenmore nodded. "Finally it was agreed that for the safety of all, the stone should be locked away."

"Where did they put it?" asked Aaron.

Bellenmore shrugged. "No one knows. The spell was designed to randomly send it to one of the places where…" He paused, then closed his eyes and moaned.

"What's wrong?" asked Aaron.

Bellenmore passed a hand across his brow. "I just had a horrible thought. What if when I banished Dark Anne I sent her to the same place as the Black Stone? She would surely have found it—or it her, for it calls to anyone with power. Found it, and freed it, and used it to make her way back. That would explain everything." His face grim, he continued, "If that **is** what happened, then the thing she will be wanting now is revenge—revenge that could take any form, come from any direction, strike at any time. We must double our guard, Aaron, be as watchful as we can. Even then we'll have but small chance of sensing her attack before it is sprung."

"Maybe we should strike first," said Aaron.

Bellenmore turned and peered at him from under thick white brows.

The forest was deep, and dark, and still, the only noise the almost unhearable rustle of softly passing feet. They traveled single file— Bellenmore (the lizard perched on his shoulder), Aaron, and, behind all three, keeping watch at the rear, a minor demon Bellenmore had summoned with a spell of service.

Clouds filled the night sky, blocking the stars and the moon. Aaron kept his hand on Bellenmore's shoulder. The demon walked backwards, the single eye in the back of its head preventing it from stumbling while the stronger eyes in its face scanned the woods behind them for any sign of menace.

The silence was broken by a screech of pain. It came from above them, seeming to fill the sky. The sound put fingers of ice to Aaron's spine.

Even as Bellenmore grabbed the boy and shoved him to the side of the path a huge shape fell from the blackness, plummeting toward them. Aaron felt the earth tremble when the thing struck the ground.

Bellenmore tapped his staff against a rock. A gentle light grew around them.

Aaron shuddered.

At their feet lay the Grangli. Its massive body was twisted, its semi-human face made more hideous than ever by the pain of its unexpected death.

"This," said the lizard, "does not look good."

"Any ideas on what could have done it?" asked Bellenmore.

The lizard blinked. Then, sounding worried for the first time since Aaron had known it, it asked, very softly, "Malefestra?"

The minor demon hissed.

III. Darkness Gathering

Malefestra!

The name burned in Aaron's mind. He had heard it whispered, of course—heard it in old tales, darker tales than he usually liked to listen to. A master of power, a master of wickedness. In the shadow of his presence, their plan to attack Dark Anne seemed like little more than a game.

"I thought Malefestra was dead," whispered the boy.

Bellenmore shook his head. "His kind never dies. They change. They wait. They go through times of quiet. But they always emerge again sooner or later, stronger than ever, ready to challenge anything that stands between themselves and the power they crave."

He paused, then added, "It would make sense, in a way. If Dark Anne did find the Black Stone and bring it back with her, that might have been enough to stir Malefestra into action. Its power would call to him as surely as it called to her."

"But why would Malefestra kill the Grangli?" asked Aaron. "Wouldn't Dark Anne be on his side?"

"On his side, but never willing to yield to him. I suspect he killed the Grangli to show her his strength, possibly even thinking he might frighten her into submission. I don't believe it will work; she is too fresh from exile, too aware of her own power. Though it could never match his, she won't surrender without a struggle. And he has managed two warnings at once with the killing of the Grangli: one to Dark Anne—and one to us."

The witch's shriek of rage echoed from the walls of her cave, so startling in its fury that it silenced the hissing of the serpents. Shaking her skinny fists, she cursed the name Malefestra.

"My Grangli is dead!" she screamed. "My beautiful Grangli dead. And it's all his fault. Oh, woe to him now, too. Woe and sorrow and pain. How he shall pay for this!"

In the heat of her anger all caution was lost. She waved her hands over her cauldron and summoned an image of Malefestra. Then through that medium she sent a bolt of power with the intention of destroying the Demon King immediately.

She realized her foolishness at once, but it was too late to call the power back. The cauldron shivered. A great gash appeared in its side. Its contents poured out across the floor, thick bubbling liquid splashing about the witch's feet. Hissing in alarm, the snakes slithered away, but several of them were too slow, and thus were boiled on the spot.

Dark Anne's eyes bloomed large with fear. For a moment she stood like an animal that has just scented a hunter on its trail. Then she snatched something from her shelves, stalked from the cave, and headed into the woods.

"I can tell you something about this," said the minor demon, its voice a raspy growl.

Bellenmore gestured for it to go on.

The creature adjusted its tail, then said, "It has long been rumored in the Otherworld that Malefestra would be on the move again. He has been gathering power and enlisting recruits—trolls, goblins, assorted monsters and creatures—for many months. Though you might think this would be our desire, many of us fear him."

"Why?" asked the lizard, which was still perched on Bellenmore's shoulder.

"We fear that if he is successful he will make our lives even more miserable than they are already."

Bellenmore nodded. "He probably would. The problem is, how do we stop him?" He tugged at his beard and scowled himself into thought.

Aaron tried to come up with an idea, too, but it was hopeless. He knew too little about all this.

He was still trying to focus his thoughts when a voice screeched, "Bellenmore!"

"As if we didn't have trouble enough already," muttered the lizard.

The call had come from Dark Anne, who was approaching through the forest. Though Aaron felt a surge of terror at the sight of her, the witch raised her hands and said, "I approach in peace."

Her voice was low and gravelly; Aaron found it somehow both terrifying and exciting.

The witch paused for a moment when she saw the crumpled form of her great flying beast, paused and closed her eyes. Then she made a sign over the broken body and walked on. Stopping a few paces from them, she said, "When the time comes we shall be enemies again, Bellenmore—unless you are willing to change your ways and hold your power less tightly. But for now, I bid you join me in confronting an enemy who would destroy us both, who has already struck at the thing I hold most—"

She paused and glanced back at the Grangli. A terrible look of grief twisted her face and a few grains of sand trickled down her withered cheek.

Aaron glanced away, embarrassed to witness such sorrow, even in an enemy. But Bellenmore was unmoved. Face stern, voice cold, he said, "I can never work with you."

"That's my boy," said the lizard, in a tone so odd that Aaron really didn't know what he meant.

The old woman sneered. "Don't be a self-righteous idiot. You know how things were the last time Malefestra's power was on the rise—the darkness that covered the land, the innocent blood that was shed. He makes no distinction between your folk and mine, Bellenmore. They suffer equally. Can you stop him by yourself? Will you risk the lives and safety of those who depend on you simply to avoid soiling your hands with the likes of me?" Gesturing to the minor demon, she added, "It's not as if you've been pure in all your dealings until now."

The minor demon hissed at her.

"Wait!" said Bellenmore, as the witch turned to go. When she turned back he nodded and said grimly, "You're right, Anne. It is the only way."

Startled, Aaron drew close to Bellenmore. "Can we do this?" he asked in an urgent whisper. "You told me there could be no compromise with her kind!"

The wizard frowned. "It is a bad idea, Aaron, and I fear it. But I see no other path. Should Malefestra conquer, there will be no choices for any of us."

It was the minor demon who gave them the next step.

"Rumors have Malefestra's headquarters in the Broken Tower," it said. After some discussion, the others agreed that the minor demon should lead them there—primarily, felt Aaron, because Bellenmore and Dark Anne wanted to keep an eye on each other and neither wished to be in front.

Now that they knew their destination, it was decided, somewhat to Aaron's dismay, that they would fly.

The night air chilled the boy as he rose into the sky at Bellenmore's side. He liked flying. Even so, it also frightened him—mostly because he had no control over his own flight. And though it was Bellenmore who lifted him and guided him, and though he trusted the old magician with all his heart, he still found it terrifying to careen through the air at such speed—and at such a dizzying height—with no control at all.

Night-dark fields streaked by below, as did cottages, huts, the occasional town or village, and here and there a large manor house—all bound in slumber and unaware of the darkness growing among them.

At last the tower rose in view. Aaron shivered at the sight of the monstrous thing. Once tall and splendid, decorated with intricate inlays of ivory and ebony, it had been charred and battered in a clash between chaos and order a millennium ago. The top of the tower had been shattered in that war, and now it rose in jagged points. Brambles grew thick around its base.

"We must not let Malefestra know of our approach," said Bellenmore as they neared the tower. "We dare go no closer without protection."

Dark Anne hesitated. Then, with a sigh, she drew from her sleeve a black stone half again the size of a man's fist. It gleamed like an ebony fire. Even Aaron could sense the crackle of power that surrounded it. "The Black Stone of Borea," he whispered in awe. "So you **did** find it!"

The hag caressed the stone. "With our combined skills, we can use this to shield ourselves from the enemy's eyes. Neither one alone, but you and I in tandem, Bellenmore, can make this magic work."

Floating high above the ground, the magician reached forward to place his hand on the powerful stone.

For a frightening moment Aaron expected betrayal. But he saw Bellenmore smile, ever so slightly, as a thrill of power raced through him. Then the wizard's brow darkened in concentration as Dark Anne began to chant. Working together, the two magicmakers threw a shield about the little group.

Moments later, they landed inside the top of the tower, on a narrow stone ledge—all that was left of its highest floor. Around them rose the jagged remnants of the wall. The pieces made Aaron think of giant teeth, as if he was standing inside some huge stone jaw. Looking down, they saw the next level, which was scorched and abandoned.

"Now what?" whispered the lizard.

"We go down, of course," replied the minor demon. "Into the tower to face Malefestra. There is no other way."

IV. The Prisoner

For a moment Aaron wondered why the demon was so intent. But Bellenmore and Dark Anne nodded their agreement, and so the demon started out. Together the mortal three—and the lizard—followed their guide onto a crumbling stair that wound a slow, spiral descent into the tower.

Darkness swallowed them as they passed out of the open area at the tower's shattered top. The walls were dank, yet Aaron pressed against them, for fear of falling off the stair and plummeting into a void for which he could see no bottom. As they continued downward the air began to change, growing cold and foul, and heavy in the lungs. Aaron wanted desperately to cough, but feared he would give them away if he did. So he held it in, though the urge grew until it was like a torment.

Once something fluttered close to him, the sound of wings in the darkness so startling that he nearly leapt away from them. He only saved himself from hurtling into the darkness by an enormous effort of will.

At last Bellenmore whispered, "The floor is solid here. We can stop for a moment."

"A bit of light would be safe," said the demon.

Bellenmore's staff began to glow. In the dim light he examined the walls, then nodded in satisfaction. "I have studied this tower in my books. We are near the room where Malefestra would most likely seat himself, on a throne that once held the high kings."

"What are you going to do when we get to that room?" asked Aaron.

Bellenmore glanced at Dark Anne, but directed his answer to Aaron. "This will be a battle of power. Skills, some, but mostly raw power. And every bit we have on our side will be important. We will spend it, spend it all. That is the reason you are here, Aaron, for I do not like to put you in harms' way like this. But if Anne and I win, and still live, we will surely need you to minister to us, since a victory here will come only at great cost. You are to stay out of the throne room until then, well away from the battle. If we win, but do not survive— well, at least there will be someone to tell the story." He paused, then added grimly, "And if we lose, then you must flee—flee as fast and as far as you can."

Despite his terror, Aaron ached with shame that he had nothing more to contribute to the battle, no power, no magic to throw against their enemy.

Bellenmore turned to Dark Anne. "Are you ready?"

Her answer came in a scratchy whisper. "As ready as you, wizard. And we need to take him by surprise, so no more chatter. Let us move on."

Another flight of steps led them to a set of doors three times Aaron's height. They were made of bronze and worked with evil figurings. Witch and wizard each took one of the handles, then chanted spells to loose all locks.

With a nod to one another, they threw wide the doors and burst through to meet Malefestra.

The room was huge and high, and empty. As they looked around in bewilderment a shimmer of grey light fell from the ceiling, wrapping itself around Bellenmore and Dark Anne.

The minor demon broke into wild laughter. Then, as Aaron watched in horror, their guide began to change, throbbing and growing until it was revealed at last in its own true shape: The Demon King, Malefestra.

Bellenmore and Dark Anne shouted in rage, but were held by a band of shimmering grey light that wrapped around them. The lizard leaped upward, but the light caught and held him. As they struggled against the grey light, Malefestra stepped into the throne room, towering over them. Huge, bat-like wings sprouted from his powerfully muscled shoulders. His legs were like flaming tree trunks, his chest as broad as the hearth in Bellenmore's cottage. But of his face Aaron saw nothing, for resting on the Demon King's shoulders was a cloud of smoke, from which licked an occasional tongue of fire.

Out of that smoke rolled a deep, oily voice, rich with satisfaction: "Oh, my fine sheep. How easily you were led to the slaughter!"

At that moment, Bellenmore and Dark Anne burst free of the grey light. They flung their strongest magics at the Demon King. But surprise they had none, and he was well armored against their attack. Though light and power sizzled and struck around him, it could not touch him.

Then he made a gesture. Green smoke began to curl about the witch and the magician. Dark Anne twisted, then cried out in pain and rage. The Black Stone of Borea fell from her hand and began to roll across the floor.

Aaron dived for it. With a flick of his finger, Malefestra unleashed a force that sent the boy crashing against the nearest wall.

The demon king spoke a word that sounded like thunder. An enormous sphere of liquid scarlet appeared and wrapped itself around Bellenmore and Dark Anne. The crimson globe shimmered evilly for a moment, then began to shrink. It grew smaller and smaller, until finally it disappeared—taking Dark Anne, Bellenmore, and the lizard with it.

Alone with Malefestra, Aaron sprang at the Demon King, fury in his eyes. "Bring them back! **Bring them back!**"

He never touched the enemy, never came anywhere near him. The Demon King simply made a sign with his fingers, and Aaron bounced away harmlessly.

"Idiot child," murmured the monster. "Did you expect to lay hands on me? Surely your master has taught you better than that. Or do I overestimate the wisdom of Bellenmore?"

Aaron burned with shame but said nothing.

From the corner of his eye he judged the distance to the Black Stone.

Malefestra laughed. The sound boomed around Aaron, seeming to press him to the floor. With a snap of his fingers, the Demon King pulled the stone to his hand. "Idiot child," he repeated.

He gestured once more. A cage formed out of the air surrounding Aaron. Iron bars rose and curved above his head, meeting in a ring at the top. A plate of cold metal slid into place beneath his feet.

At another signal from Malefestra the cage floated slowly into the air, rising until the ring at the top slipped over a great hook embedded in the rock of the ceiling, some thirty feet above the floor.

Days dragged by, but with no way to measure them Aaron lost track of the time. Small amounts of food and water appeared in his cage every once in a while—enough to keep him alive, but never enough to satisfy his young body. He grew thin, while watching the guests of his captor feast.

And guests there were many, for the stream of visitors through the throne room seemed endless. Aaron was fascinated, and frightened, by the parade of evil things that came to pay homage to the master risen among them. Towering trolls and squat, snout-faced goblins passed below him, along with other things for which he had no name; creeping, crawling things. Even worse, in Aaron's eyes, were the humans who came to do business with Malefestra. *Traitors!* he thought furiously.

Most of these visitors snorted with amusement when they noticed the boy in his cage, dangling from the stone ceiling.

Each visitor brought some gift to Malefestra, and the pile of spoils on his left hand side grew higher by the day. But on his right side there was nothing save a seemingly empty pedestal. Aaron knew that seeming to be false. He had watched the Demon King render the Black Stone invisible and then place it lovingly on the pedestal. Ever and again, when he was alone, the Demon King would reach out to stroke the stone.

When Aaron slept he had strange dreams. Sometimes he heard Bellenmore and Dark Anne calling out for help. Sometimes the lizard whispered to him, but he could not make out the words. Other times he would see the stone rise from its pedestal and thunder toward him. Then he would wake with cold sweat running down his face, and his body trembling.

He grew obsessed with the stone. Sometimes he actually thought it was calling to him. His hands ached to hold it and he would grip the bars of his cage until his knuckles went white. He would shake it in his fury, and weep for Bellenmore. But there was nothing he could do.

He had no power.

V. The Deepest Current

A time came when Malefestra called his servants to a feast. Goblins, demons, ogres, trolls, certain wicked dwarfs, a small dragon, and a handful of ghouls gathered in the Broken Tower for a celebration that quickly fell into a drunken brawl. The trolls were beating the floor, and each other, with their clubs. Goblins leaped about on the tables, flinging food in all directions. Several ogres decided they would prefer some fresh dwarf to the meat being served. The dwarves thought this was a bad idea. The noise, and the smell, were appalling.

The Demon King watched in amusement for a time. Then, as if bored with the whole affair, he left on some private business.

In the Broken Tower the revelers reveled on. The party reached new heights of hilarity as mock battles were staged across the throne room floor. Tables and chairs were shattered. Soon clubs appeared, then rocks and spears. It was not long before the battles were no longer mock, but deadly serious, as short tempers, fueled by wine and ale, flared high.

One misplaced club, flying far from its mark, struck the hook from which Aaron's cage was suspended.

The boy held his breath. The hook, set in the stone ceiling, swung gently back and forth with the movement of the cage. And each time it swung, it pulled its way just a tiny bit farther out of the ceiling.

Aaron gripped the bars and waited without moving. Beneath him the brawl raged on, surging around the room for hours, until at last all had fallen, either from drink or from well placed clubs and fists.

Aaron leaned to his right. The cage swung. The hook moved.

He shifted his weight and the cage swung back.

He began to rock with a gentle rhythm, moving the cage back and forth, back and forth. Slowly, the hook began to worm its way free.

If only he could get it out before Malefestra returned!

Hours passed, and finally the cage did come loose. Aaron felt a moment of stark terror as he plummeted to the floor. The cage's fall was broken by the body of a sleeping troll, who would now sleep even longer. Even better, the impact of the fall jarred the door loose.

Creeping out of the cage, Aaron looked about cautiously. All were sleeping. Halfway across the room stood Malefestra's throne.

Beside it, invisible, was the Black Stone of Borea.

Aaron picked his way among the fallen creatures, stepping carefully over out-flung arms and twitching legs, avoiding for his life the various demon tails that crossed his path. Several times he slipped in puddles of spilled ale, once actually landing on the flabby green stomach of a fur clad ogre. Aaron froze, holding his breath. The monster opened its enormous single eye, belched in disgust, and fell back into slumber.

The closer he drew to the throne, and the stone, the greater was Aaron's terror. Each instant he feared that Malefestra would return.

Heart pounding, he climbed the throne. When he was finally able to reach out and touch the unseen stone, he almost fainted at the flood of power that coursed through his body.

Dizzy with strength, with uncertainty, he snatched the stone and hurried back to his cage. Climbing inside, he tucked the stone into his shirt, where it rested against his skin, comforting and strengthening him.

He needed time to think.

He had little of it; not more than ten minutes later Malefestra returned. His reaction at seeing the shambles of the feast was not the explosion of rage the boy had expected. Knowing his servants, the Demon King had known well what to expect when they convened. And it was a simple matter for him to use his power to set the room right.

He seemed more perturbed over the fall of Aaron's cage.

Trying to control his trembling, Aaron lay as though he had been knocked senseless by the fall. Without leaving his throne, Malefestra resealed the cage door and caused the whole thing to float back into the air. The hook plunged into the stone of the ceiling, jolting the cage, and Aaron with it.

Not until the Demon King reached out to touch the Black Stone of Borea was his wrath King aroused.

"**Where is it?**" he roared. Behind the rage, his voice held a scarcely detectable note of panic. But it was the power of his anger that roused every creature in the room. A frightened murmur rippled through the hall as the trolls, goblins, and ogres began stumbling nervously to their feet.

Malefestra cried out in fury once more. Now all were attentive, alert and trembling.

But Malefestra stopped his ranting and seemed to grow calm. He spread his enormous, muscular arms and stood trembling with the effort of detection. Slowly, he turned toward Aaron's cage, sniffing…

A prickle of fear slid down the boy's spine. He grabbed the Black Stone, clutching it to his stomach.

Mistake. The moment his hands touched the stone, Malefestra knew.

"**You** have it!" he cried. For the second time that night Aaron's cage crashed to the floor. With no troll to cushion its landing, the cage struck with a bone-splintering crash, shattering to pieces. Aaron was thrown free, and the Black Stone fell from his grasp. Invisible, it rolled across the floor.

"Seize it!" cried Malefestra. At the same instant he gestured for it to come to him. But Aaron was quicker this time. Almost before the stone had fallen from his hands he was after it. Ignoring his pain, he scrambled across the floor, managing to find and hold it.

The others leaped upon him. For a moment he felt as if he would be crushed.

The moment passed in an explosion of screaming and screeching as the assorted monsters were thrown from Aaron's back, flung back as if by some gigantic hand.

Aaron stood. But this was no longer Aaron, powerless apprentice to a master magician. Rather it was an Aaron whose hidden strength had been quickened by the Black Stone of Borea, an Aaron who had finally tapped the currents of magic that lay deep within him and discovered that the power he had ached so long to feel was now surging through him, joining with—and magnified by—the power of the stone. Somehow, without knowing how, he knew how to use the stone. Standing, he held it high above his head, trembling with its strength.

Power crackled through the air. Shrieking, the minions of Malefestra fell to the floor and covered their heads. The Dark Lord himself was not so easily broken. Throwing up a shield, he protected himself from the power Aaron had unleashed.

"Put it down, child," he said smoothly, the words drifting from the smoke that curled where his head should be. "Put it down, and you may be allowed to live when this is over."

But the power that had woken in Aaron was still growing. Filled with pride, he threw back his head and laughed.

His second mistake. For now the Demon King was angered indeed. Aaron's laughter had fueled Malefestra's hate, and his strength. The shield about him shattered and the power that had been Aaron's swirled madly around the room to rush back at the boy.

"No!" cried Aaron. He held the stone before him. The power struck, and was absorbed by the stone. Instantly it grew hot and began to burn against his flesh.

Now it was Aaron's turn to be frightened. Bolt after bolt of power crashed toward him. Though he used the stone to capture every one it grew hotter and hotter with each bolt of power it absorbed. Soon the boy felt his flesh begin to sear. The sickening smell of burning skin hit his nostrils. He nearly vomited in terror.

Yet he dared not let the stone go; to drop it would mean death— death not only for him, but for more and more of the people in the lands that his master had sworn to protect.

"Surrender!" roared Malefestra. Again the air was slashed with power. "Surrender!"

Aaron fell to his knees but would not let go the stone. It was glowing now with the power it had absorbed and it seemed to burn him to the very bone.

"Surrender!" bellowed Malefestra.

"Never!" whispered Aaron, his throat so tight the sound could barely pass. "**Never!**"

And then the stone erupted. All the power it had absorbed burst free, and a bolt of enormous energy shot across the room. The stone itself exploded into a thousand pieces. From somewhere far away Aaron heard a cry of anguished pain. Then there was silence.

Malefestra lay still and silent on the floor.

Unable to move, unable to speak, Aaron knelt and stared at his hands, oblivious to the chaos erupting around him.

The legions of Malefestra, which had quivered against the walls during the battle, now began to rouse themselves. Their babble grew louder, until at last it penetrated Aaron's daze. Without looking up, he waved his hand and cried, "Begone!"

The forces of darkness fled squalling into the night, scattering to their separate holes and hiding places in the darkness of the earth.

And still the boy knelt and stared at his hands, on which no burns could be seen, but which throbbed with a pain so fierce it felt as if he was holding them in a fire, and pulsed with a strength that made him weak to think of it.

At last his lips parted and he whispered, "Bellenmore, please help me."

"Alas, you'll have to help yourself, my boy," said a faint voice behind him.

Aaron turned, and saw the magician, who had been called back by the power of his words. (*By* my *power*, Aaron realized in astonishment.)

His joy faded as he realized something was wrong. Though he could see Bellenmore, the wizard's form was hazy, shimmering. Aaron reached toward him. His hand went through the image.

The wizard shook his head sadly. "There's always a price, Aaron. Always a price. You were right—I should not have joined forces with Dark Anne, even in the cause of good. I cannot come back, at least not yet. Even to speak to you like this is painful, and difficult. I will contact you when I can, my boy, and I will watch as I am able. But you must fend for yourself now. You've found your power. It's time to go back to the cottage, and learn how to use it."

His form wavered and he disappeared from view. Aaron fell to his knees moaning, "Come back, come back!"

When he finally lifted his head, he noticed the lizard coiled on the floor in front of him.

"I didn't agree to the deal with Dark Anne," it said. "So I got to come back. Come on, boy. Let's go home."

Picking up the lizard, Aaron made his way from the tower.

Aaron sat on the edge of the ravine, watching the sun rise. It had been two weeks since the battle in the Broken Tower, and though his hands still throbbed with pain now and then, he had mostly recovered.

And the land—the land that Bellenmore was sworn to protect—was peaceful. The light of the rising sun lay in golden pools among the leaves. Burnished acorns were scattered like jewels in their midst. A soft breeze washed across him, carrying news from all across the earth.

He enjoyed the quiet. And he was learning to live with the new-ness that was in him, the thing that had been struggling to be born all these years and had finally been unleashed by need and terror in the tower of the Demon King.

Aaron turned his gaze back to the ancient book of power that lay in his lap.

The lizard coiled on his shoulder whispered an explanation of what the words meant.

Deep within him, Aaron felt the surge and ebb of a power he still did not understand, but that he knew would mark the days of his life forever after. A power that he knew would someday allow him to bring Bellenmore home.

Turning the page, he continued to study.

The Metamorphosis of Justin Jones

Justin Jones shot out the front door of the house where he lived—not *his* house, just the place where he was forced to live—and ran until he could no longer hear his uncle's shouts. Even then he didn't feel safe. Sometimes Uncle Rafe's anger was so powerful it propelled the man onto the street after Justin. So the boy ran on, stopping only when the stitch in his side became so painful he could go no farther.

He was on a street corner he had never seen before. He leaned against a tree, panting and gasping for breath. The air burned in his lungs.

It was late twilight, and stars had just begun to appear, peeking out of the darkness like the eyes of cats hiding in a closet. Justin didn't see them. He was pressing his face against the tree, wishing he could melt into its rough bark and be safe.

When he finally opened his eyes again Justin noticed an odd mist creeping around the base of the tree—a mist that somehow seemed to have more light, more color, than it should.

Curious, he stepped forward to investigate.

As he circled the tree he heard an odd whispering sound, and felt a tingle in his skin. The mist covered the street ahead of him—a street he had never seen before, despite the fact that Barker's Elbow was a very small town.

He walked on.

At the end of the street he saw a strange, old fashioned looking building. In the window were the words "Elives Magic Supplies— S.H. Elives, Prop."

I could sure use a little magic about now, thought Justin. He glanced at his watch. Most of the stores in town were closed by this time of the evening. But this one had a light in the window.

He tried the door. It opened smoothly.

A small bell tinkled overhead as he stepped in.

Justin smiled. He would never have dreamed Barker's Elbow held such a wonderful store. Magician's paraphernalia was scattered everywhere. Top hats, capes, scarves, big decks of cards, and ornate boxes covered the floor, the walls, the counters, even hung from the ceiling. At the back of the shop stretched a long counter with a dragon carved in the front. On top of the counter stood an old fashioned brass cash register. On top of the cash register sat a stuffed owl. Beyond the cash register was a door covered by a beaded curtain.

Justin walked to the closest counter. On it stood an artillery shell, thick as his wrist. To his disappointment, the shell had already been fired.

On it was a tag that said, "Listen."

Remembering the big seashell his mother used to put to his ear so he could "hear the ocean," Justin lifted the empty metal shell and held the hollow end to his ear.

At once he was overwhelmed by the sound of cannons, the terrified neighs of horses, the screams of wounded men.

He put the shell down. Quickly.

Next to it stood a French doll. When Justin reached for her, the doll blinked and cried, "Oooh la la! Touch me not you nasty boy!" Then she began a wild dance. When Justin pulled his hand back the doll froze in a new position.

Deciding he should just *look* at the merchandise, Justin crossed to another counter. A broom resting against the edge of it blocked his view. Justin picked it up so he could see better.

The broom began to squirm in his hands.

Justin dropped the broom. He was about to bolt for the door when the owl he had thought was stuffed uttered a low hoot. "Peace, Uwila," growled a voice from beyond the beaded curtain, "I'm coming!"

A moment later an old man appeared. He was shorter than Justin, with long white hair and dark eyes that seemed to hold strange secrets. His face was seamed with deep wrinkles. The old man looked at Justin for a moment. Something in his eyes grew softer. "What do you need?"

"I don't think I need anything," said Justin uncomfortably. "I just came in to look around."

The old man shook his head. "No one comes into this store just to look around, Justin. Now what do—"

"Hey, how do you know my name?"

"It's my job. Now, what do you need?"

Justin snorted. What did he need? A real home. His mother and father back. He needed—

"Never mind," said the old man, interrupting Justin's bitter thoughts. "Let's try this. Have you ever seen a magician?"

Justin nodded.

"All right, then what's your favorite trick?"

Justin thought back to a time three years ago, back before his parents had had the accident. His dad had taken him to see a magician who did a trick where he locked his assistant in handcuffs, put her in a canvas bag, tied up the bag, put it in a trunk, wrapped chains around the trunk, and handed the keys to a member of the audience. Then he had climbed onto the trunk, lifted a curtain in front of himself, counted to five and dropped the curtain. Only when the curtain fell, the assistant was standing there, and the magician was inside the bag in the trunk, wearing the handcuffs. Justin had loved the trick, half suspected it was real magic.

It had had a special name, something scientific.

"The metamorphosis!" he said suddenly, as his mind pulled the word from whatever mysterious place such things are kept.

The old man smiled and nodded. "Good choice. Wait there."

Justin felt as if his feet had melted to the floor. The old man disappeared through the beaded curtain—and came back a moment later carrying a small cardboard box. Clearly it didn't have a big trunk in it. What, then? Probably just some instructions and…what? Justin was dying to know.

But he also knew the state of his pockets.

"I don't think I can afford that," he said sadly.

The old man started to say something, then paused. He looked into the distance, nodded as if he was listening to something, then blinked. His eyes widened in surprise. After a moment he shrugged and turned to Justin.

"How much money do you have?"

Though he was tempted to turn and run, Justin dug in his pocket. "Forty-seven cents," he said at last.

The old man sighed. "We'll consider that a down payment. Assuming the trick is satisfactory, you will owe me…" He paused, did a calculation on his fingers, then said, "Three days and fifty seven minutes."

"What?"

"You heard me! Now do you want it, or not?"

Something in the old man's voice made it clear that "Not" was not an acceptable answer. Swallowing hard, Justin said, "I'll take it."

The old man nodded. "The instructions are inside. We'll work out your payment schedule later. Right now it's late, and I am tired. Take the side door. It will get you home more quickly."

Justin nodded and hurried out the side door.

To his astonishment, he found himself standing beside the tree once more. He would have thought the whole thing had been a dream …if not for the small cardboard box in his hands.

Justin walked home slowly. The later it was when he got there, the greater the chance his uncle would be asleep.

Luck was with him; Uncle Rafe lay snoring on the couch, a scattering of empty beer cans on the floor beside him.

Justin tiptoed up the stairs to his room. He set the box on his desk, then used his pocket knife to cut the tape that held it shut. He wasn't sure what he would find inside; clearly it was too small to hold the entire trick. Probably he'd have to go out and buy the trunk and stuff, which would mean that he'd never get to try it.

The box contained two items: a small instruction book, and a bag that—to his astonishment—shook out to be as large as the canvas sack the magician had used. The reason this astonished him was that when rolled up the bag could easily fit in his shirt pocket.

The fabric was smooth and silky, and the colors shifted and changed as he looked at it. It was very beautiful, and at first he was afraid that it would be easy to tear. But it felt oddly strong beneath his fingers.

He opened the instruction booklet.

The directions were written by hand, in a strange, spidery script. On the first page of the booklet were the words

>   WARNING: *Do not attempt this trick unless you really mean it.*
>   *Do not even turn the page unless you are serious.*

Justin rolled his eyes…and turned the page.

The directions here were even weirder:

"To begin the metamorphosis, open the bag and place it on your bed. Being careful not to damage the fabric, climb inside before you go to sleep. Keep your head out!

"After you have slept in the bag for three nights you will receive further instructions."

Justin stared at the bag and the booklet for a long time. He was tempted to just stuff them back in the box and take the whole crazy thing back to the old man. Only he wasn't sure he could find the store again, even if he tried.

He rubbed the whisper-soft fabric between his fingers. It reminded him of his mother's cheek.

He climbed inside the bag, feet down, head out, and slept. That night his dreams were sweeter than they had been in a long, long time. But when he woke he felt oddly restless.

And his shoulders felt funny.

Justin slept in the bag for the next two nights, just as the directions said. In his dreams—which grew more vivid and beautiful each night—he flew, soaring far away from his brutal uncle and the house where he had felt such pain and loss. Justin came to long for the night, and the escape that he found in his dreams.

On the morning of the fourth day Justin felt as if something must explode inside him, so deep was the restlessness that seized him. Eagerly, fearfully, he turned to the instruction booklet that had come with the silken sack. As he had half expected, he found new writing on the page after the last one he had read—the page that had been blank before.

"Sometimes a leap of faith is all that's needed."

Wondering what that was supposed to mean, he went to the bathroom to get ready for school.

His shoulders itched.

The next morning they were sore and swollen.

The morning after that, Justin Jones woke to find that he had wings. They were small. They were feeble. But they were definitely there.

Justin had two reactions. Part of him wanted to shout with joy. Another part of him, calmer, more cautious, was nearly sick with fear. He knew Uncle Rafe would not approve.

He put on a heavy shirt, and was relieved to find that the weight of it pressed the wings to his back.

The next morning the wings were bigger, and the morning after that bigger still. Justin wouldn't be able to hide them from his uncle much longer.

The wings were not feathered, nor butterfly delicate, nor leathery like a bat's. They were silky smooth, like the sack he slept in. More frustrating, they hung limp and useless. Late at night, when his uncle was asleep, Justin would flex them, in the desperate hope that they would stretch and fill, somehow find the strength to lift him, to carry him away from this place.

Exactly one week after the first night he had slept in the sack, his wings became too obvious to hide. When he sat down to breakfast that morning his uncle snapped, "Don't slouch like that. Look how you're hunching your shoulders."

Justin tried sitting up straighter, but he couldn't hide the lumps on his back.

"Take off your shirt," said his uncle, narrowing his eyes.

Slowly, nervously, Justin did as he was told.

"Turn around."

Again, Justin obeyed. He heard a sharp intake of breath, then a long silence. Finally his uncle said, "Come here, boy."

Turning to face him, Justin shook his head.

His uncle scowled. "I said, come here."

Justin backed away instead. His uncle lurched from the table, snatching at a knife as he did.

Justin turned and ran, pounding up the stairway to his room. He paused at the door, then went past it, to the attic stair. At the top he closed the door behind him and locked it.

A moment later he heard his uncle roaring on the other side of it. For one foolish moment Justin hoped he would be safe here. Then the door shuddered as his uncle threw himself against it. Justin knew it would take only seconds for the man to break through.

He backed away.

Another slam, another, and the door splintered into the room. Stepping through, Uncle Rafe roared, "Come here, you little heathen!"

Shaking his head, mute with fear, Justin backed away, moving step by step down the length of the attic, until he reached the wall and the small window at the far end. His uncle matched his pace, confident in his control.

Justin knew that once Uncle Rafe had him the wings would be gone, ripped from his shoulders. Pressing himself against the wall, letting all his fear show on his face, he groped behind him until he found the window latch. With his thumb, he pulled it open, then began to slide the window up. It hadn't gone more than a half an inch before his uncle realized what he was doing and rushed forward to grab him.

"Don't!" cried Justin, holding out his hands.

The wings trembled at his shoulders, and he could feel some strange power move out from them. His uncle continued toward him, but slowly now, as if in a dream. Moving slowly himself, Justin turned and opened the window.

He glanced behind him. His uncle's slow charge continued.

Taking a deep breath, Justin stepped out.

He fell, but only for a moment. Suddenly the wings that had hung so limp and useless for the last few days snapped out from his shoulders, caught the air, and slowed his fall.

They stretched to either side of him, strong and glorious, shining in the sun, patterned with strange colors. As if by instinct he knew how to move them, make them work. And as his uncle cried out in rage and longing behind him, Justin Jones worked his wings and flew, rising swiftly above the house, above the trees, his heart lifting as if it had wings of its own as he soared skyward.

Justin flew for a long time, as far from the town and the home of his brutal uncle as he could manage to go. He changed course often, preferring to stay above isolated areas, though twice he flew above a town, swooping down just so that he could listen to the people cry out in wonder as they saw him. Once he flew low over a farm, where an old woman stood in her yard and reached her arms toward him, not as if to catch him, but in a gesture that he knew meant that she wanted him to catch her up. He circled lower, and saw with a start that tears were streaming down her face. Yet when he flew away, she made no cries of anger as his uncle had, only put her hand to her mouth, and blew him a kiss.

And still he flew on.

Though Justin had no idea where he was heading, he could feel something pulling him north, north and west. After a time he saw a cloud ahead of him. It was glowing and beautiful, and without thought, he flew into it.

The air within seemed to be alive with light and electricity, and as Justin passed through the cloud he felt a tingle in his skin—a tingle much the same as the feeling he had had just before he found the magic shop.

When he left the cloud, he had come to a different place. He had been flying above land when he entered it, a vastness of hills and forest dotted by small towns that stretched in all directions for as far as he could see. But though it had taken no more than a minute or two to fly through the cloud, when he left it he was above water—a vast sea that, like the hills and forest, stretched as far as the eye could reach. Panic stricken, Justin turned to fly back. But the cloud was gone, and the water stretched behind him as well.

Justin's shoulders were aching. He wasn't sure how much longer he could stay aloft.

And then he saw it ahead of him: a small island, maybe two or three miles across, with an inviting looking beach. The wide swath of sand gave way to a deep forest. The forest rose up the flanks of a great mountain that loomed on the island's far side.

With a sigh of relief, Justin settled to the beach. He threw himself face forward on the sand to rest.

Soon he was fast asleep.

When Justin opened his eyes, he saw three children squatting in front of him.

"He's awake!" said the smallest, a little girl with huge eyes and short brown hair.

"I told you he wasn't dead," said the largest, a dark-haired boy of about Justin's age. "They never are, no matter how bad they look."

"Come on, then," said the girl, reaching out to Justin. "Lie here in the sun all day and you'll get burned."

Justin blinked, then glanced back at his shoulders. The wings were still there. Why didn't these strange children say anything about them?

"Maybe I should just fly away," he muttered, pushing himself to his knees. He did it a little bit to brag, a little bit to see if he could get the children to say something about the wings.

"Oh, you can't do that," said the little girl, sounding very sensible. "Well, you could. But it wouldn't be smart. Not until you've talked to the old woman."

"She's right," said the biggest boy. "Come on, we'll show you the way. But first you ought to eat something."

"So you've seen people with wings before?" asked Justin.

"Silly!" giggled the girl. "We all had wings when we came here. Were you scared when you went through the cloud? I was."

Justin nodded, uncertain what to say. He realized someone else seemed to be in the same condition. "Doesn't he ever talk?" he asked, gesturing to the middle child, a dark-eyed boy who looked to be about nine.

"Not yet," said the girl. "I think he will someday. But he was in pretty bad shape when he got here."

"Come on," said the biggest boy. "The old woman will tell you all about it."

Justin followed the three strange children up the beach and into the forest, a forest so perfect that it almost made him weep. It was not that it was beautiful, though it was. Nor that the trees were old and thick and strange—though they were. What made it so wonderful, from Justin's point of view, was that it was filled with tree-houses…and the tree houses were filled with children. Happy children. Laughing children. Children who scrambled along rope bridges, dangled from thick branches, and swung from tree to tree on vines.

"Hey, new boy!" they cried when they spotted him. "Welcome! Welcome!"

No one seemed to think it odd that Justin had wings, though a few of them gazed at the wings with a hungry look.

Justin's own hunger, which he had nearly forgotten in the strangeness and the wonder of this new place, stirred when the children led him to a platform built low in a tree, where there were bowls of fruit and bread and cheese. He ate in silence at first, too hungry to talk. But when the edge was off his appetite he began to ask questions.

"Ask the old woman," was all they would tell him. "The old woman will explain everything."

"All right," he said, when his hunger was sated. "Take me to this old woman, will you please?"

"We can't take you," said the boy. "You'll have to go on your own. We can only show you the way."

Justin walked through the forest, following the path the children had shown him. The trees were too thick here for him to spread his wings, which annoyed him, because the path was steep, and his legs were beginning to grow tired. He wanted to fly again. Where did this old woman live, anyway? A tree-house, like the children? That didn't seem likely. Maybe a cottage in some woody grove or beside a stream? Maybe even a cave. After all, he did seem to be climbing fairly high up the mountainside.

It turned out that all his guesses were wrong. The path turned a corner, and when he came out from between two trees he found himself at the edge of a large clearing where there stood a huge, beautiful house.

The door was open. Even so, Justin knocked and called out. There was no answer.

Folding his wings against his back, he stepped through the door.

"Old woman?" he called.

He felt strange using the words instead of a name, but that was the only thing the children had called her.

"Old woman?"

"Up here!" called a voice. "I've been waiting for you."

Justin climbed the stairs, flight after flight of them, going far higher than the house had looked from the outside. At each level he called, "Old woman?" And at each level the voice replied, "Up here! I'm waiting for you!"

At last the stairs ended. Before him was a silver door. He put his hand against it, and it swung open.

"Come in," said the old woman.

She was sitting before a blue fire, which cast not heat, but a pleasant coolness into the room. Her hair was white as cloud, her eyes blue as sky. A slight breeze seemed to play about the hem of her long dress.

"Come closer," she said, beckoning to him.

He did as she said.

She smiled. "I'm glad you're here. Do you like your wings?"

Justin reached back to touch one. "They're the most wonderful thing that ever happened to me," he said softly.

The old woman nodded. "I'm glad. It's not easy getting them out there, you know. I can't do nearly as many as I would like."

"Who are you?" asked Justin.

She shrugged. "Just an old woman with time on her hands, trying to do a little good. But now listen carefully, I have to tell you what happens next. The wings will only last for one more day. However that will be long enough for you to fly home, if you should wish."

Justin snorted. "Why would I want to—"

"Shhh! Before you answer, you must look into my mirror. Then I will explain your choice."

Standing, she took his hand and led him across the room. On the far side was a golden door. Behind it, Justin could hear running water. When she opened the door, Justin saw not a room, but a cave. Four torches were set in its walls.

In the center of the cave was a pool. A small waterfall fed into it from the right. A stream flowed out to the left.

"Kneel," said the old woman. "Look."

Justin knelt, and peered into the water. He saw his own face, thin and worn, with large eyes where the fear was never far beneath the surface. From his shoulders sprouted wings, huge and beautiful.

The old woman dipped her finger in the water, and stirred.

The image shifted. Now Justin saw not a boy but a man. Yet it was clearly his face.

"The man you will become," whispered the old woman.

Justin stared at the face. It was not handsome, as he had always hoped he would become. But it was a good face. The eyes were peaceful and calm. The beginning of a smile waited at the corners of the mouth. Laugh lines fanned out from the eyes. It was a strong face. A kind face.

Outside, far away down the mountain, Justin could hear the laughter of the children.

The old woman stirred the water again. The man's face disappeared. The water was still, showed no image at all.

"Come," she said quietly.

Justin followed her back to the room.

"Now you must choose," she said. "You can stay here. This place is safe and calm and no one will hurt you, ever again."

Justin felt his heart lift.

"But...you will stay just as you are. Never change, never grow any older." She sighed. "That's the trade. There's always a trade. It's the best I can do, Justin."

He looked at her, startled, then realized that given everything else that had gone on, the fact that she knew his name should be no surprise at all.

Justin went to the window. It looked out not onto forest or mountains, but clouds. He stood there a long time, looking, listening. Finally he turned to the old woman.

"Can I ask a question?"

"Certainly—though I can't guarantee I will know the answer."

He nodded. "I understand. Okay, here's the question. The man I saw in the pool. Me. What does he do?"

The old woman smiled. "He works with children."

Justin smiled too. "And what about my uncle?" he asked. "Will things be better with him if I go back?"

The old woman shook her head sadly.

Justin blinked. "Then how is it possible I can turn out the way you showed me? How can that be me?"

The old woman smiled again. "Ah, that one is easy. It is because no matter what happens, you will always remember that once upon a time...you flew."

Justin nodded and turned back to the window. Far below he could hear the sound of the children at play.

He ached to join them. But then he thought of the others he knew.

The ones who never laughed.

The ones who still needed wings.

"How would I find the way back?"

"Take the side door," said the old woman softly. "It will get you home a little more quickly."

Tucking his wings against his back, Justin stepped through the door—and found himself on top of the mountain. He could see the entire island spread out below him, could hear, even from this height, the laughter of the children.

Justin took a deep breath. Then he spread his wings and leaped forward. Catching the air in great sweeps, he soared up and up, then leveled off and flew.

Not toward home; Justin had no real home.

Flexing his wings, he pointed himself toward tomorrow. Then he flew as hard as he could.

Acknowledgments

This book would not have been created without:

Bruce Coville, an incredibly talented writer and crafter of worlds, who is a complete joy to work with.

Cover artist Omar Rayyan, who painted the beautiful art you see on the dust jacket in jig time, and insisted on creating new work despite a very tight deadline.

Sheila Rayyan, who kindly agreed to design the gorgeous dust jacket that graces this book.

My sincere thanks to Katherine Coville for allowing us to reprint her delightful illustrations for *The World's Worst Fairy Godmother*.

Mark Olson, who answered every one of my annoying questions and whose guidance on all matters technical made it possible to get this to the printer intact.

This book was typeset in Adobe Garamond (with titles set in Jenkins 2.0) using Adobe InDesign 3.0, and printed by Sheridan Books of Ann Arbor, Michigan, on acid-free paper.

—Deb Geisler

The New England
Science Fiction Association (NESFA)
and NESFA Press

Recent books from NESFA Press

All titles are hardback unless otherwise noted, and printed on long-life acid-free paper. NESFA Press accepts payment by mail, check, money order, MasterCard, or Visa. Please add $5 postage ($10 for multiple books) for each order. Massachusetts residents please add 5% sales tax. Fax orders (Visa/MC only): (617) 776-3243

Write for our free catalog, or check out our online catalog by directing your Internet web browser to: **www.nesfapress.com**.

The New England Science Fiction Association

NESFA is an all-volunteer, non-profit organization of science fiction and fantasy fans. Besides publishing, our activities include running Boskone (New England's oldest SF convention) in February each year, producing a semi-monthly newsletter, holding discussion groups relating to the field, and hosting a variety of social events. If you are interested in learning more about us, we'd like to hear from you. Write to our address above!